LOVE ME WITH LIES

DIRTY
RED

BOOKS BY TARRYN FISHER

LOVE ME WITH LIES SERIES

The Opportunist
Dirty Red
Thief

Mud Vein

Marrow

F*ck Love

Bad Mommy

Atheists Who Kneel and Pray

NEVER NEVER SERIES

LOVE ME WITH LIES

DIRTY
RED

NEW YORK TIMES BESTSELLING AUTHOR
TARRYN FISHER

For Maryse—
Thanks for changing my life.

ONE

I stare down at the screaming, pink creature in my arms, and I panic.

Panic is a maelstrom. It churns to life in your brain like a whirlpool, gaining speed as it funnels down into the rest of the body. Round and round it goes, causing your heart to race. Round and round twisting, knotting, and sickening the stomach. Round and round, it hits your knees, weakening them before creating a cesspool in your toes. You curl up your toes, take a few deep breaths, and grab onto the life-preserving ring of sanity before the panic can suck you in.

These are my first ten seconds of being a mother.

I hand her back to her father. "We have to hire a nanny."

I fan myself with a copy of *Vogue*, until it becomes too heavy, then I let my wrist go limp, dropping it to the floor.

"Can I have my Pellegrino?" I wiggle my fingers toward my bottled water, which is out of my reach, and lean my head back against the flat, hospital-issued pillow. These are the facts: a human being just fell out of my body after I grew it there for nine months. The parasitical similarities are enough to cause me to grab a doctor by his lapels and demand he tie my tubes into a pretty bow. My stomach—which I have already examined—looks like a deflated, skin-toned balloon. I am tired and sore. I want to go home. When my water doesn't come, I crack open an eye. Aren't people supposed to be running circles around me after what I just did?

Baby and father are standing in front of the window, framed by the dim afternoon light like a cheesy hospital advertisement. All they need is a pithy hospital catch phrase to caption the moment: *Start your family with our family*.

I make the effort to study them. He is cradling her in his arms, his head bent so low their noses are almost touching. It should be a tender moment, but he is gazing at her with so much love, I feel jealousy do a little squeeze-squeeze on my heart. Jealousy has a hell of a strong hand. I squirm underneath its touch, uncomfortable for letting it in.

Why couldn't it have been a boy? It…my child. Fresh disappointment makes me press my face against the pillow, blocking out the scene in front of me. Two hours earlier, the doctor had said the word *girl* and tossed her blue, slime-covered body onto my chest. I hadn't known what to do. My husband was watching me, so I reached a hand up to touch her; all the while, the word *girl* was crushing down on my chest like a thousand-ton elephant.

Girl

Girl

Girl

I am going to have to share my husband with another woman…again.

"What are we going to name her?" He doesn't even look at me when he speaks. I feel I've earned a little eye contact. Mon pied! Already I was an afterthought.

I hadn't chosen a girl's name. I had been so sure it was a boy. Charles Austin—after my father.

"I don't know. Any suggestions?" I smooth out my bed sheets, study my fingernails. A name is a name, right? I don't even go by the one my parents gave me.

He looks at her for a long time, his hand cupping her head. She has stopped thrashing her fists around and is still and content in his arms. I know the feeling.

"Estella." The name rolls off his tongue like he's been waiting to say it his whole life.

My head jerks up. I was expecting something less…ancient. I scrunch up my nose.

"That sounds like an old lady's name."

"It's from a book."

Caleb and his books.

"Which one?" I don't read…unless you count magazines, but chances are if it was made into a movie, I probably saw it.

"*Great Expectations.*"

I narrow my eyes and get that sinking feeling in my stomach. It has something to do with her. I know it.

I do not verbalize these thoughts. I am too clever to call attention to my insecurities, so I casually shrug and smile in his direction.

"Any specific reason?" I ask sweetly.

For a minute I think I see something pass across his face, a shade coming down over his eyes like he's seeing a movie play out on his eyeballs. I swallow hard. I know that face.

"Baby—?"

The movie ends, and he comes back to me. "I've always liked that name. She looks like an Estella."

A catch in his voice.

She looks like a bald, old man to me, but I nod. I am incapable of saying no to my husband, so it looks like the kid just got screwed.

When he leaves for home to take a shower, I pull my phone from underneath my pillow and google "Estella from *Great Expectations.*"

One website calls her an enchanting beauty, says she has a cold-hearted personality and a superiority complex. Another says she was the physical representation of

3

everything Pip wanted and could not have. I put the phone away and peer into the bassinet beside me. Caleb does everything with purpose. I wonder how long he's wanted a girl. I wonder if the nine months I planned on having a son, Caleb was planning on having a daughter.

I do not feel anything—none of the gushing, maternal things my friends relayed to me about their own children. They had used words like: unconditional, all encompassing, love of my life. I had smiled and nodded, storing the words away for reference when I had my own child. And now here I am, emotionless. Those words mean nothing to me. Would I have felt differently if she were a boy? The baby starts to wail, and I jab at the nurse's call button.

"Need some help?" a mid-fifties nurse wearing Care Bear scrubs walks briskly into the room. I eye her gappy smile and nod.

"Can you take her to the nursery? I need to get some sleep."

Estella is wheeled out of my room, and I breathe a sigh of relief.

I am not going to be good at this. What was I thinking? I breathe in through my nose, out through my mouth like I do in yoga.

I want a cigarette. I want a cigarette. I want to kill the woman my husband loves. This is all her fault. I got pregnant to secure the man that I had already married. A woman shouldn't have to do that. She should feel safe in her marriage. That's why you got married—to feel safe from all the men who were trying to siphon your soul. I'd yielded my soul to Caleb willingly. Offered it up like a sacrificial lamb. Now, I was not only going to have to compete with the memory of another woman, but a shriveled-up baby. He was already staring into her eyes like he could see the Grand Canyon tucked away in her irises.

I sigh and curl into a ball, tucking my knees under my chin and gripping my ankles.

I have done a number of things to keep this man. I have lied and cheated. I have been sexy and meek, fierce and vulnerable. I have been everything but myself.

He is mine right now, but I am never enough for him. I can feel it—see it in the way he looks at me. His eyes are always probing, searching for something. I don't know what he's looking for. I wish I did. I cannot compete against a baby—my baby.

I am who I am.

My name is Leah, and I will do anything to keep my husband.

TWO
PRESENT

After forty-eight hours, I am discharged from the hospital. Caleb is with me while I wait to be discharged. He holds Estella, and I am almost jealous, except he touches me constantly—a hand on my arm, his thumb rubbing circles on the back of my hand, his lips on my temple. Caleb's mother came earlier with his stepfather. They stayed for an hour, taking turns holding the baby before sweeping off to lunch with friends. I was relieved when they left. People hovering over me while my breasts slowly leaked made me squirm in discomfort. They brought a bottle of Bruichladdich for Caleb, a Tiffany piggy bank for the baby, and a Gucci sweat set for me. Despite her uppitiness, the woman has excellent taste. I am wearing the set. I rub the material between my fingers as I wait to be wheeled downstairs.

"I can't believe we did this," Caleb says for the millionth time, looking down at her. "We made this."

Technically, I made this. It's convenient how men get to sign their names to these little creations without doing much more than having an orgasm and assembling a crib. He reaches out a hand and tugs on my hair playfully. I smile weakly. I can't stay mad at him. He's perfect.

"She has red hair," he says as if to establish her credibility as my child. She's a ginger all right. Poor kid will have her work cut out for her. It's not easy to pull off red.

"What? That fluff? That's not hair," I tease.

He brought a plush lavender blanket with him. I have no idea where he got it since most of our baby things are green or white. I watch him swaddle her in it, like the nurses taught him.

"Did you call the nanny agency?" I ask timidly. This is a sore subject between us, along with breastfeeding, which Caleb strongly promotes and I couldn't care less about. Our compromise consists of me pumping for a few months and then getting an augmentation.

He frowns. I don't know if it's because of what I've said or because the blanket is giving him problems.

"We're not getting a nanny, Leah."

I hate this. Caleb has all of these ideas about how things are supposed to be. You'd swear he was raised by Betty Fucking Crocker herself.

"You said yourself that you're not going back to work."

"My friends—" I begin, but he cuts me off.

"I don't care what those spoiled voids do with their children. You are her mother, and you will raise her, not a stranger."

I bite my lip to keep from crying. By the look on his face, I know I'm not going to win this battle. I should have known someone like Caleb Drake stands over what he owns, teeth bared, not allowing anyone to touch it.

"I don't know anything about babies. I just thought I could have someone to help…" I throw my last straw…pout a little. Pouting usually works in my favor.

"We'll figure it out," he says coolly. "The rest of the birthing world does not get the option of a nanny—they figure it out. So will we."

He is done swaddling Estella. He hands her to me, and a nurse comes in to wheel me to the car. I keep my eyes closed all the way, afraid to look at her.

When Caleb pulls my new "mommy car" to the curb, we discover that you cannot get a swaddled baby into the car seat. I would have immediately turned sour. When things don't go my way, I lose it. Instead, Caleb laughs, talks to the baby about how silly he is while he unwraps her. She is fast asleep, but he keeps up a dialogue. It's silly, a grown man carrying on like that. When she is strapped, he helps me in. Before he closes the door, he kisses me softly on the lips. I close my eyes and savor it, tasting his attention. There are so few kisses that make me feel connected to him. He is always somewhere else…with someone else. If the baby can bring us together, then maybe I was right to do what I did.

It is my first time in my new car, which Caleb picked up from the dealership this morning. My friends all have less expensive SUVs. I got the best. It feels like a ninety-thousand-dollar prison sentence, despite my initial excitement to have it. He points things out as we drive. I listen intently to the sound of his voice, but not the actual words. I keep thinking about what's in the car seat.

At home, Caleb lifts Estella out of her seat and places her gently in her new crib. He is already calling her Stella. I laze on my favorite chaise lounge in our big living room, flicking through channels on the television. He brings me a breast pump, and I flinch.

"She has to eat, unless you want to do it the traditional way…"

I snatch the pump and get to work.

I feel like a cow being milked as the machine hums and purrs. How is this just? A woman carries a baby for forty grueling weeks, only to be hooked up to a machine and forced to feed it. Caleb seems to enjoy my discomfort. He has a strange sense of humor. He is always teasing and delivering some witty quip that I often fail to respond to, but now as he watches me with that little smile playing on his lips, I laugh.

"Leah Smith," he says. "A mother."

I roll my eyes. He likes those words, but they give me heart palpitations. When I am done, there is a large amount of watery-looking milk in both bottles. I expect him to do the rest, but he returns with a wailing Estella in his arms and hands her to me. This is only the third time I have held her. I try to look natural to impress him, and it seems to work because when he hands me the bottle, he smiles and touches my face.

Maybe that is the key—pretending to love this motherhood deal. Maybe that's what he needs to see in me. I stare down at her as she sucks on the bottle. Her eyes are closed and she is making horrible noises like she's half-starved. This isn't terrible. I relax a little and study her face, looking for some trace of myself in her. Caleb was right; she has the makings of a redhead. The rest of her looks more like him—full, perfectly defined lips underneath a weird little nose. Surely, she will be beautiful.

"You remember I have a business trip on Monday?" he asks, sitting down opposite me.

My head snaps up, and I do nothing to disguise the panic on my face. Caleb is often away on business trips, but I thought he would take a few weeks off to let me settle in.

"You can't leave me."

He blinks at me slowly and takes a sip of something in a snifter glass.

"I don't want to leave her yet, Leah. But, she came early. No one else can go; I've already tried to find someone." He leans down in front of me, kissing my palm. "You'll be fine. Your mother is coming in on Monday. She can help you. I'll only be gone for three days."

I want to wail at this bit of information. My mother is a drama addict on top of being an insufferable narcissist. A day with her feels like a week. Caleb sees the look on my face and frowns.

"She's trying, Leah—she wanted to come. Just go easy on her."

I bite my lip to keep from saying something really nasty. I have a malicious side to me that Caleb finds offensive, so I curb it when he is around. When he is *not* around, I swear like a sailor and throw things.

"How long is she staying?" I grumble.

"Burp her…"

"What?" I am so distracted by my mother's imminent visit, I do not notice Estella is half choking, milk bubbling from between her rosebud lips.

"I don't know how."

He comes over, takes her from me, and places her against his chest. He pats her back in short little taps that make a heartbeat sound.

"She'll be here for a week."

I roll over and hide my face in a pillow, with my butt sticking up in the air. He smacks me on the rear and laughs.

"It won't be that bad."

I grit my teeth. "Nope."

I feel the couch give as he sits next to me. I peek at him through my hair, which is wrapped around my face in a red mask. He holds the baby with one hand and uses the other to clear my face, swiping hair gently over my shoulder.

"Look at me," he says. I do, keeping my one exposed eye away from the little lump against his chest.

"You okay?"

I swallow. "Yup."

He purses his lips and nods. "Nope and yup. Have I ever told you, you only say 'nope' and 'yup' when you're vulnerable?"

I groan. "Don't psychoanalyze me, Boy Scout."

He laughs and pushes me over so that I roll onto my back. I love it when he plays with me. It used to happen a lot more, but lately...

"It's gonna be okay, Red. If you need me, I'll jump on a plane and come home."

I smile and nod.

But, he is wrong. It will not be okay. The last time I saw my mother was when I was seven months pregnant. She flew down for my baby shower and complained the entire ride there about the horrible venue my girlfriends had chosen.

"It's a tearoom, Mother—not a bar."

At the shower, she refused to speak to anyone and sat in a corner sulking because no one had announced her as mother to the mother-to-be. A fistfight almost erupted with the tearoom's owner because they did not serve organic Brazilian honey. I have refused to see her since.

Caleb—ever forgiving, ever understanding—encourages me to see past her flaws and help her understand how to be a better mother to me. I love this about him, but I learned long ago that trying to be like him is beyond my reach. I pretend to understand what he is directing me toward and then do my own thing, which usually entails some sort of passive aggression. So, I agree with him wholeheartedly. I promise to make an effort with my mother and retire upstairs to get away from him and the noisy baby. I want a cigarette so badly it's killing me. I go to the bathroom and strip, then I look at myself long and hard in the mirror. My stomach has thankfully deflated. A few more pounds and I'll be back to normal. Now all I need to do is get my life back to normal.

THREE
PRESENT

My mother arrives on Monday as scheduled. We all go to the airport to pick her up. Caleb is wary about taking the baby out in public so soon, but I convince him that she'll be fine if we keep her in the stroller. I'm tired of sitting at home, tired of holding bottles, and tired of pretending that eight pounds of screaming human flesh is cute. Besides, I want a Jamba Juice. I'm sipping on my juice and following Caleb and the stroller around baggage claim when we spot her obnoxious blonde head coming down the escalator. I roll my eyes. She is wearing an all-white pantsuit. Who travels in all white? She waves at us brightly and trots over, first hugging Caleb and then me.

She leans over the stroller and claps a hand over her mouth like she's wrought with emotion.

God, I want to be sick.

"Ooooh," she coos. "She looks like Caleb."

This is absolute bullshit. I decided a day ago that she looks exactly like me. The kid has fluffy red hair and a heart-shaped face. Regardless, Caleb smiles broadly, and they engage in a five-minute conversation about Estella's eating and pooping habits. I'm confused as to how she knows anything about babies eating and pooping since a nanny raised my sister and me. I tap my foot impatiently on the tacky tropical carpeting and look longingly at the exit. Now that I'm here I just want to leave. Why did I think this was a good idea?

When Caleb's attention is diverted with the baby, my mother pokes me accusingly in my stomach and shakes her head. I suck in my belly and look around guiltily. Who else noticed? True, I had a baby only three days ago, but I was being so careful to stand up tall—suck in the belly fat. My momentary lapse embarrasses me. It's all I can think about on the ride home. I make a pact with myself to stop eating until I reassume my former figure.

At home, my mother insists on taking the room next to Estella's, even though I had the larger guest room prepared for her.

"Mother, what is the purpose of having this room?" I ask as Caleb deposits her bag next to the bed.

"I want to help you, Leah. Get up with her in the middle of the night and all that good stuff." She bats her eyelashes at Caleb, who smiles at her.

I hold my eye roll.

She is pretending to be enamored with the baby, but I know better than that. Public doting is what she does to spunk up her image, and when her audience is gone—so is the love. I remember being a child, having her stroke my hair, kiss my face, comment on how pretty I was—all in front of her friends. After they left, I would be sent back to my room to study or practice the violin—basically get out of my mother's hair, until the next of her "good mommy" performances.

"Really, Mother?" I say through my teeth. "How will you hear her after you've taken your sleeping pills?"

Her face becomes splotchy. Caleb elbows me in the ribs. We're not supposed to talk about her addiction to sleep aids.

"I won't take them tonight," she says decidedly. "I'll do the feedings so you can rest."

Caleb gives her a quick side hug before we all go downstairs.

I watch suspiciously from my barstool in the kitchen as she carries Estella around and sings show tunes to her. We small talk, or they do. I pick at my split ends.

"We're going to have a wonderful time while Daddy is gone," she coos to the baby. "You, Mommy, and I."

Caleb shoots me a warning look before going upstairs to get the last of his things for the trip. I am itching to make a snarky comment, but I remember my promise to him and hold my tongue. Besides, if she wants to play "Grandmother" and take care of all of Estella's needs while Caleb is gone, so be it. It would save me the trouble.

"Her hair is red," my mother says as soon as he's out of earshot.

"Yes, I noticed."

She clucks her tongue. "I always imagined that my grandchildren would be dark like Charles."

"She's not," I snap, "because she's mine."

She shoots me a look out of the corner of her eye. "Don't be so touchy, Johanna. It doesn't become you."

Always critical. I can't wait until she's gone.

But, then it hits me. When she's gone, Caleb isn't going to be staying home with the baby. I am. This business trip is the first of many during which I am going to have to pull all-nighters and change…human excrement…and—oh God—give baths. I almost fall off my barstool. A nanny—I have to break Caleb on this and make him see how much I need the help.

"Mother," I say sweetly—almost too sweetly because she looks at me with her eyebrows raised. "Caleb doesn't want me to get a nanny," I complain. I am hoping to get her on my side enough to talk to him about it.

Her eyes dart to the stairs where Caleb disappeared only moments before. She licks her lips, and I lean in to better hear what nugget of wisdom she is going to impart. My mother is a very resourceful woman. It comes from being married to a controlling manipulator. She had to learn how to get her way without getting her way.

When Court was eighteen, she wanted to go to Europe with her friends. My father had refused. Well, in actuality, he'd never verbally refused. He slashed his hand through the air as soon as the words were out of her mouth. The SLASH. It was a common occurrence in our Greek home. Didn't like dinner? SLASH. Had a bad day at work and don't want anyone to talk to you? SLASH. Leah crashes her fifty-thousand-dollar car for the fifth time? SLASH. At the end of all the slashing, Court had gone to Europe.

Remember when you were a poor boy? How much you wanted to travel? My mother.

She's still a child. My father.

It's good that she goes while we can still control her. We pay for the trip, the hotels, and the safest travel…much better than her going when she's in her twenties, sleeping her way through France. My mother.

My father hated the French.

He'd looked thoughtful. Mother's logic was appealing. He booked everything a week later. Court was under careful, controlled watch, but by God she got to go to Europe. I went to community college. She gave me a small painting that she bought from a street vendor. It was a red umbrella suspended in the rain like an invisible hand was holding it. I'd pulled aside the paper and had immediately known what she was trying to say. I'd started to cry and Court had laughed and kissed me on the cheek.

"Don't cry, Lee. That's the point of this painting, yeah?"

Two months in Europe and she was saying "yeah" at the end of all of her sentences.

Court is…was…so cute. I want to bring her up, but the subject is still touchy.

"What your husband doesn't know won't hurt him." My mother's voice snaps me back to the task at hand.

That's it? I stare at her blankly. How am I supposed to translate that nonsense into full-time baby help?

She sighs.

"Leah, darling…Caleb is away on business trips much of the time, is he not?"

I catch her drift and nod slowly, my eyes becoming wide at the possibility. Could I do it? Hire someone to come in and take care of the baby on the days that Caleb is gone?

My mother is an expert in the art of deceit. Once, before Caleb and I were married, we took a break at his request. He had just been in a terrible car accident and suffered major memory loss due to a blow to the head. To my absolute horror, he didn't remember who I was. I remember thinking, *How could this happen to me?* I was about to get engaged to the man of my dreams, and here he was, looking at me like I was a perfect stranger. I had quickly gathered my wits and resolved to be supportive until his memory came back. It was only a matter of time before he would remember how much he wanted to be with me and placed the huge Tiffany rock I had found in his sock drawer on my finger. But, instead of getting closer to me as we waited for his memory to come back, he pulled away, opting to spend more and more time alone. Soon, he announced that he was…seeing another girl, if *seeing* is the right word for the shadiness that was going on, and *girl* is the right word for the cunning, worthless tramp that almost ruined my life. I called my mother right away to report what he had told me.

"Follow him," she said. "Find out how serious it is, and make him end it."

I had done just that, following him one evening to a tacky apartment complex in an even tackier neighborhood. The blocky buildings were painted a bright salmon color. I glanced at the pitiful attempt at landscaping that did nothing to cheer the place up and parked my car a block away from Caleb's Audi. I was an emotional mess, knowing that he was probably going to see the girl. Through my rearview mirror, I watched as he walked right up to a door and knocked. He hadn't consulted a piece of paper or his phone to find it. It was as if he knew exactly where to go. The door opened, and though I couldn't see who was standing inside, I knew it must be her, because his face immediately broke out in a grin that was usually directed toward me: flirtatious and sexy. God, what was going on here?

I waited for several minutes before climbing out of my car and approaching the door. Just to make sure I was doing the right thing, I texted my mother, who responded with a firm: Go in there and get him before he does something stupid!

—Which was followed a few seconds later by a single word: Cry.

I did both, and Caleb left with me that night. But, it was a short-lived victory. The girl he was seeing was an old girlfriend from college. Unbeknownst to both Caleb and me, she was pretending to have just met him, trying to squeeze her way back into his life for another round. I found this out after breaking into her apartment. I went straight to his condo with the evidence clutched in my fist, ready to out her scheme. She looked like trouble. I should have known the minute I laid eyes on her that it wasn't a casual thing by some unsuspecting girl he'd met. It took me some time to figure out. He wasn't home when I got there. I let myself in with a key that he didn't know I had and studied the mess he left behind like I was a fucking CSI. He had obviously cooked dinner for two. There was still the unmistakable smell of steak lingering in the halls. Had she been here with him? I felt sick. I found two wineglasses in the living room, and in a panic, I rushed to the bedroom for evidence that they had been together. His bed was unmade, but I saw no sign of sex anywhere in the room. What traces would he leave behind anyway? Caleb didn't—wouldn't use condoms. I'd gone on birth control shortly after we started dating because of this. He said the sight of them turned his stomach, so I wasn't going to find any wrappers lying around.

Breathing a sigh of relief, I went to his dresser and opened a drawer, running my hands along the back of it until I found the square Tiffany box that held my engagement ring. I cracked it open and felt tears spring to my eyes. It had almost happened. He was getting ready to propose when that damn accident wiped me from his memory. I deserved to be with him, wearing my two-carat, princess-cut diamond ring.

I got rid of her.

For a while.

After I drop Caleb off at the airport, I go shopping. Seems sort of shallow, like I should feel guilty…but I don't. I want to feel the buttery silks beneath my fingers. I decide that since I no longer have a basketball attached to my waist, I need a whole new wardrobe.

I pull my new SUV into a spot at the Gables and head right for Nordstrom. In the dressing room, I avert my eyes away from my belly. It feels good to slide into dresses with cinched waists. By the time I head for the doors, I am carrying over three thousand dollars in merchandise. I toss everything on the backseat and decide to meet Katine for a drink.

"Aren't you nursing?" she asks, sliding into the seat next to me. She eyes my burgeoning breasts as she plucks a cherry from the bartender's garnish tray.

I shrug. "Pumping. So?"

She smiles all condescendingly and chews on her cherry. Katine looks like a blonde, botoxed Newt Gingrich when she's being snotty. I lick the salt from the rim of my margarita glass and feel sorry for her.

"So. You're not supposed to drink when you're nursing."

I roll my eyes.

"I have plenty of stock in the fridge at home. By the time I need to pump again, the alcohol will be out of my system."

Katine widens her eyes, which makes her look even dumber than a blonde should.

"How's Mommy Dearest?"

"She's watching Baby Dearest," I say. "Can we not talk about that?"

She shrugs like she couldn't care less anyway. She orders a gin and tonic from the bartender and drinks it entirely too quickly.

"Have you had sex with Caleb yet?"

I flinch. Katine has no filter. She tries to blame it on the fact that she's from a different culture, but she's been here since before she could walk. I motion for another margarita. The bartender is attractive. For some reason I don't want him to know I'm a mother. I lower my voice.

"I just had a baby, Katine. You have to wait at least six weeks."

"I had a C-section," she announces.

Of course I know this. Katine has regaled me with her disgusting birth story over a dozen times. I look away, bored, but her next words make my head snap around.

"Your vagina is going to be all stretched out and useless now."

First, I check to see if the bartender heard her, then I narrow my eyes. "What are you talking about?"

"Birthing naturally. What? Do you think everything just snaps back into place?" She laughs a true hyena laugh. I watch her exposed throat as she throws her head back to finish her cackling. How many times have I wondered what it would feel like to slap my best friend? When she calms down, she sighs dramatically.

"God, I'm just kidding, Leah. You should have seen your face. It was like I told you your kid died."

I toy with my drink napkin. What if she's right? My fingers begin itching to pull out my phone and google. I do some Kegels for good measure.

Would Caleb notice a difference? I break out in a sweat just thinking about it. Our relationship had always been about sex. We were the sexy couple; the ones who kept things alive when all of our friends were retiring into a life of half-lucid missionary sex after the kids went to sleep. For months in the beginning of our relationship, he would get this relieved look on his face when he reached for me and I responded. I never pushed him away. I never wanted to. Now, I had to consider that he might push me away.

I order another drink.

This was going to cause all kinds of new anxiety. I would have to schedule an appointment with my therapist.

"Look," says Katine. She leans toward me and her overly sweet vanilla perfume creeps into my nose. "Things change when you have a baby. Your body changes. The dynamic between you and your husband changes. You have to be inventive, and for the love of God, lose the baby weight…fast."

She snaps her fingers at a server and puts in an order for a basket of fries and fried calamari.

Bitch.

FOUR

I met Caleb at Katine's twenty-fourth birthday party. It was held on a yacht, which was significantly better than my twenty-fourth birthday venue at one of South Beach's swanky nightclubs. I invited two hundred people; she invited three. But, being that my best friend's birthday is four months after mine, she has the advantage of outshining me every year. I call it even since I am prettier and my father placed twelve spots above hers in Forbes.

I was wearing a black silk Lanvin dress that I'd seen Katine eying the week before as we shopped in Barney's. Her hips had been slightly too wide to accommodate the slim cut of the dress, so I scooped it up when she wasn't looking and bought it. She would have done the same to me, of course.

After making rounds among our friends, I headed to the bar for a fresh martini. I spotted him sitting on one of the barstools. His back was toward me, but I could tell by the width of his shoulders and the cut of his hair that he was going to be beautiful. I slid into the available seat next to him and shot him a look out of the corner of my eye. I noticed the strong jaw first. You could crack walnuts on that jaw. His nose was kind of weird, but not in an unattractive way. The bridge was curved, a slight bend in the road. It was elegant, the way an old revolver would be.

His lips were too sensual for a man. If it were not for his nose—that incredibly elegant nose—his face would have been too pretty. I waited a few customary minutes for him to look at me—normally I didn't have to work very hard to garner male attention—but when he didn't, I cleared my throat. His eyes, which had been focused on the television above the bar, turned slowly toward me like I was an imposition. They were the color of maple syrup if you held it up to the light. I waited for him to get that lucky look that all men got on their faces when they stumbled upon my attention. It didn't come.

"I'm Leah," I said finally, holding out my hand.

"Hello, Leah." He sort of half smiled as he shook my hand and then dismissively turned back to the television. I knew his type. You had to play hard to get with boys that had crooked grins. They liked the chase.

"How do you know Katine?" I asked, suddenly feeling desperate.

"Who?"

"Katine...the girl whose birthday party you're crashing?"

"Ah, Katine," he said, taking a sip from his glass. "I don't."

I waited for him to explain that he came with a friend or his distant relation to someone at the party, but he offered no explanation. I decided to try a new route.

"Do you need bourbon and a beer to go with that Scotch?"

He looked at me for the first time, blinking as if he was clearing his vision.

"Is that your best pickup line? Lyrics from a country song?"

I saw a hint of laughter in his eyes, and I smiled, encouraged.

"Hey, we've all got a vice and mine is country music."

He studied me for a minute, his eyes roving over my hair and stopping on my lips. He ran his fingers across the condensation on his glass, collecting the moisture on the tips of his fingers. I watched in fascination as he used his thumb to rub the moisture from his fingertips.

"Okay," he said, turning toward me. "What other vices do you have?"

I could have answered *you* right then and there.

"Uh-uh," I said, seductively shaking my head and leaning forward just enough to give him a bird's eye view of my cleavage. "I already let one out of the bag. Your turn."

He harrumphed and glanced at his sweaty glass. He spun it slowly as he looked back at me, like he was deciding whether or not it was worth it to continue the conversation. After a long pause, his eyes iced over and he said—"Poisonous women."

I sat back, startled. This was perfect. I was about a ten on the poison scale. If he needed venom, I could inject it directly into his neck.

He took a long, hard sip of his Scotch. I evaluated the situation. It was clear that this man had just played emotional dodgeball with a professional. He was nursing a very strong and expensive drink at a yacht party he'd rather not be attending. Despite the fact that I was offering up my goods, wearing a dress that left little to the imagination, he barely looked at me. Normally, a man on the rebound would not scare me. They could provide passionate, casual sex in the wake of their heartbreak. They see only the best things about you—the things that remind them of the better days with their ex, showering you in compliments, and clinging to you gratefully for a fun-filled week or two. I relish rebound men. But, this one was different. This one wasn't questioning his worth as a human because his relationship ended. He was questioning her sanity. Trying to figure out at exactly what point things had started to unravel.

He was immaculately dressed, without trying. He dressed that way by nature—which meant that he had money—and I loved money. I recognized the royal sign of the Rolex, the fine thread of Armani, the easy way he looked at the world. I also recognized the way he said "thank you" when the bartender refilled his drink, and how when the couple next to him swore repeatedly, he flinched. His type was hardly ever single. I wondered what stupid bitch let him go. Whoever she was, I would wipe her from his memory in no time at all. Why? Because I was the best of the best: the Godiva, the Maserati, the perfect colorless diamond. I could improve anyone's life—especially this man's.

With my newfound confidence in our future relationship, I smiled at him and crossed my legs so that my skirt hiked up my thigh.

"Okay," I said slowly. "Today happens to be your lucky day."

"Why is that?"

He didn't even look at my legs. I sighed.

"Well, I was going to say something smart ass about being poisonous too, but I think by the looks of you, you need a good dose of Jamba Juice or something."

He cracked up.

"See, I'm funny," I quipped.

"Yeah." He smiled. "A little."

Emboldened, I tucked my elbows back to my sides and twisted my barstool to face him. My knees were now touching his outer thigh, and he made no attempt to move away.

Sucker.

"So—" I pulled a pearl cigarette case from my pursette. "This is my other vice, do you mind?" He looked at the cigarette poised at my lips and shook his head. I lit and inhaled in one smooth move I'd managed to perfect.

"What's your name, Mr. Sad Eyes?"

His mouth twitched at the corners as his eyebrows did a little dance upward.

"Caleb," he said. "Caleb Drake."

I tried Drake on with my name and decided I liked it.

I blew my mouthful of smoke toward the ocean.

"I'm Leah…and if you play your cards right, I could be Leah Drake." I raised my eyebrows.

"Wow. Wow…" he said again. "That's almost refreshing."

"She didn't want to marry you?" I asked sympathetically.

"She didn't want to do a lot of things," he said, swallowing the last of his Scotch and standing up. He was wonderfully tall. I mentally placed myself right underneath his arm, which must make him at least six one.

I waited for his next move. Whatever he did, he was mine anyway.

He stood up and kissed my hand. I was confused.

"Good night, Leah," he said. Then to my utter astonishment, he walked away.

Confounded.

I thought we had chemistry.

I thought about him the following day as I nursed my hangover. Who was he? Why had he come? What had she done to him to make him pass me up? Me! I briefly entertained the idea that his ex was a celebrity. God knows he was good-looking enough to break a celebrity's heart. I thought about his cool nonchalance, the flutter I felt when he finally looked at me. Had I ever had to work that hard to make a man look at me? No. And when he did look, you wanted him to stop. He looked at you like he already knew you—direct, slightly bored, judgmental. He made you wonder how it would feel to be on the other side of that look, to have his eyes on you because he wanted them there.

I dug around a little bit, tried to find out who he was and where he hung out. I was a talented sleuth. My social network was broad and within two phone calls, I knew where to find Caleb Drake. Two more phone calls and I had someone setting us up on a blind date.

"Wait at least a month," I said to my cousin. "Give him more time to lick his wounds before I save him."

One month later, I was walking up to a sushi joint called Tatu, the heat clinging to my bare legs, my heart boom-booming against my ribs.

"No way," he said as soon as he saw me.

I feigned surprise. Dipping my head down, I asked, "Single and British, looking for a redhead?"

He laughed a stomach laugh and hugged me.

He was wearing a white button-down, rolled to the elbows with khaki shorts. He was golden bronze, like he'd been tanning every day since I last saw him.

"How do you know Sarah?" He held open the door for me, and I stepped past him.

"My cousin," I smirked. "How do you know her?"

Of course I already knew the answer. Sarah's boyfriend and Caleb were frat brothers. The night of Katine's party he'd tagged along with them.

I listened as he explained the connection. His accent was sexy. When we followed the host to our table, he put his hand on my lower back. It was familiar and possessive. I liked that. I wondered if he would have done that if this were our first time meeting.

"You know how Sarah lured me into this blind date?" he asked.

I shook my head.

"She told me you had good legs."

I smiled and bit my lip. "And?" I extended them out from under the table, ankles together. My dress was dangerously short. Of course I knew he liked a good pair of legs. I'd grilled Sarah's stupid boyfriend for an hour to find out everything I could about him.

He grinned. He looked me in the eyes when he said, "Not bad."

I felt the tingle all the way down to my toes. That was the look I was waiting for.

The next morning I woke up in his bed. Stretching, I looked around his room. My muscles were luxuriously sore. I hadn't been bent that many ways since I was a gymnast in high school.

I heard the shower in the adjoining bathroom, and I rolled over to see if I had a view of him through the open door. I did.

The previous night we made it through three drinks and dinner without a pause in conversation. It was like talking to someone I had known for years. I was so comfortable with him, and I presumed he was with me, because he answered any questions I had without hesitation. When we left the restaurant, there was no doubt whether or not I would go home with him. I hopped into his convertible, and we drove the short fifteen minutes to his high-rise. Our trail of clothes started at the front door and ended at the foot of his bed, where we playfully tossed aside the last of what I was wearing. It would be nice to be able to blame the alcohol for my recklessness, but truth be told, we both stopped drinking before we ate. Everything that happened…happened without the influence of liquor.

When Caleb got out of the shower, I was still leaning on my elbow. I made no pretense about watching him. He ran the towel over his hair, making it stick up. I smiled broadly and patted the bed. Dropping his towel, he climbed in next to me.

"Are you still sad?" I asked, leaning my chin on his chest.

He surrendered a half grin and tweaked my nose.

"I'm feeling a bit more cheerful."

"Oooh—a bit more cheerful…" I mocked his accent and started to roll out of the bed. He caught me by the ankles and pulled me back.

"A lot more cheerful," he offered.

"Wanna have one more go and then get lunch?" I asked, tracing my finger across his chest.

"Depends," he said, grabbing my hand.

I waited for him to continue without asking the customary "on what?"

"I'm not looking for anything serious, Leah. I'm still all messed up in the head from—"

"The last girl?" I smirked and leaned up to kiss him. "Whatever," I said against his mouth. "Do I look like a commitment sort of girl to you?"

"You look like trouble," he grinned. "When I was growing up, my mother used to tell me to never trust a redhead."

I frowned. "There are only two reasons she'd say something like that."

Caleb raised his eyebrows. "And they are?"

"Your father either slept with one, or she is one."

I buzzed under his crooked smile. It extended all the way to his eyes this time.

"I like you," he said.

"That's swell, Boy Scout. Real swell."

FIVE

Two days after Caleb leaves for his business trip, my mother packs her bags and informs me she's leaving as well.

"You can't be serious," I say, watching as she zips up her suitcase. "You said you wanted to stay and help."

"It's too hot," she says, lightly touching her hair. "You know I hate the summers here."

"We're in air conditioning, Mother! I need your help."

"You'll be fine, Johanna."

I notice the slight tremor in her voice. She's slipping into one of her depressions. Courtney was the one who knew how to deal with her when she got like this. I always seem to make it worse. But, Courtney isn't here; I am. Which makes Mother Dearest my responsibility.

I shrug. "Fine, let's get you to the airport. Caleb comes back at midnight, anyway."

Let her scuttle home to her Michigan McMansion and pine away, popping pills into her mouth like Tic Tacs.

On the way back from the airport, I crank up the radio and feel like a bird out of her nest for the first time. Estella starts screaming from her car seat five minutes into my bliss. What does that mean? She's hungry? Carsick? Wet?

I had almost forgotten she was there...here...on this planet...in my life.

I do some Kegels and think bitterly of Caleb—baby-free Caleb, who is basking in the Bahamian sun, drinking snifters of his damn Bruichladdich and eating crab cakes. It isn't fair. I need a nanny; why can't he see that? Caleb is such a stickler for what is right and wrong. With all of his old-fashioned values, I should have known that he would insist on me staying home and raising her myself. He is such a Boy Scout. Who raises their own children anymore? White trash, that's who—because they can't afford the help.

I bite my lip and turn up the volume on the radio to drown out the wailing. Right now she sounds like a tiny, shrill alarm, but what will happen in a few months when her lungs are stronger? How will I tolerate that noise?

I am trying to figure out how to get her to stop crying when something yellow catches my eye. To clarify, yellow is a terrible color. Nothing good comes from a color that represents egg yolks, earwax, and mustard. It's the color equivalent of a disease—festering sores and pimple puss, nicotine-stained teeth. Nothing, nothing, nothing should be yellow, which is precisely why I turn my head to look. Immediately, I swerve my car into the far-right lane and whip my steering wheel around like I'm on the teacups at Disney World. Choruses of car horns beep as I cut across two lanes of traffic to get to the plaza. I roll my eyes. Hypocrites.

Driving in Florida reminds me of navigating a crowded grocery store—either you're stuck behind an old fart schlepping along at a mile an hour, or you're being pushed into a cereal display by a hooligan. I am a good driver, so they can go screw themselves.

I follow the yellow sign into a strip mall and peer into the empty storefronts as my car edges through the parking lot. Crooked vacancy signs hang in most of the windows. The old store names still tacked above the doors are a depressing reminder that a recession is tiptoeing across the nation. I point a gun finger where a nail salon used to be and pull the imaginary trigger. How many little dreams had hit the dust in this crap-hole plaza? In the far-right corner near a gargantuan dumpster sits the Sunny Side Up Daycare. I pull my car underneath the grungy egg-yolk sign and tap my fingers on the steering wheel. To do or not to do? Might as well go take a look.

I jump out, head for the door, and remember that there is a baby in the car. Sons of guns and motherfuckers. I retrace my steps, making sure no one has seen my blunder, and creep back to unlatch Estella's car seat. She is mercifully silent as I haul her through the doors of Sunny Side Up Daycare. The first thing I notice is that anyone can just walk into this crapstablishment and steal a kid. Where are the key-card locked doors? I eye the receptionist. She is a frumpy twenty-something wearing blue eye shadow over dull brown eyes. She wants a boyfriend. You can tell by her overzealous use of perfume and cleavage. She has eyeliner on her bottom lid. Everyone knows you don't put liner on your lower lid.

"Hellooo," I chirp cheerfully.

She smiles at me and raises her eyebrows.

"I need to speak with your director," I say loudly, just in case she is as slow as she looks.

"What's it about?"

Why do people always staff their front desks with half-wits?

"Well, I have a baby," I snap, "—and this is a day-care."

Her nose twitches. It's her only indication that I've royally pissed her off. I tap my foot on the linoleum as she pages the director of the daycare. I take a look around while I wait. Pale yellow walls, bright orange suns painted across them, a stained blue carpet scattered with this morning's Cheerios. The director emerges minutes later. She is a midlife-crisis blonde wearing a Tickle Me Elmo T-shirt, scuffed pink Keds, and two melon-sized breast implants. I eye her in disgust and paste on a smile.

Before I can utter a word, she says: "Wow, that's a new one."

"She was premature," I lie. "She's older than she looks."

"I'm Dieter," she says, holding out her hand. I take it and shake.

"Would you like a tour of Sunny Side?"

I want to say "Hell no," but I nod politely, and Dieter leads me through a set of double doors that she opens with a key card.

The place is dingy, even Dieter must see that. Every room has its own unique pee smell, ranging from *Oh my God* to a subtle piney/pee combo. Dieter is either immune to the smell or she's choosing to ignore it. I can barely contain my gag. She highlights the student/caregiver ratio, which is six to one and points gaily to a classroom of singing four-year-olds who all have snot dribbling from their noses.

Sharing is caring.

"Our playground equipment is brand new, but of course your little one won't need that for a while." She opens a door marked "Teenies" and steps inside.

Immediately, I am greeted with multiple infant voices all braying like little baby donkeys. It is quite unnerving, and almost instantly, Estella wakes up and joins the donkey chorus. I swing her car seat back and forth, and surprisingly, her crying tapers off until she's quiet again. It is clean. I'll give Dieter that. There are six cribs pushed against the walls. Each one has a crocheted Muppet hanging over it.

"We just said goodbye to one of our babies," Dieter tells me. "So we have room for little—"

"Estella." I smile.

"This is Miss Misty," she says, introducing me to the caregiver. I smile at another dumpy girl, shake another hand with chipped nail polish.

In the end, I decide to leave Estella there for a test run. Dieter suggests it. "Just for a few hours to see how you feel—" she says. I wonder if it's normal—leaving your baby with strangers to *see how you feel*. I could slice myself open with a knife and I wouldn't feel a thing. I nod.

"I've never left her with anyone," I say. It is the truth...mostly.

Dieter nods sympathetically. "We will take good care of her. I'll just need you to fill out some paperwork in the front."

I hand the car seat to Miss Misty and make a show of kissing Estella's forehead, and then I run to the car to fetch the diaper bag that a good mother would have carried in with her.

Thirty minutes later, I am finally free—free of the insufferable belly, free of the noisy baby...free, free, free. Just then my phone rings. I collect it from the passenger seat where I'd tossed it earlier and see that Caleb is calling me. I smile despite myself. To this day, when Caleb calls I get butterflies in my stomach. I am about to answer it when I realize that he is probably calling to ask about Estella. I bite my lip and send him to voicemail. I can't ever tell him what I just did. He'd probably jump on the first flight available and storm into Miami clutching divorce papers. Maybe he'd even get *her* to draw them up for him. I know that I am being unreasonable and that he hasn't spoken to her since my trial ended over a year and a half ago, but thoughts of that raven-haired witch plague me every day. I push thoughts of my trial and my attorney to the back of my mind to rehash later.

I am determined to enjoy my baby-free time. I stop at home to change out of my jeans and put on something chic. I choose white linen pants and a Gucci blouse from my shopping trip, and I slip into a pair of kitten heels. By the time I am back in the car and halfway to the restaurant, I realize that I forgot my phone on the kitchen counter.

I meet Katine and a few of our friends for sushi and sake. When I walk into the restaurant, they all clamor around me like I've been gone for a year. I air-kiss each of them, and we sit down to order. Either Katine has warned them not to ask me about the baby, or they don't care because none of them breathes a word about her. Part of me is relieved because had I been called upon to discuss my feelings as a new mother, I would have burst into tears...though there is a slight annoyance there, as well. Even if Estella has been made a no-no topic, they could at least ask how I am feeling.

I let it slide. I drink four of those mini glasses of sake and then order wine.

Katine raises her glass to me. "To having you back!" she bellows, and we all take a drink.

I feel fantastic. I am officially back, though it has been a tough decade. In my sake-induced haze, I vow to make my thirties the best years of my life. By three o'clock, lunch is over and we are all sloshed, but not ready to head home.

"So," Katine whispers to me as we eventually exit the restaurant. "Where's the kid?"

"Daycare." I giggle and cover my mouth with my hand.

Katine winks at me conspiratorially. It had been her idea after all.

"Does Caleb know?" she asks.

I look at her like the dumb blonde that she is. "Seriously, Katine? Would I be wearing this if Caleb knew that his little precious was in a stranger's care?" I wiggle my wedding band at her.

She widens her eyes and puckers her lips like she doesn't believe me. "Come on. Caleb would never leave you. I mean, he had his chance with that Olivia girl and—" She slaps her hand over her mouth and looks at me like she's said too much.

I stop dead in my tracks, ready to slap her. The bitch. How dare she bring her up!

I am breathless, full of sake and anger, when I say: "Caleb never ever considered leaving me. She was nothing. Don't you go telling people those lies, Katine."

I know my face is red. I can feel it burning under the resentment. Katine's eyebrows unhinge. They dip down, giving the impression that she's genuinely sorry.

"I…I'm sorry," she stammers. "I didn't mean anything by it."

I know this pretty, blonde devil too well to buy into her Emmy-worthy apologies. I give her a disdainful look, and she smiles at me with saccharine sweetness.

"I just meant that he loves you. Not even that hot little piece of ass could take him from you."

Now I am seething. It is one thing to mention that trash's name, but to give credence to her obvious good looks crosses the girlfriend/loyalty line.

"Leah, wait," she calls after me as I storm off. I don't wait to hear her excuse—her favorite one being that she is from Russia and doesn't always understand the right way to communicate since English is her second language. I have heard them all before, and I know my slithering best friend. She likes to sugarcoat slurs, slander, and underhanded insults. *You are so courageous to wear that skirt; I'd be afraid my cellulite would show.* Katine is bulimic and doesn't have a stitch of cellulite. So, obviously she was referring to mine.

Katine Reinlaskz is as fun as a monkey at the zoo, but cross her and she'll rip you to shreds. Our relationship, which has existed since middle school, has been a vicious tug of war to possess things greater than the other. My first car cost sixty thousand—hers cost eighty. My sweet sixteen had three hundred guests—hers had four. I won with Caleb, though. Katine has been divorced twice. The first was a Vegas wedding, which lasted approximately twenty-four hours before it was annulled, and the second was to a fifty-year-old oil tycoon who ended up being a complete miser after they were married. She drips jealousy when it comes to Caleb—handsome, rich, gentlemanly, sexy Caleb. Every girl's dream and I got him. I use every opportunity to flaunt my major life triumph, but ever since that trouble with Olivia, Katine's envy has been replaced with smugness. She even had the gall to tell me once that she admired Olivia's gumption.

I take short, choppy steps to my car, being careful not to fall in my heels, and slide into the driver's seat. The clock on the dash says it's six o'clock. I am in no position to drive, but I don't even have my cell phone to call someone to pick me up. And who would I call, anyway? My friends are all similarly drunk and the ones who aren't here would raise their eyebrows and gossip if they caught me like this.

Suddenly, I remember Estella.

"Shit," I slam my hand against the steering wheel. I was supposed to pick her up at five, and I have no way of calling the daycare. I start the car and reverse out of the spot without looking. I hear a car horn and then the jarring crunch of metal. I don't even need to look to know that it's bad. I jump unsteadily out of the driver's seat and make my way to the rear of the car. An old Ford is folded around the bumper of my Range Rover. It looks almost comical. I suppress the urge to laugh, and then I have to suppress the urge to cry because I see the flickering blue and red lights of a police car approaching us. The driver is an older man. His wife sits in the passenger side of the car, clutching her neck. I roll my eyes and cross my arms over my chest, waiting for the inevitable ambulance siren that signifies sue-happy opportunists.

I lean down so I can see the old hag. "Really?" I say through the window. "Your neck hurts?"

Sure enough, an ambulance follows the patrol car into the parking lot. The medics jump from the cab and race to the Ford. I don't get to see what happens next because a mean-looking officer is approaching me, and I know I have seconds to get it together and act sober.

"Ma'am," he says over dark lenses. "Do you realize you backed into them without even looking? I watched the whole thing happen."

Really? I was surprised he could see anything through his Blade-wannabe sunglasses.

I smile innocently. "I know. I was in a panic. I have to pick my baby up from the babysitter," I lie, "and I am running late…"

I bite my lip because it usually excites men when I do it.

He considers me for a minute, and I pray he won't smell the liquor on my breath. I watch his eyes drift to my backseat where the base of Estella's car seat sits.

"I'm going to need to see your license and registration," he says finally.

This is standard procedure—so far, so good. We go through the accident process that I am all too familiar with. I see the old lady being loaded into the ambulance, and I watch as they drive away with the lights flashing. Her husband, callously enough, stays behind to take care of matters.

"Damn fakers," I whisper under my breath.

The officer shoots me a half smile, but it is enough to tell that he is on my side. I sidle up to him and inquire when I will be able to leave to get my daughter.

"It was so hard to leave her," I tell him. "I had a business dinner." He nods like he understands.

"We're issuing you a ticket—seeing that it was your fault," he says. "After that you are free to leave."

I breathe a sigh of relief. The tow truck comes and cranks apart the vehicles. The damage to my Range Rover is minimal compared to the Ford, which is practically folded in half. I am told that the Bernhards' insurance company will be contacting mine, and I am fairly certain that they will be hiring a lawyer in the next few days as well.

I pull out of my spot, relieved that the Rover is driving the same as it was when I pulled in. Aside from a dented bumper and some minor scratches, my pricey car came out unscathed. But, better yet, I came out unscathed. I could have been arrested and issued a DUI. Thanks to some great acting and a smitten cop, I am getting away with minor costs.

I feel almost sober as I drive carefully toward Sunny Side Up Daycare. When I pull into the parking lot, it is empty. I glance at the clock on the dash nervously. It reads seven ten. Someone must have stayed late with her. They will probably be angry, but surely after I explain what happened with the phone and the accident, they will understand. I push the buzzer on the door before I notice that it is completely dark inside. Pressing my hands to the glass, I peer in. Empty. Locked up; shut down. I panic. It's the type of panic I felt when I learned that I might go to prison for pharmaceutical fraud. The panic I felt as I stood in front of the judge expecting to hear the "guilty" verdict that would give me twenty years in state prison. It is purely selfish panic. The *ohmyword Caleb is going to divorce me for losing his daughter* panic. I have been a mother for less than two weeks, and I have already lost my baby. That's the shit that gets you on *Nancy Grace*. I hate that blonde bitch.

Pacing back and forth on the sidewalk, I contemplate my options. I could call the police. I mean, what is the policy on parents who fail to pick up their children from daycare? Do they send them to social services? Does the owner take them home? I struggle to remember the director's name—Dieter. Did she even give me her last name? Either way, I need to get to a phone and fast.

I drive home like I am in *The Fast and the Furious*—and careen my car into the driveway. My urgency is audible as I run through the door, not bothering to close it, and head for the kitchen counter where I left my phone. It's not there. My head swims. I was so sure that's where I'd left it. I am going to have a killer hangover tomorrow. *Think!* For the first time, I regret not having a landline. *Who needs a landline anymore?* I remember saying to Caleb right before we got rid of it. I spin around to head for the stairs, and my heart seizes in surprise.

"Looking for this?"

Caleb is leaning against the doorframe watching me. In his hand is my precious iPhone. I study his face. He looks calm—that means he doesn't know that I don't have Estella with me—or maybe he thinks she's with my mother. I haven't told him that I took her to the airport this morning.

"You're home early," I say in genuine surprise.

He doesn't smile or greet me with his usual warmness; instead he keeps his eyes trained on my face—the phone pinched between his fingers and extended toward me. I take a few precautionary steps in his direction, being careful not to let my remaining buzz show. Caleb reads me like a low-grade novel. I stand on my toes to give him a quick peck on the cheek before plucking the phone from his fingers. Now, if only I could get outside, I might be able to figure something out, call someone…FIND THE BABY!

I back up a few steps.

"You missed a call. Fourteen, actually," Caleb says casually—too casually—like the calm before a storm. The low, rumbling growl before the wolf rips out your trachea.

I swallow. There is sand in my throat and I'm drowning…suffocating. My eyes dart around the room. God—what does he know? How am I going to fix this?

"Apparently, you forgot to pick Estella up at daycare…" his voice trails off. An invisible hand cracks open my jaw and pours fear down my throat. I choke on it.

"Caleb—" I start. He holds up his hand for me to stop, and I do because I'm not even sure what excuse I can give.

I dropped our daughter off at a seedy daycare because...

Fuck.

I'm not that creative. My mind sieves out all of the possible excuses.

"Is she...is she here?" I whisper. The most expressive part of Caleb is his jaw. I use it to read his emotion. It is square, manly—only softened by his overly full lips. When that jaw is happy with you, you want to trace it with your fingertips, reach on your tiptoes to run kisses across it. The jaw is angry with me. His lips are white anger pulled tight. I am afraid.

Caleb doesn't say anything. This is his fighting technique. He heats up the room with his anger and then waits for you to sweat out a confession. He's never been violent toward a woman a day in his life, but I'd bet my life that little girl could make him do things he'd never considered.

I make the mistake of looking in the direction of the stairs. It makes him really angry. He bounces off the wall and walks toward me.

"She's fine," he says between his teeth. "I came back early because I was worried about you. Obviously, you were not the one I needed to be worried about."

"It was only for a few hours," I rush to say. "I needed some time alone, and my mother just up and left me..."

He studies me for a few beats, but not because he is gauging the truth of my words. He is asking himself how he could marry someone like me. I can see the utter disappointment. It scratches into the self-righteousness I am cradling to my chest. It makes me feel like a failure. Well, what did he expect—that I was going to be a good mother? That I would fall right into a role that I don't understand?

I don't know what to do. The alcohol is still babysitting my brain, and all I can think about is the fact that he's going to leave me.

"I'm sorry," I whisper, looking at the floor. Acting contrite is a cheap shot, especially since I'm sorrier for being caught than the actual deed.

"You're sorry for getting caught," he responds.

My head snaps up. *Fucking mind reader!*

How dare he think the worst of me? I am his wife! For better or worse, right? Or did the worse refer to the situation and not the person?

"You left your newborn daughter with complete strangers. She hadn't eaten in hours!"

"There was breast milk in the diaper bag!" I argue.

"Not enough for seven hours!"

I frown down at the tiles. "I didn't realize," I say, defeated. Had I really been away for that long?

I feel a surge of self-righteous anger. Was it my fault that I wasn't adhering to parental bliss like he was? I open my mouth to tell him so, but he cuts me off.

"Don't, Leah," he warns. "There are no excuses for this. If I had any sense, I'd take her and leave." He turns and walks toward the stairs.

My thoughts blur as my anger rushes in. "She's mine!"

He stops. It's an abrupt stop, like my words have just freeze-sprayed his legs.

When he turns back around, his face is red. "You pull a stunt like this again, and you'll be screaming that in court."

I feel my chest heave as his threat wraps around me like a cold wind. He means it. Caleb has never spoken to me with this much coldness. He's never threatened me. It's the baby. She's changing him, turning him against me. He stops right before he reaches the stairs.

"I'm getting a nanny."

Words I wanted, but now they don't feel like a victory. Caleb is conceding to a nanny because he no longer trusts me—his wife. Suddenly, I don't want one.

"No," I say. "I can take care of her. I don't need help."

He ignores me, taking the stairs two at a time. I trail behind, deciding if I want to be pleading or aggressive.

"I made one mistake; it won't happen again," I say, taking the pleading route. "And, you can't make that decision alone—she's my daughter, too." A speckle of aggression for good measure.

He's in our bedroom, rifling around in his bedside table. He pulls out his "little black book" which I have snooped in often. I follow him to his office, where he retrieves his cell phone from the charger.

"Who are you calling?" I demand.

He points to the door, telling me to get out. I stand firm, hugging myself, worry coiling in my stomach.

"Hey," he says into the receiver. His voice is intimate, insinuating. Obviously, he is on cozy terms with the person on the other end. I feel an icy chill hit my spine. There is only one person who makes his voice that soft, but why would he be calling her? He laughs at something the person has said and leans back in his chair.

Oh—God—oh—God. I feel sick.

"Yes, I do," he says all chummy. "Can you make it happen?" He pauses as he listens. "I trust whomever you send. No—no—I don't have a problem with that. Okay then, tomorrow? Yes, I'll forward you the address—oh you remember?" He smiles wryly. "Talk to you then."

I jump to action as soon as he hangs up.

"Who was that? Was that her?"

He pauses in his paper sorting to look at me quizzically. "Her?"

"You know who I'm talking about."

We don't ever talk about that—her. The muscles in his jaw clench. I have the urge to crawl under his desk and hide my head between my knees.

WHY

DID

I

SAY

THAT?

"No," he says, resuming his shuffling. "It was an old friend who owns a nanny agency out of Boca. Someone will be coming over to meet me tomorrow."

My jaw drops. Another secret part of his life that I know nothing about. How the hell is he connected to someone who owns a nanny agency?

"This is bullshit," I say, stomping my foot. "Are you at least going to let me meet her?"

Caleb shrugs. "Perhaps, though I assume you are going to have a hangover tomorrow…"

I inwardly shrivel. He always knows. He sees everything. I wonder if my breath gave it away, or if somehow he had seen my banged-up car bumper and guessed. I don't care to ask. I make a quick exit from the room without explaining myself and run upstairs. I stand in the door to our bedroom and glance down the hall. I feel a pang of something. Should I go check on her? I did practically desert her today. I should at least make sure she is okay. I am glad she is not old enough to realize what I did. Kids hold things against you.

Walking quietly down the hall, I push the door to the nursery open with my toe and peer in. I don't know why I feel so guilty looking at my own baby, but I do. I cross the space to her crib, holding my breath. She is asleep. Caleb has bathed and swaddled her, though she has managed to wiggle one of her hands free and is sucking on it. I can smell her from where I stand—the lavender soap Caleb bought for her mixed with the oatmeal smell of a new baby. I reach a finger down and touch her fist, and then I bolt from the room.

SIX

PAST

"Why do you have this?" I held up a pint of ice cream that had been sitting in his freezer since we met. It was Ben and Jerry's Cherry Garcia. I pried open the lid and saw that it was half eaten with a serious case of freezer burn. "You don't like cherries. Can I throw it out?"

Caleb launched himself from the couch where he was watching TV and took the container from my hand. I blinked at him in surprise. I'd never seen a man move that quickly for ice cream.

"Leave it," he said.

I watched him shove it behind a couple of frozen steaks and shut the door.

"That wasn't creepy at all," I said.

He looked seriously disoriented for a minute before taking my hand and leading me to the couch. He started kissing my neck, but my mind was still on the ice cream.

"Why don't we move in together?" I asked casually.

He paused what he was doing and rested his forehead in the curve of my neck.

"No," he said.

"No? Why not? We've been seeing each other for nine months. I'm here practically every night."

He sat up and ran his fingers through his hair, making it stand on end.

"I thought we weren't doing anything serious?"

My eyes bulged. "Yeah, in the beginning. You don't think this is serious? We've been exclusive for five months now."

That wasn't true. I had been exclusive from the day I met him. I hadn't so much as looked at another guy since the yacht. Caleb had admittedly gone on a few other dates, but in the end, he always landed back in my bed. What could I say? Sexually, I was a force to be reckoned with. Obviously, not enough of a force.

"Why is that ice cream in your freezer?"

"That's where you keep ice cream," he said dryly.

Caleb had a scar near his eye. I'd tried to get him to see my plastic surgeon about it, but he'd refused. Scars should stay where fate put them, he'd said. I laughed at the time. It was one of the most ridiculous things I'd ever heard.

Now, staring at my almost boyfriend, I knew I was right. Scars should be removed. Ice cream scars especially. I reached up and ran my finger across it. I didn't know where he got the scar. I'd never asked. What else did I not know about him?

"Was it hers?"

We rarely spoke about his ex, but when we did, Caleb's mood became damp and remote. Normally, I tried to avoid the subject—not wanting to look like the jealous new girlfriend, but if the guy couldn't get rid of her ice cream...

"Caleb?" I crawled onto his lap and straddled him. "Was it hers?"

He couldn't get away from me, so he opted to look me right in the eyes. That always made me nervous. Caleb had very intense eyes—the kind of eyes that stripped you right down to your sins.

He sighed. "Yes."

I was a little taken aback that he actually admitted it. I shifted uncomfortably on his lap, not sure whether I should ask the inevitable follow-up questions.

"Okay," I said, hoping he'd offer some sort of explanation. "Can we talk about this?"

"There's nothing to talk about," he said with finality.

I knew what that meant. There's nothing to talk about meant—I can't talk about it because it still hurts. And—I don't want to talk about it because I haven't dealt with it yet. Swinging my leg around, I slid off his lap and onto the couch. I felt paper-thin. I am seasoned in the art of men, and I know from experience that nothing can compete with a memory. It is uncharacteristic for me to not be the memory, so I was unsure of how to act.

"Am I not enough for you?" I asked.

"You're more than enough," he said seriously. "I was completely empty until you came along."

Normally, something like this coming from any man would sound cheesy…cliché. I've dated poets and musicians, all of whom were verbally gifted enough to give me goosebumps, though none ever had. But I felt warmth saturate my heart when Caleb said it.

"But, I told you from the start that I am not ready. You can't fix me, Leah."

I registered what he'd just said, but I didn't believe him. Of course I could fix him. He'd just told me that I filled his empty. What I didn't want to think about was who had created the empty…and how big of a hole she had left.

"I'm not trying to fix you," I said. "But, I am developing serious feelings for you, and you're basically rejecting me for a tub of Cherry Garcia."

He laughed and pulled me back onto his lap.

"I'm not moving in with anyone until I marry them," he said.

49

I hadn't heard anyone say this since I was fifteen and my parents forced me to go to Bible camp. "Swell," I said. "And I'm not sleeping with anyone until I marry them."

Caleb turned his best *I can have you whenever I want you* look on me, and I got so flustered I didn't know whether to kiss him or blush. He outplays my seduction attempts every time. *Power*, I thought with only half-dipped interest because he was kissing me. *He has power over me.*

We didn't mention the ice cream again, though every time I was in the vicinity of the fridge I felt like a base-dwelling bottom-feeder. The stupid Cherry Garcia turned into a body part to me. It was like he was keeping her finger in the freezer instead of just shitty ice cream. I imagined the finger wore black nail polish and scooted around the house when we weren't home. It was after my ring, I knew it. Ex-girlfriends have a way of keeping their fingers in things, long after they're gone.

It worried me at first, but Caleb was so present in our "non-serious" relationship that I forgot about it. I had more pressing matters vying for my attention, like my job at the bank and the everyday drama between my co-workers, and my upcoming vacation with Caleb to go skiing in Colorado. Everything needed my attention, and I was more than willing to spread my ear, input, and good-times expertise all around. We went another three months without talking about the finger. What we did talk about was us—what we wanted, where we wanted to go, who we wanted to be. When he talked about having children, instead of bolting from the room, I sat up and listened with a half-smile on my face.

We were three days into our ski trip when Caleb's college roommate called to tell him that his wife was in labor. As soon as he hung up the phone, he looked at me. "If we leave now, we can be there by tomorrow morning."

"Are you crazy? We have the cabin for two more days!"

"I'm the godfather. I want to see the baby."

"Yeah, you're the godfather—not the father. The baby will still be there in two days."

He didn't mention it again, but I could tell he was disappointed. When we finally did make it to the hospital, he was grinning from ear to ear, his arms loaded with ridiculous presents.

He held that damn baby for thirty minutes before he had to give him back to his mother to be fed. When he tried to pass him to me, I pretended to have a cold. "I'd love to," I'd said. "But, I really shouldn't."

The truth was, babies made me nervous. People were always shoving them at you, trying to get you to hold them and coo at them. I didn't want to hold someone else's spawn. Who knows what you could be holding? The kid could be the next John Wayne Gacy and you'd never know it.

Caleb was nuts for that baby. It sent him into baby-talk overdrive and got to me after a while. I started picturing little sandy-haired Calebs running around. I'd rewind a little to our picture-perfect wedding and rewind some more to the romantic proposal he'd deliver on the beach. I was planning out our lives and that goddamn finger was still in the freezer. If I could just get a little glimpse of her, maybe I'd understand.

Turns out I didn't have to wait long.

SEVEN
PRESENT

I wake up to the sound of an alarm. It is broken, obviously, because the beeping is not constant but wailing like a siren. Everything feels thick, as if my brain has been dipped in honey. I reach for the alarm—to turn it off—and then my eyes snap open. That is not an alarm. I jump up and look around my dimly lit bedroom, the covers slipping to my waist. According to my cell phone it is three o'clock in the morning. Caleb's side of the bed has not been touched. I wonder if he's in the guest room, and then I hear it again—the sound of a baby crying. I stumble toward the nursery. Where is Caleb? He must be with her. I walk into the nursery to see him pacing the room with her in his arms. His cell phone is pressed between his shoulder and ear and he's speaking rapidly. The baby is not just crying, she is screaming like she's in some sort of pain.

"What's—?" I stop when he holds up a finger to shush me.

He finishes off the conversation and tosses the phone aside. "Get your things. We're taking her to the emergency room."

I nod, cotton-mouthed, and run to throw on some clothes. Sweatpants, his Pink Floyd T-shirt...I race down the stairs and meet him at the door. He is strapping the baby into her car seat. She has not stopped crying since I left them in the nursery.

"What's happening?" I say. "Is she sick?"

He nods grimly and walks out the door with her. I follow on his heels and jump into the passenger seat.

I remember the things I've read about a baby's immune system. How you shouldn't have them around other children, foreign places. Keep them at home until they've had time to build antibodies to the many floating viruses.

Shit. He's going to hate me even more.

"She has a fever of a hundred and five." He jumps into the driver's seat, gunning the engine.

"Oh."

He looks at me out of the corner of his eye as we pull out of the driveway. What was that? Frustration? Disappointment?

I squirm for the entire ten-minute ride, shooting glances to the backseat where she is strapped. Should I have sat back there with her? What is the fucking protocol for being a mother? When we pull up, he hops out of the car before I can even open my door. The car seat is unstrapped, and Caleb is halfway to the emergency room doors before I can straighten my hair. I follow him in. He is at the nurse's station when the automatic doors hiss open for me.

She slides over a clipboard of paperwork and tells him to fill it out. I reach out before he can and grab it from the counter. He is in no state to fill out paperwork. I carry it over to a chair and get to work.

I can see the worry on his face as he speaks to a nurse. I pause to watch him. It is such a rarity to see him this way—vulnerable, fretting—the corners of his full mouth turned down as he nods at something she says and looks into the car seat at the baby. He glances back at me and disappears behind the emergency room doors with the nurse, not bothering to ask me if I want to come. I'm not sure what to do, so I ask the nurse at the desk if I can go back with them as I hand in the forms. She looks at me like I'm an idiot.

"Aren't you the mother?"

The mother. Not her mother or the baby's mother—just the mother.

I look at her frizzy hair and her eyebrows, which are in bad need of tweezing.

"Yes, I am the uterus that carried the child," I snap. I walk through the emergency room doors without waiting for an answer.

I have to peek into several curtained partitions before I find them. Caleb does not acknowledge my presence. He's watching a nurse hook Estella up to an IV while she explains the risks of dehydration.

"Where are they going to put the needle?" I ask, because clearly her hands are too small.

She gives me a sympathetic look before telling us that the IV needle will be inserted into a vein in Estella's head. Caleb's face drains of color. He won't be able to watch this, I know him. I straighten my back importantly. At least I can be of some use. I can stay with her while they do this procedure while Caleb waits outside. I am neither squeamish nor prone to tears, but when I suggest this, he looks at me coldly and says:

"Just because it makes me uncomfortable doesn't mean I'm going to leave her by herself."

I shut my parted lips. I can't believe he said that. I didn't leave her by herself per se. She was in the care of professionals.

I sulk in my hard, miserable chair while Estella wails down the emergency room. She looks pitiful and tiny beneath the beeping machines and wires that are snaking out from her small head.

Caleb looks like he's on the verge of tears, but he has her in his arms, careful not to disturb the wires. Once again, I am struck by how natural he is. I thought it would be this way for me—that the minute I laid eyes on my baby, I would know what to do and feel an instantaneous connection. I bite my lip and wonder if I should offer to hold her.

It *is* sort of my fault that she's here. Before I can stand up, the doctor pulls aside the curtain that separates us from the busy ER room beyond. He is middle-aged and balding. Before he greets us, he consults a clipboard in his hand.

"What do we have here?" he asks, touching Estella lightly on the head. Caleb explains her symptoms, and the doctor listens while examining her. He mentions that she was taken to daycare, and I shoot him a dirty look.

"Her immune system needs time to develop," he says, removing his stethoscope from her chest. "In my opinion, she's too young for daycare. Usually women take a short maternity leave before putting their child into full-time care."

Caleb shoots *me* a look. Seething. He is absolutely seething.

I focus on a box of latex gloves. He's going to yell at me. I hate when he yells at me. I can guarantee my skin has already erupted into a splotchy mess—a telltale sign that I'm shitting myself.

"I'm going to admit her so we can monitor her for forty-eight hours. She could dehydrate otherwise. Someone should be in to take her up to pediatrics in a few minutes."

As soon as he leaves the room, Caleb turns to me.

"Go home."

I stare at him with my mouth open.

"Don't you take that self-righteous tone with me," I hiss. "While you go traipsing all over the country, I'm stuck at home—"

"You carried this little girl, Leah, in your body." He makes a motion with his hands that makes it look like he's holding an invisible ball. Then just as suddenly, he drops his arms to his sides. "How can you be so calloused?"

"I—I don't know." I frown. I had never thought of it like that. "I thought it was a boy. I would have felt differently if—"

"You were given something…a life. That is so much more important than shopping and drinks with your fucking girlfriends."

I jerk at his F-bomb. Caleb hardly ever uses profanity.

"I'm more than that," I say. "You know I am."

His next words spear through my soul, laying me out in the most profound hurt I have experienced.

"I think I've fooled myself into believing you are."

I spring to my feet, but my knees fail me. I have to lean against the wall for support. He's never spoken to me this way.

It takes a few seconds to coerce the words from my tongue. "You said you would never hurt me."

His eyes are frigid. "That was before you fucked with my daughter."

I leave before I explode.

Forty-eight hours later, Caleb returns from the hospital with the baby. I saw him twice while he was there—both times to drop off breast milk. I am sitting at the kitchen table, reading a magazine, and eating green beans straight from the freezer when he walks in carrying her car seat. He has more hair on his face than I've ever seen him with, and his eyes are dark and tired. He takes her up to her room without saying a word to me. I expect him to come right back down and give me a rundown of what the doctor said. When he doesn't, I sneak upstairs to see where he is. I hear the shower running, so I decide to wait on the bed.

When he comes out of the bathroom, he has a towel wrapped around his waist. My first thought is of how gorgeous he is. I want to jump his bones despite what he said to me. He kept his facial hair. I kind of like it. I watch him drop the towel and pull on his boxer briefs. The best thing about Caleb is not his perfect body, or his half-smiles, or his even sexier voice…it's his mannerisms. The teasing, the way he runs his thumbnail across his bottom lip when he's thinking, the way he bites his tongue when he's turned on. The way he makes me look at him when I have an orgasm. He can undress you with one look, make you feel like you're standing naked in front of him. I know from experience, it's a pleasure to be naked in front of Caleb. I think of the angles I could go with—an apology and make-up sex…a slap to the face and angry sex. I am extremely proficient at seducing him. It's likely that he won't believe any apology I try to offer. I go for something new.

"I'll try harder."

He continues getting dressed without looking at me…jeans, T-shirt. I don't know what to do, and for the first time, it occurs to me that I may have taken things a little too far. I guard my true self so well from Caleb. I try to live up to his expectations. This time, he caught me with my panties down.

"I think I have postpartum," I blurt.

He looks at me. I breathe a sigh of relief. The best way to manipulate Caleb is by lying about medical conditions. He's had stress- and shock-induced amnesia. If anyone could relate to an uncontrollable medical condition, it should be him.

"I'll…I'll go see a doctor about it. I'm sure they can prescribe something…" I let my voice trail off.

I can see his profile in the mirror. His Adam's apple bobs as he swallows, and he rests his forehead on his thumb.

"I have to interview the nanny," he says. "We'll talk about this later."

He strides from the room without a backward glance.

I refuse to hide when Caleb interviews Estella's potential nanny. I dress in a blush-colored Chanel suit and park myself in the formal living room to wait. Whomever Caleb called the other night is coming with the nanny candidate, and I want to see whom he was speaking with so much familiarity. I wonder if this person was a part of his life when he had amnesia. There is so much I still do not know about that time in his life, and I'm constantly wondering what he got up to without my supervision.

The doorbell rings. I stand to my feet, smooth out my skirt. Caleb eyes me suspiciously as he walks through the foyer. I hear him greet them warmly, and then seconds later, he appears around the corner. I see the man first. He is shorter than Caleb and stocky. He bears a striking resemblance to Dermot Mulroney—that is, if Dermot had a goatee and shaggy hair, and dressed like a slob. I eye his jeans and tucked-in button-down. He has one of those distasteful sleeve tattoos—which is peeking out of his cuffs. I immediately dislike him. He is a most unlikely owner of a nanny agency. He should at least iron his clothes.

The girl that follows behind him gets my catty seal of approval. She is a petite blonde with a pretty oval face. She looks innocent enough, except that she has heavily lined come-hither eyes. Unlike her sloppy employer, she is wearing Dolce's newest pantsuit in sage green with an exact pair of snakeskin Louboutins that I have in my closet. How can a nanny afford to buy such expensive clothes? And then I realize she probably has one nice suit that she saves for interviews to impress potential employers. I won't let her wear makeup like that when she's with Estella. I don't want my neighbors thinking that I got my nanny from an escort service. And besides, in my house, I get to be the most beautiful woman. I make a mental note to tell her that her uniform needs to be khaki pants and a white polo, and then I smile at them politely.

"Leah," Caleb says in a clipped voice. "This is Cammie Chase." The nanny smiles—one of those smug, puckered smiles where one corner of her mouth dips in. I immediately dislike her, too.

"And this is Sam Foster."

Sam extends his hand toward me.

"How do you do," he says slowly, maintaining uncomfortable eye contact with me. His hands, I notice, are rough and calloused—something I'm not used to feeling. The men who run in my circles have the smooth skin of businessmen, their only work being to type rapidly on keyboards. His hand lingers in mine, and I have to pull away first.

I offer them something to drink. Sam declines, but Cammie smiles boldly at me and requests a Perrier. I look from her employer to her and wonder if he will reproach her for such a rude request, but he is talking to Caleb and doesn't notice. I decide to play nice. I'm not going to give her the job anyway, so why not send her away with a few sips of Perrier.

I excuse myself to the kitchen and come back with a tray carrying the green bottle of sparkling water, a glass, and two frosty beers—one for Caleb and one for Sam— even though he declined a beverage. They look at me as I set it down on the table.

As soon as I've taken a seat, Cammie looks at me expectantly and asks: "Do you happen to have a wedge of lime?"

It takes all of my control to keep my mouth from falling open. Surely this time Sam will say something. But, he smiles at me politely and ignores the little witch's outlandish request.

"We have some in the drawer of the fridge," Caleb presses. I glare at him for encouraging this sort of behavior from the potential help and stand up to get it.

When I return with my neatly sliced wedge of lime, Cammie takes it from me without even saying thank you.

I sit down in a huff, not even bothering to smile.

"So—" I say, turning my body away from Cammie and directing my attention to Sam, "—how do you know my husband?"

Sam looks confused. His brows dip together and his gaze shifts from Caleb to me.

"I don't," he says. "This is the first time we're meeting."

I blink in confusion.

Caleb, who is reclined casually on the love seat like he is visiting with old friends, smiles at me knowingly. I know that smile. He is amused at my expense.

I look at everyone's faces and slowly the picture pieces together. Cammie's audacity, the expensive clothing...

I try not to let my shock show as everything suddenly makes sense. We are not interviewing Cammie for the position of Estella's nanny—we are interviewing Sam!

I can see on their faces that they know about my mistake. It's embarrassing. The little blonde bitch, who I see in a new light now that I know she owns her own company, smiles, showing her teeth for the first time. She is evidently delighted by my blunder. Sam looks slightly more abashed. He looks away from me politely, and I clear my throat.

"Well, I suppose I got it all wrong," I say generously, though I am inwardly fuming.

There is collective laughter—the loudest being from Cammie—and then Caleb turns to Sam.

"Tell me about your experience," he says.

Sam rises to the challenge, listing his childcare experience. He has a master's degree in child psychology from the University of Seattle. He practiced clinically for two years before deciding that he didn't like the politics of being a counselor—how cold and impersonal it felt. He decided to move somewhere sunny—South Florida—and get a new degree in music, which he intended to use when he opened a rehabilitation center for abused children.

"Music heals people," he says. "I've seen what it can do for a broken child, and I want to heavily incorporate it into the center, but I need to have a degree in it first."

"So," I say more skeptically than I intend. "You spent seven years getting a master's degree and now you want to be a nanny?"

Caleb clears his throat and takes his arms off the back of the sofa where they were resting. "What Leah means is, why not practice part-time while you finish up the degree? Why nanny when the financial benefits aren't nearly as great?"

I lift my nose and wait for his answer.

Sam laughs nervously and rubs the hair on his face.

"Actually, being a counselor doesn't exactly line your pockets, if you know what I mean. I did it for reasons other than money. And, I don't come cheap as a child-care provider," he says honestly. "Notice I'm sitting in your living room, which is a significant step up from middle-class America."

I sniff at his mention of our money. I was taught it was bad manners to point such things out verbally.

"I have a daughter," he adds. "Her mother and I split up two years ago, but you can say I am well versed in taking care of babies."

"Where is your daughter?" I ask.

Caleb shoots me a warning look, but I ignore him. I don't want some wild kid running around my house on the days that he has her. And besides, she might get the baby sick. Something I can't point out in lieu of my latest escapade.

"She's in Puerto Rico with her mother," he says.

I picture a beautifully exotic Latin woman that shared his home, but not his last name. Their daughter would probably have her mother's hair and her father's light eyes.

"Her mother moved back there after we split up. That's part of the reason I chose to come to Florida—so on weekends I can fly over to see her." I wonder what type of woman takes her child so many hundreds of miles away from her father, especially when she can use him as a babysitter on the weekends.

"Sam," Cammie finally speaks up, "is my cousin. I promised him my best job, and when Caleb called I knew it would be a perfect fit."

"And, how do you know Caleb?" I say, finally getting the opportunity to address the question that's been on my mind.

For the first time, Cammie looks unsure of how to answer. She looks to Caleb, who smiles at me indulgently.

"We went to college together," he provides simply. "And, frankly, Sam, if Cammie recommends you—family or not—I believe you're the best." He winks at Cammie, who raises her eyebrows and smiles.

An alarm goes off in my head. Caleb was a hotshot basketball player in college. He slept his way through the cheerleading squad, and then went on to meet that home-wrecking bitch Olivia. I narrow my eyes at Cammie. Did she know Olivia? Had they competed for my husband? My questions are left unanswered, as money becomes the topic of conversation.

I half listen as Caleb offers Sam a generous salary, which he accepts, and before I can protest that I would prefer a traditional female nanny—preferably one with both a large ass and a large facial wart—Caleb is standing up and shaking Sam's hand.

It is decided. Sam will take care of Estella five days a week, with evenings off to attend class. He will start tomorrow, as Caleb leaves in two days on another business trip and he wants to make sure Sam is settled before he goes. Which is code for: My wife doesn't know what she is doing, and I have to teach you how to coerce her to use the breast pump.

I sigh, defeated, and remain seated as Caleb walks them to the door.

Well, I got my way—kind of.

EIGHT

I was not a commitment girl. Until Caleb rejected me—then I was. We'd had the talk, the one where I asked him where we were going, and he looked at me like I was a space alien.

"You knew," he'd said. "You knew when you got involved with me that I wasn't looking for commitment."

I countered that I hadn't been looking for anything, either. That things change when people *click*.

But, Caleb had remained firm. He wasn't ready. He didn't want me. He wanted her. He hadn't exactly said that, but I knew it down to my marrow. I knew it by the way he always looked away when I brought her up. He wouldn't even tell me her name. Whoever had ruined him had ruined everything for me.

I felt like a small piece of regurgitated potato skin. He just wanted to fuck me. I was curled up on my own sofa, after leaving his place in a fit of rage. I wanted to do something destructive. I called every single one of my slutty, ho-bag friends and arranged to meet them for drinks.

I walked into the bar and had three numbers within an hour. Normally, I didn't give any of the douchebags who approached me the time of day, but there was a doctor with an accent I found attractive. I tucked his number into my purse and had another drink.

By the time I left the bar, I was sufficiently sauced. Nothing new for me. I climbed into my car after bidding my girlfriends good night and hadn't driven five blocks when I crashed into a parked SUV. I sped off before anyone could notice me, but I was severely shaken.

I called my mother.

Her voice was impatient when she answered.

"Mom, I got into an accident. Can you come get me?"

"I'm in bed."

"I know. I'm sorry. I'm drunk. I need you, Mom."

She sighed heavily. I heard my father's voice in the background and her snap—"It's Leah. She's gotten into some sort of trouble. She wants me to go get her."

They exchanged words I couldn't hear, and then she was back on the line. "Did anyone see you?"

I told her no.

"Good," she said.

They spoke some more. My father sounded angry.

I waited patiently, massaging my head. It had hit the steering wheel on impact, and I felt the beginnings of a headache.

Her voice came back on the line. "Daddy is sending Cliff. He'll bring you to the house."

Cliff was my father's driver. He lived in a little apartment on their twelve-acre property. I thanked her, trying to hide the disappointment in my voice, and gave her directions to where I was.

What had I expected? My mother hopping in her little, red Mercedes and driving to my rescue? A hug? I wiped the tears from my face and shrugged away the hurt feelings.

"Don't be such a fucking little baby," I told myself.

Cliff arrived ten minutes later. He parked his pickup in an empty lot and jumped in the driver's seat of my car. I looked over at him gratefully.

"Thanks, Cliff."

He nodded and shifted the car into drive. The good thing about Cliff was that he wasn't a talker. When we pulled through the gates of the mansion, all of the lights were out. I stumbled through the front door—which was left open for me—and felt my way up to the spare room. No mother waiting, no father waiting.

I cleaned up in the bathroom, put a Band-Aid on the cut on my forehead, and swallowed three Advil for my headache. Crawling into bed, I drifted off, thinking of Caleb.

I woke up to the sound of my name. It was my mother's voice, impatient. I sat up quickly and flinched at the pain that zigzagged across my scalp. She was standing next to my bed, fully dressed, her hair coiffed on top of her head in a perfect chignon. Her lips were ruby red and pulled tight. She was angry with me. I flinched again and pulled the sheet up to my chin.

"Hi, Mama."

"Get up."

"Okay…"

"Your father is very angry, Johanna. This is the third time this year you've had an incident with your car."

I shifted uncomfortably. She was right.

"He's having breakfast. He wants you to come down so he can speak to you."

I nodded. Of course he would send my mother. My father never spoke to me unless my mother—ever his envoy—summoned me for a meeting. Even when I was a little girl, I remember being called this way when I did something naughty.

I hurriedly dressed in my clothes from the night before and followed her down the stairs to the dining room. He was sitting in his usual spot at the head of the table, with the paper spread out in front of him. At his elbow was a cup of coffee and a goat cheese and spinach omelet. He didn't look up when I walked in.

"Sit," he said. I scooted into a chair, and the housekeeper brought me a coffee and a small, white pill.

"Johanna," he said, snapping his paper closed and peering at me with his hard, grey eyes. "I've decided that it's in your best interest to come work for me."

I started. I already had a job. I worked as a teller at a local bank. My father did not employ family; he called it a conflict of interest. Just last year, my cousin begged to be taken on as an accountant and my father refused.

"W-why?"

He frowned. *Why* was not a word my father enjoyed hearing.

"I mean—you don't believe in mixing family and work," I rushed. My palms were sweating. God, why did I drink so much last night?

My father was handsome. He had olive skin and greenish grey eyes. He had spent ten hours a week in the gym for years and had the physique to show for it. With my flaming red hair and pale skin, I look nothing like him.

His eyes locked onto mine and in that moment, I knew what he was saying.

A dull ache worked its way across my chest as if it was searching for something. It found my heart, ripped it open, and climbed inside. I picked my emotions up from the floor and looked my father in the eyes. If he wanted me to leave my job and work for him, I would leave my job and work for him.

"Yes, Daddy."

"You'll start Monday. You can take the Lincoln while your car is in the shop. Leave your keys with Cliff."

He reopened his paper, and I knew I'd been dismissed.

I stood up, wanting to say something else, wanting him to say something else.

"Bye, Daddy."

He didn't even acknowledge I'd spoken.

My mother was waiting for me in the hall. She handed me the keys to the Lincoln. This was such a well-oiled operation.

I drove straight to the bank and informed them I would not be returning to work. Then I headed to my townhouse with the full intention of drinking a bottle of wine and going to sleep. When I got home, Caleb was sitting on my doorstep. I stopped short. He was in his work clothes: grey pants and a white button-down, sleeves rolled to his elbows. He was sitting with his legs spread, elbows resting on his knees and looking at the ground, seemingly deep in thought. When he heard my heels on the concrete, he looked up…smiled. It was his crooked smile. It reached all the way to his eyes and made you wonder if he was picturing you naked. God, I was so lost to this man. I walked right past him and unlocked the door. When I opened it, he stood and followed me inside.

Afterward, we ordered Thai food and sat in bed eating it. I was still a little raw from my conversation with my dad—not to mention, I'd just slept with Caleb, again, after he told me he didn't want me.

"Why did you come here? You can't come for booty calls and then tell me I'm not good enough to be your girlfriend."

He set his container down on the side table and turned to face me.

"That's not what I said."

"You didn't need to, asshole. Actions speak louder than words."

He nodded. My chopsticks froze on the way to my mouth. I had expected him to at least put up a fight…deny it.

"You're right. I'm sorry."

He took my container of curry and my chopsticks and put them next to his. I wiped my mouth with the back of my hand while he was distracted. Something big was happening. I could feel it.

He pulled me onto his lap so that I was straddling him.

"I'm only going to talk about this once. No questions, okay?"

I nodded.

"I was with her for three years. I loved her…love her," he amended. Jealousy rushed. That's all it did—rushed through me with nowhere to go. It felt like I was going to pop from the pressure. I bit the insides of my cheeks.

"You never quite stop loving someone when you're in that deep." His eyes kind of glazed over at that point. "Anyway, we were really young…and stupid. I couldn't control her the way I wanted to; she was too strong for me. I made a really bad decision one night and she caught me."

"You cheated on her?" Up until that point I had kept my mouth shut, too afraid to speak in case it broke the rare chatty moment he was having.

The muscles in his jaw clenched, and his nostrils flared.

"Yes—no." He rubbed his forehead. "I was…" He dropped his hand to my hip. He looked so tortured that I reached up to put my palm against his cheek. I knew a little about Caleb's father. He was a notorious womanizer. Currently, he was married to a woman younger than me. It was his fourth marriage. From what I gathered from Caleb, he highly disapproved of his father's behavior, so cheating was coming as quite a surprise to me.

"I'm not a cheater, Leah. But, God, that woman doesn't trust anyone…"

I took a deep breath and let it ooze from between my lips. He watched me carefully, trying to gauge my response.

"But, did you do anything with her?"

"Not technically—no."

I didn't understand what he was saying. Did he think that he cheated just because he wanted to cheat? Did he want to cheat?

"Leah," he swiped my hair over my shoulder, his fingers brushing against my skin. I shivered. We were having a serious discussion and all I could think about was—

I shook my head in frustration. "Either you fucked her or you didn't."

He sighed. "I never cheated on her. Not in the traditional sense of the word."

"God, I don't even know what that means."

He tilted his head back and laughed. "Obviously our moral compasses do not point in the same direction."

I blushed. A rare thing for me to do.

"Leah," he said. "I like you. More than I should at this point. But, I'm still a mess. I can't be in a relationship if I'm only in halfway. I still love her."

My eyes filled with tears. He was telling me that he couldn't even try to love me because he loved someone else.

"Fuck." I swung my legs off of him and sat on my side of the bed. The sheet was pushed down to his waist. I looked at him out of the corner of my eye. His face was wiped of emotion.

"So what are you saying? May I remind you that you showed up on my doorstep, not the other way around?"

He laughed and, tackling me to my back, leaned over me.

"I am very attracted to you." He kissed my nose. "I care about you. When you left the other night, you were hurt."

"Yes, I was."

"And now?"

I smiled up at him. "Now, I'm hurting in a different way."

He laughed. He had a great laugh. It started as a rumble in his chest and then rolled out in a smooth, raspy wave. Every time I made him laugh, I felt triumphant.

I suddenly grew serious. "I can make you forget her."

His lips were still curled in a half-smile. His eyes grew foggy as he looked down at my mouth.

"Yeah?"

I nodded. "Yeah."

"Okay, Red," he said, softly winding a piece of my hair around his finger.

I giggled—also an unusual thing for me to do. *Red.* I liked that.

He kissed me softly and slid on top of me.

We made love. It was the first time in my life that someone made love to me. It had always just been sex.

I fell hard that day.

NINE

I am in my Juicy sweats and a tank top, making a smoothie in the kitchen, when Sam arrives for work the next day. I am supposed to be watching Estella—who is napping in her movable bassinet—while Caleb takes a shower, but by the time I let Sam in the front door, I have forgotten where I parked her.

"How are you?" Sam greets me warmly, carrying a duffel bag over his shoulder. I wonder if he is planning on spending the night. I am creeped out by the thought of it.

"So, where's my charge?" he says, rubbing his hands together and smiling. For a minute, I think he is referencing a credit card—because it's something I say often as I browse the mall and scrounge around in my purse for my American Express—and then I realize he's talking about the baby. It takes everything in me not to roll my damn eyes.

The baby's insatiable hunger rescues me as she begins to mewl from somewhere over my shoulder. It is then that I remember wheeling her into the dining room. I glance toward her bassinet in annoyance.

"I'll get her," Sam says, taking control and walking past me. I shrug with indifference and wander toward my laptop. He walks back into the room, cradling her in his arms, just as Caleb bounds down the main staircase—his hair still damp from his shower. I feel a surge of lust just looking at him. Caleb ignores me and walks over to slap Sam on the back like they're old friends. He hasn't spoken to me since our late night trip to the hospital, other than to ask a question about the baby or to spout an instruction. I turn away and sulk while they discuss things that don't interest me. I am planning a trip to the spa and deciding how many treatments I can fit into eight hours when Caleb calls my name. Desperate to be the center of his attention, I forsake my computer and look up at him hopefully.

"I won't be home until later," he says. "I have a business dinner."

I nod. I remember when I used to accompany him on those business dinners. I open my mouth to tell him that I'd like to come, but he's kissed the baby and is halfway to the door. I sigh and turn my attention to the manny.

"So you're related to your boss," I say lamely, biting into an apple. Sam raises an eyebrow at me, but doesn't respond. My mind goes to that place where I wonder if Caleb ever slept with Cammie.

"Do you…um…do you hang out with her much?"

He shrugs. "Cammie has a lot of friends. Martinis with the girls really isn't my thing."

"But, don't you want to meet someone?" I ask, getting sidetracked. He's pretty good-looking if you're into the grungy musician type. Hellooo, grunge died with Kurt Cobain.

"Is that where you'd hang out if you were single?" He looks directly at me when he asks. It's a simple question, but the look in his eyes makes me feel like I'm being interrogated.

"I'm not single," I snap.

"Proof," he holds the baby up. I look away.

"Have you met any of her friends?" I am hoping for a reference of some sort to Olivia. It would be nice to know if she plays into this somehow.

Sam plays dumb. I can't tell whether or not he knows something.

"Eh, a couple here and there," he says dabbing Estella's mouth with a burp rag. "Are you sure you don't want to do this?" He nods toward the baby. "I don't want to take away your time with her."

When he looks down at her, I roll my eyes.

"Nope, I'm good," I say pleasantly.

"You're not bonding with her, are you?" he says, without looking at me.

I'm glad he can't see my face. My face is smeared in shock. I force my features into neutrality.

"Why would you say that?" I narrow my eyes. "You've known me for what? Five minutes?"

"It's nothing to be ashamed of," he says ignoring me. "Most women experience some form of depression after they give birth."

"Okay, Dr. Phil. I am not depressed!" I turn away and then spin back around. "How dare you judge me—you think you're qualified to 'diagnose' me, psych boy? Why don't you take a good square look at your own parenting skills? You have a kid in Puerto Rico, buddy…without you."

Sam seems unfazed by my words. Instead of recoiling like I want him to, he looks at me thoughtfully.

"Caleb is a pretty nice guy."

I stare at him. What did that matter? Was this some type of psychological trick? Some sort of trap that will confirm to him that I suffer from the baby blues? I lick my lips and try to see his angle.

"Yes? And?"

He takes his time answering me, setting the bottle on the counter and positioning Estella on his shoulder for another round of burping.

"Why would he marry a girl like you?"

At first, I think I hear him wrong. Surely not…he couldn't have said what I think he did. He's the help—a lowly manny. But, when he looks at me expectantly, waiting for an answer, my eye begins to twitch—an embarrassing reaction. I feel heavy under my rage. Like I can lift it from my shoulders where it landed and throw it at him.

So rude! So inappropriate!

I briefly consider firing him, and then I see milk erupt from Estella's mouth and run down the back of his shirt. I scrunch up my nose. Better him than me. I turn on my heel and charge up the stairs, as if motherhood herself is chasing me.

When I shut my bedroom door, the first thing I think about is sex. I have the urge to rip someone's clothes off—someone being Caleb, of course. When I was seventeen, my therapist told me that I use sex to validate myself. I promptly had sex with him.

The second thing that enters my mind is the box of Virginia Slims I keep stashed in my lingerie drawer. I go there now and run my hand across the wood paneling at the back. It is still there, half full. I pull a lighter out of an arrangement of silk flowers and head for the balcony that sits off my bedroom. I have not had a cigarette since my sixth month of pregnancy, when I sneaked one after a particularly stressful night at my in-laws' house. I light up while replaying Sam's grody comments in my mind. I would have to talk to Caleb. Obviously, Sam could not continue to work for us after saying such terrible, degrading things to me.

I wonder what he meant by "a girl like you"? People had used that line on me many times in my life, but it was usually to deliver a compliment or to grease the prospects of my bright future. A girl like you can go far in the world of modeling. A girl like you can be anything she wants. A girl like you can have any guy she wants.

Sam had said it differently. There was no compliment, just…why would he marry a girl like you?

I suck on my cigarette, relishing the comfort it brings. Why did I ever give these things up? Oh yeah—because I wanted to have a damn baby. I stub out what's left of it on the stone edging of the balcony and toss it expertly into some bushes on the ground level. Caleb cannot stand the smell of cigarette smoke; in fact, it was his one and only complaint about me when we were dating. He begged, pleaded, and went on sex strike to get me to stop smoking, but in the end it took getting pregnant for me to kick the habit. I was going to have to shower if I didn't want to get busted. I'm already in enough trouble. I strip down to my bra and panties and head toward the bathroom, when I see Sam appear in the garden with Estella. He's wheeling her in her carriage—a three-thousand-dollar purchase I have yet to even touch. I watch him with narrowed eyes, trailing him as he winds along the garden path, wondering if he saw me smoking. It doesn't matter, I decide. By the end of the day, he will be gone for good.

"Your days are numbered, buddy," I say tersely, before closing the bathroom door.

Caleb comes home after Sam is already gone, which has both foiled my plans and left me alone with the baby. I am chewing on celery, when he walks in the door carrying take-out.

He drops the bag on the kitchen counter and goes straight upstairs to check on the baby. I ignore them and dig around in the bag to see what he's brought me. When he comes back down, he's holding her.

"Wha—? Why did you wake her up?"

I was hoping to spend some time with him without her butting in.

He sighs, opens the fridge. "She's a newborn. She eats every three hours, Leah. She was awake."

I glance at the baby monitor and remember that I turned it off to take a nap. I must have forgotten to put it back on. I wonder how long she's been awake.

"Oh."

I watch as he puts the cold breast milk into the bottle warmer. I can count on one hand the times I've fed her. So far, either Caleb or Sam has done her feedings.

"She's six weeks old today," I say. I'd been counting down the days until I could sleep with him again. I almost hadn't made it to the six-week mark when he came back from his run the week before. He is at his best when he's sweaty.

The food in the bag is making my mouth water. I start eating without him. He brought chicken masala from my favorite little place. We eat from there so often I have the calories all worked out. If I eat one full chicken breast, five mushrooms, and scrape off most of the sauce, I can get away with two hundred calories. I have to force myself to stop eating. I want the last piece of chicken, but if I'm trying to lose the baby weight...

He still hasn't looked at me.

"Thank you for dinner," I say. "My favorite."

He nods.

"Are you just never going to talk to me again?"

"I haven't forgiven you."

I sigh. "Really? I hadn't noticed."

His lips pinch together. I hop off my barstool and make a brave move. He raises his eyebrows as I gently take the baby from his arms and lay her across my forearm as I've seen Sam do.

"She burps quicker this way," I tell him, imitating Sam's movements. The baby plays along brilliantly, burping loudly seconds after I do the little pat-pat. I relocate her to the crook of my arm and reach for the rest of her bottle. Caleb watches it all without uttering a word.

I smile at him sweetly.

Come on, you bastard. Forgive me.

I feed her the rest of her bottle and repeat my burping trick.

"Do you want to put her back, or should I?"

He takes her from me, but this time he holds my eyes for one…two…three seconds.

SCORE!

While he puts her to sleep, I run upstairs to put on something sexy. I am so nervous when I get back to the kitchen, I rip open a bag of frozen broccoli and cram a handful into my mouth.

I'm wearing a black nightie. It's not presumptuous. I don't want Caleb to know I'm trying to have make-up sex. I saunter around the kitchen until he comes back down. When I hear him on the stairs, I make a show of rewashing the bottles Sam cleaned earlier. I hear him behind me. He pauses in the doorway, and I smile knowing that he's looking.

When he moves to the living room, I follow him. When he sits down, I crawl onto the couch next to him.

"It'll never happen again. I was having trouble bonding with her. Things are much better. I need you to believe me."

He nods. I can tell that I haven't convinced him, but he'll come around. I'll play mommy, and soon he'll be looking at me like he used to. I kiss his neck.

"No, Leah."

I jerk back, narrowing my eyes. Who was using sex as a weapon now?

"I want to say sorry." I pout a little, but he only looks annoyed.

"Then say it to Estella." Then, he gets up and walks away. I roll onto my back and stare up at the ceiling. Rejection. Had that ever happened to me before? I couldn't remember a time. This was getting out of hand.

I want to call someone—a girlfriend…my sister. I need to talk about what just happened, gain some perspective. I reach for my cell and scroll through my contacts. I pause when I reach Katine. She'd only half listen to what I said, and in five minutes we'd be talking about her. I keep scrolling. I reach Court and my heart throbs. Court! I dial her number. Before it can go through, I hang up.

TEN

I remember humid summers, with air so thick it felt like you were breathing soup into your lungs. We'd get restless at home—my sister and I, running up and down the corridors of our big house, screaming and chasing each other until we'd get in trouble. My mother, exasperated, would send us outside with our nanny, Mattia, while she rested. Mattia made frequent trips to the dollar store for things to do outside. Courtney and I, who spent most shopping excursions at stuffy boutiques, found it endlessly amusing that you could go to a store and everything inside was a dollar. She'd bring us sidewalk chalk, jump ropes, hula hoops, and of course, our favorite—bubbles.

Mattia always saved them for last. She'd pretend that she forgot the big pink container inside, and we'd sigh and pout. At the last minute, she'd pull it out from behind her back, and we'd jump and cheer like she was so clever. We called the bubbles "empty planets" and the game was to pop as many empty planets as you could before they could self-implode and send their debris hurtling toward Earth. Mattia would stand underneath a tree for shade and blow them for us. Our legs were perpetually covered in bruises from this game. We got into the habit of tripping each other to reach the empty planets first. We'd run so fast Mattia said we looked like blurs. She called us the Red and the Raven for our respective hair colors. At the end of the game we'd tally up how many bubbles we'd popped. Twenty-seven for Red, Twenty-two for Raven, she'd announce. Then, we'd limp inside happily, rubbing our bruised shins and asking for Popsicles. My mother hated the bruises. She made us wear hose to cover them. My mother hated most things associated with me—the tangles in my hair after a bath, the color of my hair, the way I chewed, the way I laughed too loud, the way I flicked my fingernails across my thumb when I was in trouble. If you asked me, then or now, what she actually liked about me, I wouldn't be able to tell you. What I could tell you was that my childhood was the cool pop of bubbles on my skin. Court and I laughing and breathing soupy air. Mattia giving me hugs to compensate for the sharp words of a distant mother.

My mother loved my sister. My sister was worthy of love. I remember walking in on them once, as she was brushing Courtney's hair after her bath. She was telling her a story about when she was a little girl. Courtney was giggling, and my mother was laughing along with her.

"We would have been good friends if we'd grown up together. You are just like me when I was your age." I sat on the edge of the bathtub to watch them.

"What about Jo?" Courtney asked, shooting me a smile that was missing its two front teeth. "Would you have been good friends with her too?"

It was like she hadn't even noticed I was in the room until Court said my name. She blinked at me slowly and smiled at her youngest daughter. "Oh, you know Johanna and her books. She wouldn't have had time to play with us, all that reading she does."

I wanted to tell her that I would burn every book I owned to be a part of their little mother/daughter club. Instead, I just shrugged. Courtney was a lot like my mother, the only difference being that she actually liked me.

I should have been jealous of her, but I wasn't. She was the kind one in my family; the one who got up early on my birthday and piled a plate with Little Debbie snack cakes and sneaked them into my room singing "Lake of Fire" by Nirvana. My birthday was on the Fourth of July— a huge imposition to my parents who hosted a party for the company on that day. But, Court always made sure the day was special. When my straight A's went unnoticed, she would pin my report card to the refrigerator and circle my GPA in red marker. She was the love in my otherwise loveless life...the warm blanket in a household that valued frigid emotional temperatures. When everyone else skimmed right over me, my sister zoned in. We had a bond and bonds were hard to come by.

When I brought Caleb home for the first time, my father noticed me. It was as if he could finally look at me now that I had secured a man of Caleb's caliber. Not only was my new beau from money, he was well spoken, respectable, and ambitious...and he knew a damn lot of sports trivia.

They'd invited us for dinner. I watched them from my perch on the sofa. My dad laughed at everything Caleb said, and my mother buzzed around him like he was a blue blood. My sister was sitting next to me—so close our legs were touching. When we were together, we were always this close. It was a quiet rebellion against our parents. You try to create a divide between us, but we resist. When my parents were distracted with Caleb, Court elbowed me in the ribs and wagged her eyebrows. I burst into laughter.

"Methinks you did *good* on this one," she said. "Any good in bed?"

I pulled a face at her. "Why would I be with anyone who was not?"

She raised her eyebrows. "I dunno, Lee, remember that guy from high school? The one with the chin dimple?"

I snorted into my glass of wine. Kirby, that was his name. The name in itself should have told me everything. You could not take a man whose name sounded like a video game avatar seriously. Especially when his head was between your legs and he started humming Kiss while making aggressive jabbing motions with his tongue.

"Women, not girls, rule my world, I said they rule my world..." My sister sang the lyrics, squeezing her eyes shut and biting her lip like Kirby used to do.

We erupted into laughter, earning a disapproving look from my mother. I swear that woman still had the ability to make me feel fifteen. I looked at her defiantly and laughed louder. I was twenty-eight fucking years old. She couldn't control me anymore.

I thought everything went splendidly until we climbed into the car. Caleb was holding the door open for me when he suddenly said, "Your dad's a chauvinist."

I blinked in surprise. He didn't say it as an accusation. It was more of an observation. It was a true observation. I shrugged.

"He's a little old-fashioned."

Caleb pulled me into a hug. He was looking at me strangely, his eyebrows drawn and his mouth pulled into a thoughtful pucker. I'd come to know this as the "I'm psychoanalyzing you" face. I wanted to pull away so he couldn't see into me, but pulling away from Caleb was like shutting yourself in a freezer. If he was shining on you, you wanted to stand under his warmth, soak it all up. Pathetic. It was also beautiful. No one had ever given me as much warmth. I clung to his arms and let him psychoanalyze to his heart's desire. I wanted to know what he was seeing when he looked at me so intensely. He broke the spell, suddenly grinning.

"So, I guess you'll be staying home, barefoot and pregnant?"

I raised my eyebrows. When he said it, it didn't sound so bad. "Will this be in your home?" I asked. I was being coy. He kissed the tip of my nose.

"Maybe, baby."

He let me go too soon. I wanted to stay there and talk about whose baby I was pregnant with, if the floor my bare feet were standing on was hardwood or tile? If we'd be living in a two-story or a ranch house? My head was spinning. That was as good as a proposal for me. The man was golden. He even made my father look at me like I was human. We'd only been together around eight months, but if I played my cards right I could have my ring by spring. That was a happy night for me.

It didn't take me long to realize that Caleb was my empty planet.

ELEVEN

I jump up when I hear Caleb's car in the driveway. We've been together for more than five years, but I still get butterflies whenever he walks into a room. I try not to look needy, but when his key turns the latch and he steps inside, I fling myself at him. I need him to forgive me. I've been in perpetual twilight since he stopped smiling at me.

I catch him off guard, and he laughs as my weight slams him into the wall. I have my legs wrapped around his waist and my nose pressed to his. I want to make out with him like we used to do when we first met, but the first thing he says is—"Where's Stella?"

The smile drops from my face. I hate that. How am I supposed to know?

I sigh and slide down his body, disappointed. "Probably with whatshisname."

Caleb narrows his eyes at me; his mouth is a straight line.

"Did you spend any time with her today?"

"Yes," I snap. "I fed her this morning because the manny was late."

The muscles in his jaw pop as he grinds his teeth. They pop. I flinch.

Pop…flinch…pop…flinch.

I feel self-righteously angry. It wasn't unusual for mothers to rely on nannies to take care of their babies. In my circle, it was perfectly normal. Why did he always have to make me feel inferior?

I curl my upper lip across my teeth. "Do you think Olivia would have made a better mother than me?"

For a second, undisguised anger flashes across his eyes. He turns away, turns back to me, and turns away again like he doesn't know whether or not to confront the fact that I said her name.

I want a fight. Every time he looks at me like I'm a big, fat disappointment, my mind goes to Olivia. It's like shifting gears for me; Caleb's disappointed eyes trigger it. Suddenly, I'm in that magical place where I release the clutch, the gas pedal goes down, and my mind is racing toward Olivia. Fuck. That. Bitch. What power does she have over him? I want to run at him, pound my fists against his chest for always mentally comparing me to her. Or am I the one mentally comparing myself to her? God, life is so messed up.

Just then, Sam comes into the room with the baby. The anger on Caleb's face melts away, and all of a sudden, he looks like he's about to cry. I know that look; he is relieved—relieved to have something other than me. I turn and walk toward the door.

"Where are you going?" Caleb asks.

"I'm hanging out with Sam tonight," I say. I avoid Sam's face and snatch up my purse.

"Let's go, Samuel," I snap. I see him stifle a smile as he ducks his head obediently and walks to where I am waiting. I am out the door and down the stairs before Caleb can say anything. I hear them exchange words behind me, but I am halfway to Sam's car, and I decide that stopping to eavesdrop will ruin my credibility. Caleb is probably warning him about my tendency to become belligerent when drunk. Sam comes jogging out a minute later. Without a word, he opens the passenger-side door for me, and I climb in. He drives a Jeep, the kind that has no roof or real windows. I settle into my seat and stare straight ahead. I'm going to destroy Olivia. I'm going to find her and beat the crap out of her for ruining my life.

"Where to?" Sam says, looping around the driveway.

"Call that slutty-looking cousin of yours," I say. "We're going wherever she is."

He raises his eyebrows at me but doesn't move toward his phone.

"She's at Mother Gothel tonight," he explains. "You ever been there?"

I shake my head.

"Great. It's your kind of place." He shifts his Jeep into traffic, and I grab onto the door to steady myself. This was going to be a long drive.

Mother Gothel is not my kind of place. I announce this loudly as we walk through the door. A bouncer with half a dozen face piercings checks our IDs. He eyes me in a way that makes my skin crawl, and I grab on to Sam's arm.

"What the hell is this place?" I whisper as we enter into a room lit by electric blue lights.

"A hookah bar," he says. He raises his eyebrows. "An emo hookah bar."

I wrinkle my nose. "Why would she come here?" I was thinking of all the classy bars on Mizner Avenue, just a stone's throw away from this depressing rathole.

"She goes through phases," he says, nodding toward the bartender. "Last month it was tearooms."

He orders two dirty martinis. As I take mine, I wonder how he knew I drink them.

"Aren't you going to lecture me about liquorfying my breast milk?" I say over the rim of my glass. He groans and tries to take it from me.

"Shit, I forgot," he says. "It's hard to remember that a cold shrew like you is actually a mother."

I grunt and hold it out of his reach. Touché.

We make our way over to a table, where a small group of people is clustered together. I see Cammie's blonde head bobbing around animatedly, as she tells a story. When she spots Sam her face breaks into a smile...until she sees me. Her blinks come in rapid succession, like she's trying to expunge me from her vision. I smile sweetly and head in her direction. This bitch has info on Olivia. I can feel it. I bend down to kiss her on the cheek. I like to keep my greetings European.

"Sam," she says tightly, "I didn't know you were bringing a...guest." She cocks her head in a way I've only seen Southern belles do. I place her accent to Texas.

"First night out since the baby?" she asks me.

Sam grunts from behind me. I spin around to shoot him a warning look and then turn back to Cammie.

"Sure," I say. "Sam was kind enough to let me tag along. Cool bar!" I look around in mock interest. When I look back at her, she's on the tail end of an eye roll.

She motions toward two available chairs. I take the one closest to her, and Sam sits down next to me. She makes introductions around the table. The group is composed of two attorneys, a professional skateboarder that keeps shooting looks at Cammie's exposed cleavage, and a number of pierced, tattooed lesbians.

For the next hour, I listen to them prattle on about the most dull topics in the world. I play with my hair and try not to yawn. Sam watches me in amusement as he contributes to their conversation. Twice, he catches me unawares by asking my opinion on politicians.

"Really, Sam," I finally snap when no one is listening. "Can you not?"

He grins. "Just trying to be friendly."

How does someone with so many tattoos know about politics? Am I stereotyping? Too bad. I lean close to his ear so only he can hear me. Cammie frowns.

He's gay! I want to scream at her. And, even if he weren't, seriously, I don't do sloppy men.

"I'll give you a hundred bucks if you can get everyone out of here so I can talk to your slutty cousin alone."

Sam stands up and claps his hands. "I'll buy everyone a shot, except for Cammie."

Cammie rolls her eyes but stays seated. Everyone else follows Sam to the bar, laughing and clapping each other on the back.

She looks at me expectantly, like she's on to my scheme.

I swear this bitch and I speak the same language...in different accents.

"Olivia Kaspen," I say. Her face registers nothing. "Do you know her?"

Her lips curl into a smile, and she dips her head once to acknowledge that she does. I feel searing heat start in my chest and spread outward. Emotional fireworks, if you must. I knew it! I lick my lips and pull a cigarette from my purse.

"That's how you know Caleb," I say. She nods, that awful smile still on her lips. I inhale and watch her through my lashes.

"Why does he love her?" This was the first time I had ever verbalized the question, though I had pondered over it for God knows how many years. Olivia was attractive— if you were into sluts. She had too much hair and wide-spaced eyes, but I had been around her enough during my trial to know how men responded to her. She was aloof, cold. It was mysterious. Goddamn men and their goddamn mysteries. I had never seen her smile. Not once. It was hard to believe someone as alive and warm as Caleb could have feelings for an emotional prune.

Cammie is watching me, trying to decide how far she wants to go with her answer. I wonder how well she knows Olivia. It had never occurred to me, until now, that she might be good friends with her.

Eventually, she clears her throat. "Well, she's a bitch like you. Caleb has always been attracted to the Cruella de

Vil type. But, I suppose if you want an honest answer…" her voice trails off. The band comes on stage and things are starting to get loud. I lean forward, hungry for her answer.

"They spark," she says. I jerk back. What the hell did that mean? "When they're together, it's like putting a hurricane and a tornado in the same room—you can feel the tension. I didn't believe in the cliché of soulmates until I saw them together."

I've heard enough. I am sick to my stomach. I look around for my ride and can't see him anywhere, but Cammie's not done.

"I know you got pregnant on purpose," she says, plucking my cigarette from my fingers and taking a draw. I blink at her, too intrigued to argue. How could she possibly know?

"Now, you've got the guy…and the baby. You won. So, why are you asking about Olivia?"

I consider lying, telling her that I'm making sure she is gone for good or some bullshit like that.

She smirks. "You want to know why he loves her, Leah?" She overemphasizes the *ah* in my name. I flinch.

What a bitch.

I shake my head, but the little blonde is smarter than she looks.

She stubs out my cigarette. "You won't find an answer to that from anyone but Caleb. If I were you, I'd let it go. Go enjoy the life you stole for yourself. Olivia won't be showing up at *your* doorstep crying, if that's what you're worried about."

I feel my face heat as I remember the time I followed Caleb to Olivia's apartment. That was insider information. The little bitch is probably her best friend.

"He wouldn't leave me for her even if she did." I say this with more confidence than I feel.

Cammie raises her eyebrows and shrugs. "Then why do you care?"

I swallow hard. Why do I care? It isn't like I grew up in a home where my parents were madly in love. My mother married my father for money; she'd told me so on numerous occasions. I have my guy, so why am I picking at the scab?

"I—I don't know."

"It's not fun to be second choice, is it?" She plucks a piece of tobacco from her tongue and flicks it off her fingertip. "There is a possibility that you feel like you're worth more than being Caleb's marriage of pity, and if that's true then you should jump ship now. It's only a matter of time before the Caleb/Olivia saga starts up again."

Her words sting. I shift around in my chair as pain courses through me. "I thought you said she moved on?" I hiss.

"Yeah, so?" Cammie shrugs. "Their story will never be over. She's married, you know? So, technically you have some time to make your husband fall in love with you."

I can't hide my surprise. She hadn't married Turner, that's for sure. He'd blown up my phone after she broke things off with him, begging me to appeal to her on his behalf. Stupid Turner.

After the whole amnesia debacle, I broke into her apartment and found letters from Caleb, dated from his college days. It didn't take long to figure out she was his ex-girlfriend, trying to pull a fast one on him. I blackmailed her into leaving town and then hired a private detective who tracked her to Texas. A friend was attending the same law school as Olivia was, so I made a call, traded some Super Bowl tickets, and BAM! Next thing I knew, they were engaged. The luck! Turner was a tool. How a woman could go from Caleb to that half-wit was beyond me. Either way, I thought she was out of my life for good until Caleb hired her to be my attorney—and a good thing he did, because she won the case and saved me from twenty years in state prison.

I don't say any of this to Cammie, whose Southern accent is suddenly making me uncomfortable. Was she the friend Olivia had gone to live with in Texas?

Nothing further passes between us, as Sam chooses to resurface at the table at that exact moment. I stand up to leave. Cammie is no longer looking at me; she's kissing the skateboarder who is cupping her chest in one hand and holding the other above his head as he makes the Black Sabbath horns with his fingers.

I turn, disgusted, and follow Sam to his car.

"Did you get the answers you needed?" he says when we are on the road.

I look at him in surprise. "What are you talking about?"

He tucks in one side of his mouth and looks at me out of the corner of his eye. "She's my cousin, and she's a blabber mouth. She told me about that chick."

I stare at him, openmouthed. "You knew she was friends with Olivia, and you didn't tell me?"

"That's what you were hoping for, weren't you? You wanted to know if she knew her?"

He's right, but I'm still angry.

"I'm your boss," I say. "You should have told me. And, what kind of gay man are you, anyway? You're supposed to love gossip and drama."

He throws back his head and laughs. Despite the world of bad news swirling around my head, I smile. Maybe he's not so bad. I decide to stop trying to get Caleb to fire him.

When I get home, Caleb is already in bed—not ours, but the twin bed in the baby's room. I check the milk supply in the fridge; luckily there is enough frozen for a day or two—enough time for the dirty martinis to work their way out of my system. I roll my eyes. Caleb will probably check my blood alcohol level before he lets me pump again.

I go to bed, still wearing my clothes, sadder than I've ever felt.

TWELVE

My sister was so beautiful it almost hurt your eyes to look at her—and God, that's all I did in those early years. She was younger than me. Only by a year, but still. It was kind of awkward to idolize your baby sister. It was hard not to, since the minute she walked into a room, every eye was stuck to her like she had some sort of ethereal fairy magic flowing from her pores. For a long time, I believed that once I hit a certain age, I would get some of that fairy juice—no such luck. I looked like a malnourished crack ho with braces and twelve-hundred-dollar sneakers. Courtney made me want to die—especially when she dated and then disposed of all the boys I liked. I could never be mad at her for it. We were a team—Court and Jo—until Jo decided she wanted to be Leah, and then it was Court and Lee. Despite our closeness, as we got older there was no denying the chasm our differences caused. Our friendship wavered for a year in middle school. She left me for the cheerleaders. I watched her make new friends from my seat in the social bleachers, picking bread from my braces and trying to figure out why my boobs hadn't come in yet.

I am nothing like the rest of my family. Each one of them, with the exception of my mother, has raven black hair. Pair that with the Smith signature olive skin and green eyes, and they look like an army of beautiful Greeks. I was born red: my skin, my hair, and my hot, fussy attitude. My mother used to tell me that I cried for a week after they brought me home. She said I lost my voice, and all you could hear was air coming out of me as I made screaming faces.

Our mother encouraged Courtney to do all of the typical, perfect girl things—cheerleading, modeling, and stealing other girls' boyfriends. I, on the other hand, was encouraged to diet, especially during my last year of middle school. I was a little chubby. I started eating my feelings when I discovered boys, rejection, and Little Debbie snack cakes. I went from malnourished to fleshy all in a matter of months.

"You're going to seriously regret this," my mother said, upon discovering my stash. I'd hidden a dozen assorted boxes in an old Christmas popcorn tin in the pantry. "You already have red hair, now you want to add pounds of extra flesh?" To emphasize her point, she'd grabbed a handful of fat at my waist and pinched it until I'd cried out. She shook her head. "Hopeless, Johanna." And then she'd tossed all of my snack cakes in the trash.

I bit my lip to keep from crying. When she saw me struggling with tears, she'd softened a little. *Maybe she was chubby once*, I thought hopefully.

"Here." She opened the freezer and shoved a bag of frozen peas against my chest. "When you get the urge to binge on crap, eat these instead. Just think of it as a frozen treat...like ice cream." When I looked doubtful, she'd grabbed my chin and forced me to look at her. "You like boys?"

I nodded.

"You won't get them if you eat snack cakes, trust me. No one's ever hooked a man with processed cake crumbs on her face."

I'd carried my bag of frozen peas back to my room and sat down cross-legged on the floor. Staring up at my

Jonathan Taylor Thomas poster, I ate the entire bag, pea by pea.

I was kind of nerdy. I liked boys, but I also liked math and science. But, math and science didn't give you attention. It was a one-sided, dry love. I wanted people to look at me the way they did Court. I rolled onto my back and chewed on my peas. I kind of liked them.

The next day I asked Court to introduce me to her friends.

"You make fun of cheerleaders," she said.

"I won't anymore. I want people to like me."

She nodded. "They will, Lee. I do."

Court snagged me an invite to a sleepover, complete with all her giggly friends. Despite her reassurance, her friends had not liked me. They were thirteen-year-old bitches, heavily sedated by their mothers' opinions. They ended almost every sentence with the words *sweetie* or *awesome*. I didn't want to be like those girls. I didn't want to be like my mother. When one of them asked why I hung out with the math geeks, I'd snapped.

"They talk about more interesting things than you."

The girl—Britney—had looked at me like I was something detestable. She'd cocked her head and smiled at me. I could almost see her cardigan-wearing mother doing the same thing. "She's a lesbian," she'd announced to the room. The rest of the girls nodded, like it was a completely acceptable explanation for my strangeness.

Court's face had dropped. She'd looked so disappointed in me.

"I'm not a lesbian," I'd said. But, my voice had been weak, unconvincing. The girls had already taken Britney's word for it. They were already avoiding my eyes.

I'd looked around the room at their stupid, hair-sprayed, pink-lipped heads and said a loud *"Fuck you!"* before storming out. I felt mildly guilty for casting a shadow over Court's social game. She'd recover. She was too pretty not to. When she came home, she stormed into my room and folded her arms across her chest.

"Why would you do that?" she'd asked. "You ask me to help you and then you act like an idiot in front of my friends."

I shook my head. Was she kidding?

"Court, it was them. What are you talking about?"

"You made me look really bad, Leah! You're so selfish. I'm so sick of your drama."

She turned to leave, but I'd jumped up and grabbed her arm. I couldn't believe she was saying this. It's like they were slowly stealing chunks of her brain and replacing it with their lesser functioning ones.

"That's not fair! You're my sister. How can you take their side? Britney lied to everyone. You know I'm not a lesbian."

Courtney had jerked her arm away. "I don't know that."

I'd opened and closed my mouth in shock. My sister—my Courtney—had never spoken to me this way. She'd never taken anyone's side over mine. I felt like someone was burning a hole through my chest, it hurt so bad.

"You're ruining things for me," she'd finally said. "They're my friends. You're my sister. It bothers me when they say stuff about you. Just please, leave it alone and don't run your mouth anymore. You're making things hard for me."

I swallowed my response and nodded. I could do that for her.

We never spoke about what happened after that day, but she was weird with me for a long time. Her friends made a point of snickering when they walked past me in the halls of our private school. They spread rumors too—told people that they caught me masturbating at the sleepover. All this and Court never spoke a word in my defense. I never spoke a word in my defense. I started wondering if she believed them.

In a few weeks, I was declared a lesbian by every popular kid in the seventh and eighth grade. When the rumors finally made it back to my parents, they sent me to Bible camp for the summer. I loved it. I met a pastor's son and lost my V-card in the bushes behind the communal bathroom. I came back with an affirmed taste for men. Of course, that didn't stop the lesbian rumors when school started again. Britney took it upon herself to make sure every girl in her grade and mine knew that they shouldn't undress in front of me in the locker room. The boys would elbow each other in the hallways, snickering and making comments as I walked by. It was terrible. Hurtful. Courtney didn't correct them—that was the worst part. Our bond frayed and snapped, all under the cruel fingertips of Kings High School. I had become used to it in a way; I expected that it was the same way I had become used to my parents' hands-off approach with me.

I kept my head down, dated boys in the math club who could keep up with me mentally, and never stopped plotting against Britney and her lackeys. I changed that year, and no one noticed. They were too busy ostracizing me to notice that my C-cups came in. I learned how to use a blow dryer and makeup. I lost my puppy fat.

That same year, my sister and Britney had a falling out over a boy named Paul. They both wanted him. To save their friendship, both girls had sworn off him in an emotional embrace, insisting that nothing—especially a guy—could come between their friendship. Britney lasted a month before she slept with him. My sister was crushed. I didn't like seeing Courtney cry. And that's what she did for two weeks. I even caught her clutching a bottle of sleeping pills in the bathroom one day.

"Not for a boy, Courtney," I'd said, snatching the bottle from her fingers. "Seriously, when did you become so weak?"

She'd cried silent tears while staring at me with her bruised eyes. I'd realized then that she was probably always weak. She stood up to our parents when it came to me because our parents favored her. It wasn't an act of courage to defy your parents when they never so much as raised their voices to you. I'd walked her to her bedroom and tucked her into bed. Then I'd crawled in next to her so I could watch her.

The next day I'd cornered Britney at her locker. She was officially Paul's girlfriend, and now that she'd severed the bond with my sister, I didn't have to keep my mouth shut anymore.

"You are a worthless slut, you know that?" I poked her in the collarbone for emphasis.

Paul was waiting for her a few feet away.

Britney glared at me, slapping my hand away.

"Eew! Don't touch me, lesbian," she spat. I ignored her, turning my attention to Paul. I had planned this out. Paul was smiling slightly. I could see the words *chick fight* forming in his miniature, underdeveloped brain. A few people were gathering around us to see what was happening.

"And you," I said, looking at Paul. "You're gonna need this…" I tossed a condom at him. It bounced off his chest and landed between his Nikes. He looked at me, then at the red square at his feet. "She has herpes, you ass."

The look on his face was worth every lesbian comment Britney had made over the last two years. Before walking away, I glanced at Britney. Her face was ashen. I wasn't supposed to know about the herpes. The walls in my house were thin, and she'd had one too many sleepovers with my sister.

Destroying Britney's reputation like she destroyed mine was just the ax I needed to loosen my shackles. It started with Britney, but soon I was sleeping with everyone's boyfriends. I liked how easily I could make boys follow me around by dangling sex in their faces. I liked the way their girlfriends came to school with puffy red eyes from crying, after they found out their boyfriends cheated on them.

I hadn't joined ranks with the popular girls like my sister; I'd outranked them. I was flying high, and I didn't intend to stop.

THIRTEEN

PRESENT

"We've been together a long time, Caleb."

He doesn't look up when he says, "Yes."

Normally, I would get a "Yes, Red" or a "Yes, love," but this time I just get "Yes."

It feels lonely, that "Yes."

"Do you remember the time we went to Los Angeles and ate at every celebrity hotspot we could get into?"

He shoots me a look and keeps shuffling mail. Caleb is nostalgic. He likes talking about old memories.

"We didn't have reservations," I continue, "but you talked your way into every restaurant we wanted to try."

He's quiet as he listens.

"We didn't see a single celebrity, but I felt like one the entire week...just being with you."

I take the mail from his hands and set it on the counter, entwining our fingers.

"Caleb, I know I'm a mess. You know I'm a mess. But, you make me better. We have so much history...so much love. Please stop ignoring me."

His jaw is working.

"I didn't want to go to those pretentious restaurants, Leah."

"What?" I shake my head. I thought this was going to work. I don't even have a backup plan.

"I went because of you. I had a good time because of you, but that's not who I am."

"I don't understand," I say. His fingers are trying to pry themselves away from mine.

"I've been someone different with you. Someone I don't understand."

"Well, then be someone new. I don't care. We will change together."

Caleb sighs. "I don't think you'll like who I am."

"Try me, Caleb. I'll work hard to get to know him. Please. We can fix this."

"I don't know if we can do that, but we can try."

I smile tightly and hug him. I feel only the slightest hesitation before he hugs me back. I breathe in the smell of him. *We can try.* I silently repeat to myself. Words I want, but they have an expiration date. *We can try...*until we can't anymore. *We can try...*but this already feels doomed.

I will have to think of a way to make this more permanent.

The next few weeks are peaceful. I pull out all of the cookbooks I got as wedding presents and actually start making meals rather than ordering out. If my man wanted a stay-at-home mom and wife, that's what he was going to get. I could totally be traditional. I make us eat at the dining room table we've never used. I even wheel the baby's movable bassinet into the room so she can be with us. He likes my cooking, or he says he does. He eats all of it and seems genuinely happy that I'm trying. I go shopping for girl clothes for the baby and throw out all of the yellow and green. I proudly display them on the bed for Caleb to see. He picks up each one and nods in approval.

"She's not wearing this," he says, holding up a little T-shirt that says *Date me.*

"It's cute," I argue, diving for it. He grabs the shirt before I can and holds it above his head so I can't reach it.

We spend the next five minutes chasing each other around the bedroom for ownership of it. We haven't played like this in a very long time. It feels good, like it did in the beginning of "us."

Sam watches our marital transformation with amusement.

One day at breakfast, I ask Caleb where we are planning on vacationing this year.

"Our vacations will have to be kid-friendly," he says, sipping his tea. "Lots of Disney World and beach resorts, I imagine."

I balk. He has to be kidding. Sam notices my expression and has to stifle a laugh.

I look at Caleb in alarm.

He smiles crookedly. "What? Did you think we'd be taking on Paris and Tuscany with a little girl?"

I nod.

"They need things too, Leah. It's fine if we expose her to the world, but little people need Disney World and sandcastles. Don't you have those memories from when you were little?"

I don't. My school took us to Disney World my junior year. I got really drunk with a couple of guys the night before and had a hangover the whole next day at the park. I don't tell Caleb this.

"I guess," I say noncommittally. This traditional thing was really beginning to suck.

"What if she likes Paris?" I ask hopefully. "Then can we go?"

He stands up, kisses the top of my head. "Yes. Right after we give her a childhood."

"So while she's still little, can we go somewhere good? It's not like she's going to care about Minnie Mouse just yet."

"We are probably not going on vacation this year. She's too little to leave or to take anywhere." I watch incredulously as he picks up his cell phone. Did he just confiscate my vacation?

"That's ridiculous," I announce, licking my spoon clean of oatmeal. "Plenty of people have babies and go on vacation."

"There are things you have to give up when you have a family, Red. Are you just figuring this out?"

"Let's give up red meat...music...electricity! Just not vacation."

Sam drops the armful of laundry he's holding. I can see his back shaking with laughter as he bends to pick it up.

Caleb is ignoring me, scrolling through his phone.

All the men in my life treat me like I'm a joke.

"I'm going on vacation," I announce to both of them. Caleb looks up and raises an eyebrow.

"What are you saying, Leah?"

He is goading me. I don't know why I take the bait.

"I'm saying that with or without you, I'm going."

I march out of the room so I don't have to see his expression. Why do I feel like a ten-year-old? No, there is nothing wrong with me. It's him. He doesn't want me for who I am. He wants to make me someone else. This is a game Caleb and I have been playing for years. He gives me a standard by which to live, and I fail.

He follows me.

"What are you doing?" He grabs me by the arm as I try to walk away.

"You're trying to control me."

"The idea of a controlled Leah bores me, I assure you. However, being part of a family means making decisions as a unit."

"Oh please," I spit at him, "let's not pretend anyone but you is making the decisions."

I pull my arm away. "I'm tired of the dog-and-pony show I always have to put on for you."

I am at the stairs when I hear him say, "Well, there you have it."

I don't look back.

Upstairs, I pull out the street painting Courtney brought me from her trip to Europe. I keep it wrapped in wax paper in a box. I touch the red umbrella with my fingertip. Courtney said that I was her red umbrella. When she was in turmoil, all she had to do was come stand near me and I'd keep the bad stuff off of her. It wasn't true. I failed Courtney, I failed my father, and I was in the process of failing Caleb.

I shove it back in the box and swipe at the tears that are coming down my cheeks. I hear Estella cry out as she wakes up from her nap. I gather my emotions, take a deep breath, and go to her.

FOURTEEN
PAST

We fought the day of his accident. Can you imagine? Your boyfriend almost dies, and hours before, you tell him that you want to break up. I didn't mean it. It was a "shit or get off the pot" statement, a cruel attempt at strong-arming him into marriage. Except, you can't give Caleb Drake an ultimatum. I could see his face in my mind as the words left my mouth—eyebrows up, his jaw clenching like a fist. The day before he left on his business trip to Scranton, we fought about the same topic. I wanted a goddamn ring. Caleb wanted to make sure mine was the right finger to put it on.

Then the call came. I was at work when Luca's refined voice came onto the line. Luca and I had a floating relationship: sometimes things were great between us, sometimes I wanted to pour kerosene over her head and strike a match. She was saying words like *hospital* and *memory loss*. I didn't get it until she said, "Leah, are you listening to me? Caleb is in the hospital! He doesn't know his own name!"

"The hospital?" I repeated. Caleb was supposed to be ring shopping for me.

"An accident, Leah," she repeated. "We're flying out in the morning."

As soon as I hung up with Luca, I started looking for flights. If I left now, I'd be there before midnight. She was flying up with Steve, Caleb's stepfather, in the morning. I wanted to be there first. I needed to look into his eyes and make him remember me. My father strolled into my office, a stack of papers in his hands. My mouse hovered over the purchase button. He was forever needing me to sign things.

"What are you doing?" He looked at me over the rim of his glasses.

"Caleb's been in an accident," I said. "He has a concussion, and he doesn't know who he is."

"You can't leave," he said matter-of-factly. "We're in the middle of our trial run. I need you here."

He dropped the papers on my desk and strode toward the door. I blinked at his back, unclear if he'd heard me.

"Daddy?"

He paused at the door, his back still to me. This was how most of our relationship was—me talking to his back, or his bent head, or his newspaper.

"Caleb needs me. I'm going." I clicked *purchase* on the ticket and stood up to gather my things.

I didn't look at him as I walked to the door, where he was most definitely frozen in place, glaring at me.

"Johanna—"

"Don't call me that. My name is Leah."

I pushed past him, the force of my body knocking him into the doorframe. I looked braver than I felt—I was good at that. Did I just defy my father—the man whose love I was forever trying to win, earn…deserve? It took every bit of métier I possessed not to turn around and assess his anger. I knew that if I looked at him I would go running back, scrounging for the crumbs of his affection like a dog. He was furious…boiling. Walk, walk, walk—I told myself. Caleb needed me. He was the good that I owned, and I was not going to let him forget me. What did this job matter? What did my father matter? I needed Caleb more than both of them.

I drove home and threw things into an overnight bag. By the time I reached the airport, I was shaking. It was all a blur from there—going through security, finding my gate. When I reached the gate, there were still thirty minutes until the flight could board. I stood as close to the ticketing agent as possible. The marquee above her desk read Scranton, but it might as well have said Caleb. When the first boarding call was announced, I was the first one to hand her my ticket. Collapsing into my seat, I pressed my fingertips to my eyes to hold back the tears. I distracted myself by pulling out my iPhone and googling *amnesia*. I was reading through the different types when the flight attendant told me I had to turn off my phone. I hated that. My boyfriend had amnesia, my father was going to disown me as soon as I got home, and the blue-eyeshadow-wearing biotch was worried about my cell phone taking out a plane. I stowed my phone and flicked my nails over the pad of my thumb, one by one—starting with the pinkie and working my way across. I did that for the duration of the flight.

When it was finally time to land, I could barely keep from standing up and rushing to the front of the plane. I thought of all the things that could go wrong. Luca had mentioned on the phone that Caleb's memory loss was classified as retrograde amnesia—meaning he had lost the ability to recall anything that happened before the accident. How could someone just…forget everything about their life? I didn't believe it. There was no way he could forget me. We were together every day…he loved me. That was the absolute worst thing about love; no matter how hard you tried, you could never forget the person who had your heart. Until Caleb, I didn't know what that meant. I was queen of date 'em and ditch 'em.

The line moved forward and I trotted out of the terminal and to the car rental kiosk. Thirty minutes later, I was speeding toward the hospital in a Ford Focus, the heat turned all the way up and my right thumb flicking, flicking, flicking at my nails. It was snowing outside. All I'd brought was a light jacket and a couple light sweaters. I was going to freeze.

The walk up to his hospital room was the longest I'd ever taken. My chest hurt as I worried if he'd remember me or not. His doctor—an Indian man with a kind face—met me in the hallway.

"There was some bleeding to his brain that we managed to get under control. He is in stable condition, but he is very confused. Don't be upset if he doesn't know who you are."

"But, what caused it? Thousands of people get concussions and don't lose their memories," I said.

"There's never a single causal explanation for these things. All you can do is be patient and give him the support that he needs. With this type of memory loss, it usually takes time, but their memories return."

I looked fearfully toward his door. This was really happening. I was going to walk through that door, and the only man I'd ever allowed myself to love would not recognize me.

"Can I see him?"

The doctor nodded. "Give him space. To him, this will be the first time he's meeting you. If you want to hug him, ask permission first."

I swallowed the fist in my throat. Thanking the doctor, I knocked lightly on his door.

I heard him say, "Come in."

The first thing I saw when I walked in was the pretty nurse who was checking his IV line. She was flirting with him. My initial response was to walk directly up to Caleb and kiss him. My territory. Instead, I stood furtively by the door and waited for him to notice me.

Please…please…

He looked up. I smiled.

"Hi, Caleb." I walked a few steps closer. There was nothing in his eyes. My heart shook with each second of realization. There was not going to be a miracle when he saw my face; my beautiful red hair would not usher back his memories. I was made of steel. I could handle this.

"I'm Leah."

He glanced at the nurse—who was pretending not to notice me—and she nodded, touching his arm lightly before heading out the door.

"Hi, Leah," he said.

"Do you—" I caught myself before I could say any more. I wouldn't question whether he knew me or not—no, that would surely paint me as an uncertainty. I would simply assert who I was to him and demand that he mentally accept it.

"I'm your girlfriend. It's weird having to explain that to you."

He smiled—the old Caleb smile. I released the breath I was holding. God, I needed a cigarette.

I neared the side of his bed. He was pretty banged up. There were five stitches over his right eye and his face looked like a Kandinsky.

"I was so scared," I said. "I came right away."

He nodded and looked down at his hands. "Thank you."

The muscles were working in his jaw as he ground his teeth. I blinked at him, unsure of what to say next. Did we start at square one? Did I give him a summary of who we were, where we'd been?

Be still my manic heart.

"Can I...can I hug you?" I shook as I waited for his answer. They were tremors of fear, a calculation of the loss I'd feel if he rejected me.

He looked up, his brows furrowed, and nodded. It was one of those great moments of relief I would always remember. My internal knots untangled and I dove at him, wrapping my arms around his neck and sobbing into his chest. For a few seconds, it was just me holding him, and then I felt his hands rest lightly on my back. I cried harder. This was so messed up. I should be comforting him, and here I was weeping.

If he had died…oh God…I would have been all alone. His mother had told me that the driver of the car had died. I'd met him once or twice at Caleb's work functions.

When I pulled away from him, I couldn't meet his eyes. I grabbed a wad of tissues from my purse and turned my back to him as I dabbed at my eyes.

I had to keep it together. Think positive. Soon this would be over and buried in our past. For now, I needed to be there for him. We were so good together. Even if he had no memory of before, he would see it now. I needed to make him see it. I stifled a sob. Why did this have to happen? Right when our relationship had finally been moving forward.

"Leah."

I froze. My name sounded foreign on his voice, like he was saying it for the first time, tonguing the syllables cautiously. I dabbed at the last of my tears and faced him…smiling.

"Are you…? God…" He balled his fists when he saw my wet eyes. "I'm so sorry."

He looked like he was about to cry, so I sat on the edge of his bed, seeing my opportunity to be of some use.

"Don't worry about me," I said. "I'm fine so long as you're fine."

He frowned. "I'm not fine."

"Then, neither am I, but we're in this together."

FIFTEEN

I am in the living room, flipping through *Vogue* while Caleb cooks dinner. The baby is sleeping upstairs, and the television is on some grody news station, playing just loud enough so Caleb can hear it. I am thinking about changing the channel to put on *America's Next Top Model*, when I hear her name. My head snaps up. Olivia Kaspen. Her picture is on the screen, as she stands surrounded by reporters. I grab for the remote, not to turn it up, but to change the channel before Caleb can see it.

"Don't," I hear from behind me. I squeeze my eyes shut. Shrugging, I increase the volume. The newscaster is female. I once read a statistic that said sixty percent of men tune out female newscasters. Unfortunately for me, Caleb is not one of those men. He edges closer to the TV, the knife still in his hand. His knuckles are white. My eyes trace up his arm and rest on his face. From his nose down, his features are marble. Everything above that is registering emotion on a nuclear level. His eyebrows are drawn and his eyes look like a loaded gun ready to go off at any moment. I transfer my gaze to the television, afraid that if I keep watching him, I'll start crying.

"The trial for Dobson Scott Orchard will begin next week. His attorney, Olivia Kaspen, who up until this point has been mum about her client, recently made a statement, saying she took the case after the accused kidnapper and serial rapist contacted her directly, asking her to represent him. It is highly speculated that Olivia, who received her undergraduate degree from the same college as one of his victims, will be issuing a plea of 'not guilty by reason of insanity.'"

The show switches to a commercial. I flop back against the couch. The picture they had shown of Olivia was grainy. The only thing really visible was her hair, which was much longer than it had been through my trial. I slowly pivot my neck around until I can see Caleb's face. He is standing motionless behind me, his eyes slightly narrowed and glued to the toilet paper commercial, like he's suspicious of their three-ply guarantee.

"Caleb?" I say. My voice catches, and I clear my throat. Tears sting at my eyes, and I have to use all of my willpower to keep them from spilling onto my cheeks. Caleb is looking at me, but he is not seeing me. I want to throw up. How fragile is my marriage, if all he has to do is look at her and I cease to exist? I turn off the television and abruptly stand up, sending the contents of my lap crashing to the floor. I grab for my purse, feeling for where I stashed my cigarettes the night I went to Mother Gothel with Sam. I pull them out, not caring if he sees…wanting him to see.

"Are you serious?"

His voice is calm, but I can see the unbridled anger in his eyes.

"You don't own me," I say casually, but my hand is shaking as I lift my lighter. It is such a lie. Caleb has owned every one of my thoughts and actions for the last five years. Why? Was I always such a sellout to love? I think back to my other relationships as I take a drag. No, in every relationship that came before Caleb, I had the power. I blow my smoke in his direction, but he's gone. I stub out the cigarette. Why did I feel the need to do that? God.

I don't go to bed. I sit on the couch all night, drinking rum straight from the bottle. Self-reflection is not something I excel in. I think of myself as being perfectly Photoshopped. If I started scraping at the layers of what I'm suppressing—what I've put a pretty picture over— things would start looking pretty ugly. I do not like to think about who I really am, but the loneliness and alcohol are loosening my restraints. I call Sam to distract myself. When he picks up, I can hear music in the background.

"Hold on," he says.

He comes back on a few seconds later.

"Is Estella okay?"

"Yes," I say, annoyed. I can hear his sigh of relief.

"I am not a good mother," I announce to him. "I'm probably worse than my own self-absorbed, critical, gin- and-tonic-drinking mother."

"Leah, are you drinking?"

"No."

I set the bottle of rum aside. It misses the table and crashes to the floor. Good thing it was empty. I flinch.

"You better have pumped before you did that," he snaps.

I start crying. I did. Everyone is so judgmental.

He hears me sniffling and sighs. "You're a pretty bad mother, yes. But, you don't have to be."

"Also, Caleb still has strong feelings for Olivia."

"Can you just not focus on Caleb for once? You're obsessed. Let's talk about Estella—"

I cut him off. "I think I've always known this, but I'm not sure. I can pull dozens of memories from some private storage room in my brain that only alcohol has the key to unlock. Most of the memories are of looks—the ones he gives her and not me." I bite my kneecap and rock back and forth.

"You know what, I have to go," Sam says. "I'll see you tomorrow." He hangs up. I toss my phone aside. Fuck Sam.

When Caleb looks at her, his eyes shift into a different gear. It's like he's seeing the only thing that matters. I am sickly familiar with the way he looks at Olivia, because it is the way I look at him.

When I stand up, the room swings. I am so drunk I can barely understand my own thoughts. I stumble upstairs and into my closet. I pull down bags and suitcases until I am surrounded by L's and V's and the subtle rich smell of leather. I'm going to leave him. I don't deserve this. It's just like Cammie said. I'm being half loved. I stuff a few handfuls of clothes into a bag and then collapse on the floor. Who am I kidding? I'll never leave him. If I leave him, she wins.

I wake up with my face pressed to the floor. I groan and roll onto my back trying to fit the pieces of last night together. I feel worse than the day I gave birth. I wipe the drool from my face and stare around at the mess. Suitcases and duffel bags are littered around me like my closet rained them. Was I trying to reach something when I knocked these down? I have the violent urge to vomit, and I hurl myself toward the toilet, making it just in time to empty my stomach into the bowl. I am gasping for air when Caleb strolls in, smelling clean and fresh. He is dressed in shorts and a T-shirt, which is odd since he works today. He ignores me as he slips his watch over his hand and checks the time.

"Why are you dressed like that?" My voice is raspy like I spent the night screaming.

"I took the day off of work."

He won't look at me, a bad sign. I am trying to remember what I did to him, when I catch a whiff of my hair. Smoke. I inwardly groan as the memories come drifting back. That was so stupid.

"Why?" I ask cautiously.

"I need to think."

He heads out of the bathroom, and I follow him downstairs. Sam is feeding the baby; he raises his eyebrows when he sees me, and I run my fingers through my hair self-consciously. Screw him. This is entirely his fault. Ever since he showed up, my life has slowly started unraveling.

Caleb kisses the baby on top of her head and walks toward the door like he is late for something. I chase after him.

"What do you need to think about? Divorce?"

He stops suddenly, and I slam into his back.

"Divorce?" he says. "Do you think I should divorce you?"

I swallow my pride and the challenge that is on the tip of my tongue. I have to be smart. I've let myself get carried away lately. Pushed him when I had the chance to make things right.

"Let me go with you," I say evenly. "Let's spend the day together—talk."

He looks unsure, his eyes darting to the nursery door. "She'll be fine with Sam," I assure him. "It's not like I do anything anyway…"

My statement seems to seal the deal. He nods once, and I want to scream in relief.

"I'll just be five minutes," I say.

He heads out to the car to wait for me. I launch myself up the stairs two at a time and slam through the door of my closet almost falling over in the process. I put on a clean pair of jeans and pull a T-shirt over my head. In the bathroom, I splash water on my face, wiping away the smudged makeup and take a swig of mouthwash. I don't bother with new makeup.

I come running out the front door, and I have a small heart attack when I don't see his car. He left me. I am ready to fall down in the driveway and cry when his shiny BMW turns the corner. Relieved, I get in and try to play it cool.

"You thought I left you," he says. There is humor in his voice, and I am so relieved to get something other than coldness, that I nod. He looks over at me, and I see surprise cross his face. I look down at myself self-consciously. I very rarely let him see me without makeup, and I never wear T-shirts.

"Where are we going?" I say, trying to distract his attention from how disgusting I look.

"You don't get to ask questions," he says. "You wanted to come along, so here we go…"

I'll take it.

He turns the radio on, and we drive with the windows down. Normally I would have a fit about the wind messing up my hair, but I'm so beyond caring, I almost enjoy the feel of it on my face. He heads south on the highway. There is nothing but ocean in this direction. I can't even begin to guess where he's taking me.

We pull into a gravel driveway about an hour later. I sit up straighter in my seat and peer around. There is a lot of foliage. Suddenly, the trees open up, and I am staring at aquamarine water. Caleb takes a sharp left and pulls the car underneath a tree. He gets out without saying a word. When he doesn't do his usual spiel of coming around to open my door, I jump out and follow him. We walk in silence, trailing the water until we come to a small harbor. There are four boats, bobbing gently on the swells. Two of the four are newer-looking fishing boats. He passes these and heads for an old Sea Cat that is in bad need of paint.

"Is this yours?" I ask, incredulous. He nods, and I feel momentarily affronted that he never told me that he bought a boat. I keep my mouth shut and climb onboard without his help. Sea Cats are a British brand. I'm not surprised; he usually buys European. I look around in disgust. I am allergic to things that are not shiny and new. It looks like he has started to work on it. I smell the sharp tang of sealant, and I spot the can next to the hatch.

I try for a nice, neutral comment. "What are you going to call her?"

He seems to like my question, because he half smiles as he messes with the rope that holds us to the dock.

"Great Expectations."

I like it. I was prepared not to, but I do. *Great Expectations* is the name of the book where he chose Estella's name. Since I gave birth to the screaming pile of flesh, I feel pretty good about the whole thing. So long as it has nothing to do with Olivia. *Don't think about her*, I chide myself. *She's the reason you're in trouble in the first place.*

"So are we going to take her out?" I ask the obvious question. His head is still bent, but he lifts his eyes to look at me as his hands work. It is one of those things that only he does. I find it incredibly sexy, and I get butterflies. I sit down on the only available seat—which is ripped—and watch the muscles in his back as he turns on the engine and steers us out of the harbor. I am so insanely attracted to him, even in the wake of our fight, I want to rip off his clothes and climb on top of him. Instead, I sit ladylike and watch as we cruise over the water. We stay like this for a long time, him at the wheel and me waiting. He turns off the engine. The shoreline runs in a parade of sand dunes and houses to my left, the ocean dark and blue to my right. He walks to the helm and looks out over the water. I lift myself from my seat and walk the few steps to join him.

"I leave tomorrow for Denver," he says.

"I won't go postpartum and kill your daughter—if that's what you're getting at."

He tilts his head slightly and looks down at me. "She's your daughter, too."

"Yes."

We watch the waves lap against the side of the boat, neither of us speaking our thoughts.

"Why didn't you tell me about the boat?" I run my fingernails over the pad of my thumb.

"I would have eventually. It was a spur-of-the-moment purchase."

That's fair enough, I suppose. I've bought shoes that probably equaled the cost of this thing without telling him first. But, spur of the moment meant it was an emotional purchase. The kind I made when I was depressed or worried about something.

"What else are you not telling me?"

"Probably the same amount of stuff you're not telling me."

I cringe. So painfully true. Caleb could see through walls like nobody's business. But, if he really knew what I was not telling him, he'd be gone tomorrow...and I couldn't have that.

If he really was hiding more—I was going to find it.

"You know everything about me—all of my secrets and family drama. What could I have to hide?" I say.

He faces me. There is a dark cloud behind him. It seems like an omen. I shiver.

"There is a lot I don't know about you," he says.

My mind immediately goes to the fertility monitor and Clomiphene I was using to get pregnant.

His brain is working overtime. I can see the burning behind his irises. When Caleb thinks, his eyes practically glow. I hate that. The benefit is, I always know when he's on to me. His eyes now dart to mine; they drop to my mouth and then lift back to my eyes. He narrows his and tilts his head like he's reading my thoughts. Can you read a secret on someone's face? I fucking hope not.

"When you came to me that night...in the hotel...were you trying to get pregnant?"

I remove my eyes from his and stare down at the water. Goddamn, he can. My hands are shaking. I fist them. Then I fist him with the truth.

"Yes."

I don't know why I tell the truth. I never tell the truth. Dammit all! I want to suck the words back into my mouth before they reach him, but it's too late.

Caleb links his hands behind his neck. His eyebrows are up, up, up, creasing his forehead into half a dozen little lines. He's mad as hell.

I think of that night at his hotel. I went there with determination. I had a plan. My plan worked. I never thought I'd get caught. Caught I was. I flick my thumbnails across the pads of my fingers.

Flick

Flick

Flick

Caleb is biting the inside of his cheek. It looks like he wants to take off running. He runs to think. When he speaks, his words come from between his teeth.

"Okay," he says. "Okay." He looks up at the sky, the struggle evident on his face. "I love her so much…" his voice cracks. He leans an arm on the side of the boat and peers into the water with me. "I love her so much," he starts again, "I don't care how she came to be. I'm just glad she's here."

I breathe a sigh of relief and look at him out of the corner of my fearful eye.

He swallows once, twice…

"You got pregnant on purpose. And now you don't seem to want her."

It's hard to hear…both parts. Chilling and true and ugly.

"I thought she'd be a boy." My voice is so low it's competing with the waves, but Caleb hears me.

"And if she were? Would you like being a mother then?"

I hate when he forces me to think. Would I? Or was this role something I was doomed to fail at, boy or girl?

"I don't know."

He lifts his head to look at me. I eye the scruff on his face, and I want to touch it.

"Do you want her?"

Don't tell him the truth!

"I…I don't know what I want. I want you. I want to make you happy…"

"But, not Estella?"

His voice has an edge to it. The edge that usually indicates I'm in big trouble. I try to work my way out of it.

"Of course I want her. I'm her mother…"

My voice lacks conviction. I used to be such an accomplished liar.

"What you did after that…was that planned out too?"

I watch his chest play the in/out game. Rapid angry breaths…he's steeling himself for my answer.

I suck in all the air that the sky has to offer. I pull it until my lungs burn. I don't want to let it go. I want to hold that air and hold the confession he's forcing out of me. I don't have to tell him the truth.

"Caleb…"

"God, Leah, just tell me the truth…"

He runs a hand through his hair, walks a couple paces to the left so that I can only see his back.

"I was upset…Courtney—"

He cuts me off. "Did you do it to make me come back?"

I swallow. Fuck. If I say no, he'll keep asking me questions until he traps me.

"Yes."

He swears and drops to his haunches, his fingertips pressed on his forehead like he's trying to hold his thoughts in.

"I think I need time to think."

"No, Caleb!" I shake my head from side to side. He shakes his up and down. We look like a couple of distraught bobbleheads.

The whirlpool starts, panic sucking me down until I whimper, "Don't leave me again. I can't take care of her alone." I drop my head.

"You won't have to, Leah."

I look up at him hopefully.

"I'll take her with me. She's my daughter; I'll take care of her."

Oh God. What have I done now?

He gets up, turns on the Cat's engine, and we are slicing back toward shore, the remnants of my sanity shredding.

The minute he ties us to the dock, I am off the boat and racing to my phone, which I left in his car. I want to get out of here. My fingers become boneless as I fumble with the screen, jabbing uselessly. I dial a taxi service and tell them my location. I am shivering despite the heat. My God, what was I thinking telling him that? I can barely breathe as I see him walk down the dock and toward where I am perched against the hood of his car. Even in lieu of our current situation, my heart stirs at the sight of him. I love him so much my heart aches. He won't look at me. I don't know what this means, but thinking is never a good thing. Thinking stirs up a dangerous maelstrom of emotion. My emotion almost drowned me once. I don't want to go back there.

The gravel shifts beneath his feet as he walks to where I sit. My arms are wrapped around my waist as I try to press my sanity back into my torso. He stops a few feet away. He's coming to check on me. He hates me at this moment, but he's coming to check on me. "I called a cab," I say. He nods and looks out at the water, which is just visible beyond the copse of trees where he parked his car.

"I'm going to stay here," he says. "I'll call you when I'm back so I can pick up Estella."

My head snaps up. "Pick her up?" Oh yeah, that.

"I'm going to take her to stay with me for a while at my condo."

I breathe through my nose, grappling with my emotions, trying to rein back control of the situation.

"You can't take her from me," I say through clenched teeth.

"I'm not trying to. You don't want her, Leah. I need some time to think, and it's better if she stays with me." He rubs his forehead while I calmly panic.

I want to scream—*Don't think! Don't think!*

"What about work? You can't take care of her with your work schedule."

I'm trying to buy time. I messed up, but I can fix this. I can be a good mother and a good wife…

"She's more important than work. I'll take some time off. I have a trip next week; after that, I'll come get her."

My thoughts drag. I can't come up with excuses for why he can't do this to me. I can use the baby as leverage—threaten him—but that would screw me in the long run. If he wants to take some time, maybe I should let him. Maybe, I need time too.

I nod.

He presses his lips together until they burn white. Neither of us says anything for the next twenty minutes. He waits with me until the dingy-looking cab pulls up, spraying gravel at our ankles until it comes to a stop. I climb in, refusing to meet his eyes. Perhaps he is waiting for me to turn around and tell him that it was all a lie. I look straight ahead.

The drive from the Keys back to Miami is taken across narrow patches of land that stretch out over deep blue water. I refuse to think…all the way home. I just can't do it. I focus on the cars we pass. I look in their windows and judge their passengers: sunburned families coming from vacation, blue-collared workers with bored expressions, a woman crying as she sings along with the radio. I look away when I see that one. I don't need to be reminded about tears.

When I get home, Sam has just put the baby down for the night. He studies my face and opens his mouth, the questions ready to pour out.

"Don't fucking say anything," I snap. His mouth is still hanging open when I storm up the stairs and slam my door. I hear his Jeep pull out of the driveway a few minutes later, and I peek through the drapes to make sure he's gone. I pace around my room, flicking my fingernails, and trying to decide what to do about this mess Olivia created. Then almost abruptly, I jerk toward the hall and slip inside of the baby's room. Tiptoeing to her crib, I peer over the edge like I expect to find a snake instead of a sleeping infant.

She is on her back, her head to the side. She's managed to wriggle a hand free of Sam's swaddling and she has it fisted and partially in her mouth. Every few seconds, she starts sucking on it so fiercely I think she is going to wake herself up. I back up a few steps in case she sees me. I don't even know if she can see me yet. Mothers usually keep charts of these things—first smile, first burp, first whatever. I tilt my head and look at her again. She's grown, gotten a little less—yuck. I'm surprised that I can actually see myself in her face, the curve of her nose and the sharp chin. Babies usually just look like blobs until they're four, but this one has a little character to her face. I suppose that if any baby were to be cuter than the rest, it would be mine. I linger for another moment before stepping out. I close the door and then I open it, remembering that I am on my own tonight. No Caleb. No Sam. Not even my self-absorbed, alcoholic mother. I have watched Sam and Caleb enough with the baby to know the basics. You feed it, it craps the food out, you wipe away the crap, you put it in the crib...you drink.

Oh God. I slide down the wall until my butt hits the tile, and drop my head between my knees. I can't help feeling sorry for myself. I didn't ask for this life—to be loved second best and to be forced to have a baby. I wanted...I wanted what Olivia had and threw away— someone who adores me even though my insides curl and lash like a poisonous snake. *No!* I think. *I am not the poisonous snake. Olivia is. Everything that I've had to do is her fault. I am innocent.* I fall asleep that way, sniffling and wiping my nose on my pant leg, assuring myself of my innocence and listening to my daughter breathe. Maybe she'd be better off without me. Maybe I'd be better off without her.

I wake up to a siren. Fire! I jump up, my muscles unraveling in protest. I am disoriented and not sure where I am. It is dark, still night. I place a hand against the wall and sniff for smoke. Not a siren...a baby. I am not really relieved; I might have preferred the fire. I head to the kitchen, knocking things over in my haste to find a bottle and a pack of breast milk. I swear out loud. Sam must have moved things around, because I can't find anything. Then I see the note taped to the fridge.

No more breast milk.

You need to pump.

Damn. I look at the breast pump, which is sitting on the counter. It will take at least fifteen minutes to pump the amount she needs, and she is screaming so loud I'm afraid someone will hear and come to investigate. I see Child Protective Services showing up on my block, and I cringe. I can't afford any more run-ins with the law.

Taking the stairs two at a time, I pause at the nursery door, taking a deep breath before pushing it open. I flick on the light and flinch. The sudden change seems to make her angrier too, so I flick it off and put on the small lamp in the corner. I remember picking the lamp out at Pottery Barn. A brown bear...for my son. I head to the crib for my daughter. She is soaking wet. Her diaper has leaked through her clothes and onto her sheet. I set her on the changing table and pull off her onesie. Once it's off and I've re-diapered her she seems to calm down, but she's still wailing.

"Shush," I say. "You sound like a cat." I move to the five-thousand-dollar rocking chair my mother bought me and sit in it for the first time.

"You're a real pain in the ass, you know that?" I glare at her as I lift my T-shirt. I look away when she latches on. It takes all of my willpower not to yank her off. The next thirty minutes are pure torture. I am a human bottle. My legs are crossed, and I bounce my foot to keep my sanity. My eyes are closed and pressed against my fingertips. I hate this. She falls asleep still sucking. I lift her to my shoulder to burp her, but she beats me to it and burps in my face. I laugh a little because it's so disgusting and carry her to her crib.

Standing back, I feel a small sense of accomplishment. I can take care of a baby.

"Let's see you do that, Olivia."

The constant cycle of feeding continues until the sun cracks through the palm trees like an overzealous fucking spotlight. I hide my head under my arms as it shines through the flimsy nursery curtains, cutting a line straight for my eyes. I'd moved myself into her room a few hours earlier, curling up on the twin bed in the corner. There had been no sleep—none. Nothing. I roll onto my back and stare up at the ceiling. I smell like sour milk. I am just about to haul myself to my feet when her caterwauling starts up again.

"Oh God," I say, crawling toward her crib. "Please, just let me die."

SIXTEEN

He was with her. He had to be. I went to his condo, and I called his parents. No one had seen or heard from him in a few days. I left half a dozen voicemails, but he never called back. My life was starting to feel like a runaway train. I was heading toward something bad at a breakneck pace. Caleb was pulling away from me. My fingers, which used to be twined with his, were now gripping air. I needed to grab on to something, take back control. I considered asking my mother for help, but after she'd told me to follow Caleb to that bitch's apartment, I'd been too ashamed to tell her anything else about the situation.

Courtney!

I called my sister and told her everything.

"Geez, Leah. What are you going to do?" Courtney was in her first year as a teacher. She had taken a job teaching math to inner-city kids at a high school.

"Seriously, you have to find him and talk to him. Who is this girl, anyway? She obviously knows about you and doesn't care. What a heartless bitch."

"I don't know that he'd listen, Courtney. He's not himself."

I heard voices in the background.

"I have to go," she said. "I'm doing after-school tutoring. This is the love of your life. You have to fight for him."

"Okay," I said. "How?"

She was quiet for a few seconds. "Figure out who this girl is. If she's just a fling, let it go, he'll come back to you. If it's more, you have to put a stop to it. Hear me?"

"I hear you."

She hung up. I felt rejuvenated. I stopped for a Jamba Juice and drove straight to the apartment complex I'd followed Caleb to a week earlier. His car wasn't there. I knocked on the door and heard a dog barking. I knocked again, louder. If that damn animal kept making that racket, someone was going to notice. At my feet, there was a Welcome mat and a small potted plant to the left of it. It did little to brighten the dull grey corridor. Looking around, I squatted next to the plant, lifting it off the ground. Nothing.

Hmmmmm.

I stuck my finger in the soil and dug around until...I came up with a small Ziploc baggie. I dusted away the dirt with my finger and leaned in for a closer look. A key. I snorted. Standing up, I put the key in the lock, and the door swung open. My ankles were immediately under attack. I managed to dodge my way around the ugly creature and close the door to the apartment, locking it outside. I pressed my ear against the door. I could hear it whining on the other side and then the faint click of nails on concrete as it trotted away. Good.

Taking a deep breath, I turned to face the apartment. It was nice. Decent. She'd put work into making it homey. I wandered over to the living room. It smelled so strongly of cinnamon, I wanted to find the source. I followed the smell to one of those plug-in wall things and nudged it with the tip of my shoe. What type of woman used those? I had never even thought to buy one.

Fuck it. Enough screwing around.

I started in her bedroom. That's where women had been hiding their secrets since the beginning of…well, secrets. I pulled out her dresser drawers one by one, running my hands along the back of her clothes. When I reached her underwear drawer, I grimaced. Please, God, do not let Caleb have seen her underwear. She wears lace—black and white and pink. No patterns. I closed the drawer empty-handed and looked at her closet. So far, she's boring. Caleb doesn't do boring. Well, the Caleb I used to know didn't do boring. I shook my head. I had no idea who this new Caleb was. I wanted the old one back.

I clicked on the light in the closet. It was creepily organized. A shoebox rested on a shelf above her clothes. I pulled it down and slid off the lid.

I felt like I'd been punched in the stomach. Staring up at me was a picture of a much younger Caleb. He had his arm around a girl with raven black hair. I recognized her from the day I followed him to her apartment. What did this mean? They knew each other? Had Caleb reached out to her after he got amnesia? Was he trying to connect with his past? I flipped through the pictures. They were more than just friends. My God. I stopped on a picture of them kissing and flung the box away from me.

What was happening? Did he know who she was or—

No, it had to be her. She somehow found out he had lost his memory, and she showed up to mess with his head. Oh my God. Caleb had no idea.

I stopped rocking and scrambled for the box. Inside were handwritten letters in Caleb's slanted print. My eyes burned as I read through them. His words…to this girl I knew nothing about. Except this wasn't just any girl. This was Cherry Garcia. I was almost sure of it.

I had to find him, tell him what she was doing. But first things first.

I gathered what I needed into a pile and stuffed it into my pocket. Then I went to look for scissors.

135

SEVENTEEN

No one comes. By noon I realize that I have destroyed my marriage and it is Sam's day off. I break out the Scotch. I don't even like Scotch, but for some reason it makes me feel bonded to Caleb.

The little brat is finally sleeping. I don't think twice about taking two fingers of Caleb's best. She's so high-strung, a little single malt would do her good. I catch a glimpse of myself in the hall mirror as I trudge up the stairs toward the shower. I look like one of those chubby, lank-haired mothers who occupy park benches, all the hope drained from their eyes. Is that what I am destined to become? A single mother, wearing ugly jeans and doling out those disgusting goldfish cracker-things at snack time?

No—I square my shoulders. If I am going to do this, I will not go to the damn park. I will go to France, and I will feed her caviar and pâté. I can do better than a stereotype. I can be a Chanel mother.

By the time I climb out of the shower, I feel like a new woman. No wonder Caleb drinks that expensive stuff. I'm practically walking on air. When the baby wakes up, I feed her from the stock of milk I pumped earlier. She already seems fussy, like the bottle is an inconvenience instead of a meal. She screams and thrashes her head around until her skin flushes as red as the troll fluff that's sprouting on top of her head.

I wiggle it in her mouth, until finally she latches on, grunting with her eyes closed.

"Lost that battle, didn't you?" I say, resting my head back in the rocker and closing my eyes. "If you think I'm going to be doing that all the time, you're wrong. Spoiled, little, redheaded brat."

I wake up in the rocker. The baby is asleep on my shoulder. I can feel her heat seeping through my clothes and hear her little breaths in my ear. I lower her in her crib as gently as I can and check my phone.

Nothing from Caleb, but two calls from Sam. I am about to call my good-for-nothing manny when he sends me a text.

Sam: Stomach flu, need a couple days off.

Before I know what I'm doing my phone is spiraling out of my hand and toward my beautiful fucking marble staircase. I close my eyes as I hear it smash into a dozen pieces. My whole life is falling apart.

The baby starts to cry; I start to cry. I smash a few more priceless antiques and pull myself together. I have a gosh-darn baby to take care of. When I march back into her room, my sobbing has subsided to a whimper and I already have my boob out.

Sam finds me in my usual spot on the floor next to her crib. He nudges me in the ribs with his foot, and I shove his leg away.

"Did you stop bathing?"

When I don't respond, he pulls me to my feet, casting a quick glance into the crib before ushering me out.

"I didn't kill her," I sputter, "if that's what you're thinking."

He ignores me, pushing me toward my bedroom.

"Just because you're a mother doesn't mean you can't take care of yourself."

I shoot him a nasty look. Obviously, he has no idea what it is to take care of a baby. He shoves me into the bathroom and turns on the shower.

"Caleb called to say he won't be coming home," he says without looking at me. I slap his hands away. "What else did he say?"

Sam won't answer me. This is bad. This is really bad. Caleb doesn't air his dirty laundry. If he's telling the damn manny something, it must be because he's made up his mind. I climb into the water and let it roll across my face.

God—why didn't I think of these nasty consequences before I flung that at him? Did I really think I'd be hurting only Caleb? I pretty much screwed myself from here to Mars, and now that poor, little brat isn't going to have a father.

Unless.

I shake my head. How could I even think that?

EIGHTEEN
PAST

Caleb came back to me. I knew he would. Not because we had something irreplaceable, but because I was true blue. I fought for what I wanted, and I drove his past out of town. She wouldn't come back. I was fairly certain of this. She was too much of a coward. I knew on some level, when I found those letters and pictures, that she had deep feelings for him. A woman didn't keep a box of mementos unless the flame was still burning strong. I used that to my advantage. I played on her guilt, and thank God, she responded. If she had fought harder, something told me I would have lost.

He retreated into himself after she left. I had to watch his heart break…silently. It was awful. I was so jealous I could barely breathe. He didn't tell me what happened between them, and why would he? He was confused. I had no choice but to wait. It ground at me—the fact that he had obviously cared very much for her before the amnesia, so much so that the feelings were all there, even though his memory was not. It would have made for an interesting psychological study had it not been so incredibly fucked up. He stared off into space a lot after I put an end to their little romance. I could have stood right in front of him during those days, and he wouldn't have seen me. I wondered what he would say when his memory came back. Would he tell me that she was a girl from his past, or would he pretend it never happened?

And then his memory did come back. It happened suddenly, on a Tuesday in April. I was at work when he called to tell me.

"Oh my God," I said, standing up. I was having lunch with a colleague in the break room, but I wanted to go to him right away.

"How do you feel?" I asked, cautiously. I stepped into the hall for privacy. Would he mention Olivia? Was he angry?

"I'm fine," he paused. "Relieved that it's over."

"We should celebrate. As soon as I'm done with work, I can meet you."

He hesitated. "Sure, Leah. There's a lot I want to talk to you about."

My heart fluttered. What did that mean? Now that he remembered who I was, maybe he wanted to move forward with me. I pushed the thought away. No use getting my hopes up for nothing.

"Okay, I'll see you after work. And Caleb…" I held my breath. "I love you."

There was a brief pause, during which my heart went to battle with my stomach for who felt sicker.

"I love you too, Leah." He ended the call. I slouched against the wall.

He remembered that he loved me. I'd been waiting to hear those words for months. I started crying, and then I called Katine and Courtney. Katine was ecstatic, Courtney, not so much.

"So he just remembered everything…out of the blue?" my sister said after I told her.

"Yes, that's how it works."

"I guess I'm just finding it hard to believe that you can forget your girlfriend for months and then, BAM! All of a sudden, it all comes back."

"Can you just be happy for me?" I snapped. "We can finally move forward in our relationship."

"What if he doesn't want to move forward?" she asked. My heart plummeted. He had said he wanted to talk to me. Weren't those infamous breakup words?

"Courtney," I hissed, "you're really pissing me off."

"I'm just trying to look out for you. The guy was having a relationship with another woman for goodness' sake. Wake up, Leah. He's not as perfect as you think he is."

I hung up on her. Courtney was bitter. She'd recently broken up with her boyfriend and was taking it out on Caleb. I wasn't going to let anything dampen my spirits. He was back, and he was mine.

I walked into his condo without knocking. Now that he remembered who I was, there was no need for pretenses. He was standing in the kitchen, drinking a beer, his hair still wet from his shower.

I dropped my purse and ran to him. He just managed to set his bottle on the counter when I launched myself at him. He caught me, laughing.

"Hi, Red."

"Hi, Caleb."

We looked at each other for a good minute before he set me down.

"How do you feel?"

"Fine…great. I just…there is so much…"

I put my hand over his mouth. "You don't have to say anything. I'm just glad you're back."

Before he could argue, I reached up on my tiptoes and kissed him. He was surprised at first. I felt his hands on my arms, trying to pull me away. I wrapped my hands around his neck. I was being territorial. God knows what he had been doing with that woman. I needed to reclaim him, have him kiss me like he did before the accident. He didn't. When I backed away, he wouldn't look at me.

"Caleb, what's wrong? You remember everything, right?"

"Yes."

"I feel like you're still treating me like you don't know who I am."

He walked away, went to stand at the window with his back to me. I wrapped my arms around myself, squeezing my eyes shut. Why did I suddenly feel so cold?

"You're breaking up with me, aren't you?"

He kept his body stiff, but turned his head to look at me. "Were we still together? The way I remember it, you broke up with me the morning of the accident."

I swallowed. That was true.

"The accident put things into perspective for me," I said, carefully. "I almost lost you."

"The accident put things into perspective for me too, Leah. It changed everything—what I wanted…what I thought I could have…"

I shook my head. I didn't understand what he was saying. Was he referring to her?

I squeezed in between him and the window so he was forced to look at me. "Caleb, before the accident you wanted me. Do you still want me?"

The longest two minutes of my life came next. I started to walk away. He grabbed my arm.

I was already crying. I didn't want him to see.

"Leah, look at me."

I did.

"I've been really selfish—"

"I don't care," I rushed. "You were confused."

"I knew what I was doing."

I stared at him. "What do you mean?"

He swore and ran his hand through his hair.

There was a knock at the door.

"Dammit…dammit!" He pressed the heels of his hands to his eyes, before stalking off to answer it.

It was Luca and Steve. I grabbed my purse and ran to the bathroom to fix my face before they could see me. If my mother had taught me anything in life, it was not to get caught with your emotions out.

"Leah!" she exclaimed when I walked out of the bathroom. She moved like a cat toward me. I resisted the urge to back up. The difference between Luca and my mother was a tremendous amount of sincerity and maternal love. This woman loved her son in ways I was completely unfamiliar with. It was unconditional. I envied him that. Something about her need to always embrace me, made me uncomfortable. I felt sized up every time she did it, like she was testing my bones to see if they were worthy of her son. I let her, looking at Caleb over her shoulder. He watched us with a strange expression on his face.

When she pulled away, she kept a hold on my upper arms and looked me in the eyes.

"Caleb, this girl..." She looked over her shoulder at him, then back at me with tears in her eyes. "This girl is a rarity."

My surprise must have been evident on my face. She hugged me again. "Thank you, Leah. You have been so loyal to my son. A mother couldn't ask for anything better."

I wasn't the only one in shock. Caleb's face ranged between full-on astonishment and confusion.

When I caught his eye, he shrugged and smiled.

They stayed for the majority of the night, talking and drinking champagne—which they'd brought to celebrate. I left when they did. At the door, Caleb caught me by the wrist before I could walk away.

"Leah," his voice was husky. "My mother was right. No matter what, you stuck with me. Even when..."

I shook my head. "I don't want to talk about that." Her.

He narrowed his eyes. I felt like he was seeing me for the first time in months.

"You didn't have to. It's a shame it took my mother to point that out to me."

"What are you saying, Caleb?"

"I've taken you for granted. Your loyalty. Your trust. I'm sorry."

He pulled me toward him and wrapped me in a hug. I didn't know what his words meant for us, but I was sure as hell going to stick around to see.

"I'll walk you to your car."

I nodded, swiping at my tears with my fingertips.

Please, God, don't let him hurt me.

NINETEEN

PRESENT

Sam is on my side—or at least I think he is. He doesn't judge me. I like that. He knows the basics of what happened between Caleb and me. So far, he hasn't asked any probing questions. I almost want him to.

I feel like we're a team. He cleans the house, keeps me fed, does the laundry, and tells me when to feed the baby.

I feed the baby.

Sometimes I watch when he gives her a bath and hand him the towel.

Motherhood isn't nearly as hard as I thought. Except when it is.

Caleb doesn't call.

Caleb doesn't call.

"What's with all the tattoos?" I ask him one day. He has his sleeves rolled up to the elbows and he's gently rinsing the soap from the baby's hair. He looks at me out of the corner of his eye. I trace the pictures with my finger, something I've never done before…to anyone. It's a mess of artwork: a pirate ship, a lotus flower, and an incredibly tacky spiderweb. When I reach his elbow, he raises his eyebrows. "Would you like me to take my shirt off so you can continue?"

"There's more?"

He smirks and lifts the baby out of the bath. "If I didn't know better, I'd think you were attracted to me."

I cackle. Really. It's kind of embarrassing.

"You're gay, Sam. And no offense, but I'm not really into the Kurt Cobain, tattooed look."

Sam carries the baby into the nursery and sets her on the changing table. "I hope you're at least into the Kurt Cobain sound, then."

I swallow. God. I feel dizzy all of a sudden.

I'm shaking my head before words can make it past my lips. "I listened when I was younger."

He looks at me quizzically.

"I'm gonna go get something to drink…" I slip out of the room before he can say anything else, but instead of going to the kitchen, I head for my bedroom. I shut the door as quietly as possible and crawl onto my bed.

Breathe, Leah.

I am trying to think of happy things, things my therapist gave me to focus on, but all I can hear are the words to a Nirvana song, echoing so loudly in my head I want to scream.

I scream into my pillow. I hate that. I'm a goddamn mess and there is nothing I can do about it. When my heart stops racing, I go downstairs and get a drink of water.

I am channel surfing a few hours later when I hear Olivia's name. I flick past the channel and have to backtrack. Since Caleb's been gone, I am desperate for any news on her. I know he's watching. I pluck at my eyelashes and watch as Nancy Grace gives me an update on what's happening in Dobson's trial preparation. She's on a tirade. I snicker. When is she not on a tirade? She moves on from Dobson and it takes me a few minutes to figure out that her sharp Southern accent is directed at Olivia. I turn up the volume and lean forward. Yes! Olivia bashing! This is exactly what I need to feel better about myself.

I snuggle down in my seat to watch, a full glass of Scotch sweating in my hand. One corner of the screen is reeling footage of Dobson's victims. They range in age and appearance, but they all have the same haunted look in their eyes. When a video clip of the rapist comes on the screen, I scrunch my nose. He's in an orange jumpsuit, handcuffed and shackled. Officers wearing plain clothes surround him as he walks the short distance from the vehicle to the courthouse. He gives me the heebie-jeebies. He's huge—linebacker size. The cop next to him looks puny. How this buffoon managed to get girls to come within five feet of him astounds me.

Suddenly, the screen flashes to Olivia. I want to change the channel, but as usual, I can't pull my eyes from her. Nancy is waving her bejeweled hand in the air. Her voice is rising in crescendo, and she's told three people on her panel that they're idiots for defending Olivia's case. I reach over for a handful of popcorn, not taking my eyes from the screen. Nancy is right. I feel a sudden fondness for her. She obviously knows how to read people. Then I hear my name. I spit out my popcorn and lean forward.

She won a case a year ago, defending an heiress on clinical fraud charges. Nancy calls to someone on her panel. *Did she win that case, Dave?*

Dave gives a brief summary of my case and affirms that yes, indeed, Olivia did win the case.

Nancy is disgusted.

The evidence against that girl was overwhelming, she says, stabbing the desk with her finger.

I change the channel.

But, the following night, I turn it on again and watch all fifty-two minutes of blonde fury. By night three, I've called into the show as a Ms. Lucy Knight from Missouri, and expressed my disgust with Olivia too. I make sure to tell her that I appreciate what she does for women, that's she's a goddamn hero. Nancy tearfully thanks me for being a fan.

By the end of her show, I am usually drunk. Sometimes Sam stays to watch it with me.

"She's really pretty," he says about Olivia. I spit an ice cube at him and he laughs. The baby is almost sleeping through the night now. I still sleep in her room, just in case she wakes up. Sam thinks I'm finally bonding with her, but I only do it so I don't have to walk far in the middle of the night. Caleb is supposed to be back from his trip late the following day. He sent me a text saying he'd pick up Estella as soon as he got back. I plan a trip to the spa in the morning. If everything goes my way, he won't be going anywhere.

"So, they were together in college?"

I look over to where Sam is sipping on his soda. "What the hell?"

"What?" He shrugs. "I feel like I'm watching a soap opera without all of the backstory."

I sniff. "Yes, they were together for a few years in college. But, it wasn't that serious. They never even slept together."

Sam raises his eyebrows. "Caleb stuck around for a girl who wasn't having sex with him?" He lets out a low whistle.

"What does that mean?" I curl my feet under my body and try not to look too interested. The lack of sex between Caleb and Olivia always confused me. I had wanted to ask questions on the rare occasion it came up, but never wanted to seem like the jealous girlfriend. Besides, Caleb protected his past like it was the goddamn Crown Jewels.

Sam looks thoughtful as he chews on a mouthful of beef jerky. He eats so much of the stuff I've come to associate the smell with him.

"Seems like a long time to ask a college-aged guy to wait. The only way I see someone doing that is if they are crazy in love...addiction love."

"What do you mean *addiction love*?" Caleb has the most non-addictive personality I've ever seen. In fact, it bothers me. One year he will be a full-fledged skier and the next year when I book a trip to the lodge, he'll tell me he's not interested anymore. It's happened countless times throughout our relationship—with restaurants, clothes...he even trades his car in every year. It almost always starts with him loving something intensely and then gradually becoming bored with it.

"I don't know," Sam says. "I guess it sounds like he was willing to do anything for her...even if it meant going against what he was used to."

"I hate you."

He slaps my leg playfully and stands up. "Just trying to clear your head a little, Mommy Monster. Seems like he's your addiction, and it's not a healthy one."

I glare after him as he heads for the door. He's such a pompous ass.

"See you tomorrow," he calls over his shoulder. "When Mr. Perfect returns..."

But, the next day Sam calls to say he's having car problems. I cancel the spa. I haven't spent an entire day alone with the baby since Sam's run with the flu. I eat a mini bag of frozen corn before going up to get her. For most of the day, I repeat everything I see Sam do. We have tummy time in the living room. I wipe her face after she's done eating. I even splurge and take her for a mini walk in the stroller I have never used.

When I discover I'm out of diapers, I call Sam in a panic. He doesn't answer, because no one is ever around when you really damn well need them! How am I supposed to take a baby to the store with me? There has to be some kind of service that runs errands for new mothers. After debating for more than an hour, I pack the baby in the car and head to the nearest grocery store. It takes me ten minutes to figure out how to load her car seat onto the cart. I swear under my breath, until a more seasoned mother comes over to help me. I thank her without meeting her eyes and steer my cart into the store just in time to miss the rain. The minute the cold air conditioning blows on the baby, she starts wailing. I push the cart haphazardly to the kid aisle and toss in five packages of diapers. Better safe than sorry.

By the time I've raced back to the register, people are looking at me like I'm a bad mother. I load everything onto the conveyor and lift her out of the car seat. Holding her against my chest, I pat her back awkwardly. I am fumbling with my wallet and trying to bounce her when the cashier—a bubble-popping juvenile delinquent—asks me, "Will that be all?" I look at the bags of diapers that are now bagged in my cart and then at the empty belt. He is staring at me with his watery marijuana eyes, waiting for my answer.

"Um no, I'd like all of this invisible shit too." I wave a hand at the conveyer, and he is actually dumb enough to look.

"God," I say, viciously swiping my credit card. "Lay off the pot."

The baby chooses that exact moment to have a bowel movement. Before I've pocketed my credit card, the contents of her diaper have leaked onto my hands and shirt. I look around in horror and bolt from the store.

Without the diapers.

I send Sam to go back for them later when he finally calls me back. When he shows up at the front door, I still haven't changed my crapped-on shirt, and in addition to my daughter's brown artwork, both of my breasts are leaking. He shakes his head.

"You look worse every time I see you."

I burst into tears. Sam sets the diapers on the counter and hugs me. "Go shower while she's sleeping. I'll make us something to eat."

I nod and head upstairs. When I come back down, he's made spaghetti.

"Sit." He points to a barstool. I obey, pulling in the plate he slides toward me.

"You're losing it," he says. He wraps spaghetti around his fork without looking at me.

I use a knife to cut mine into little pieces so that they fit onto my fork.

"How do I get him to come home?"

"Get a new personality and learn to shut the fuck up."

I give him a dirty look as I dab at my mouth.

"Are you attracted to me?"

There is a long pause.

"I'm gay, Leah."

"What? I never *really* thought you were."

"You've been saying it all along!"

"But, you have a daughter…what's her name, again?"

He laughs. "Kenley. And, I guess I only figured it out later in life."

I drop my head in my hands. This is an all-time new low for me, seducing a gay man. I take a deep breath and look up.

"Caleb's going to leave me again. I know it."

For a second Sam looks taken aback, and then he scoots over and puts an arm around my shoulders.

"Probably," he says. My head snaps around to look at him. Weren't gay men supposed to be sensitive? The minute he announced he was gay, I was planning on using him to replace Katine. "Probably. I can't believe he's stayed with you for this long." He smiles at my expression.

"Did you really just say that?"

He nods. "Maybe the guy loves a good bitch—but you're treading a thin line between attractively bitchy and psycho. You messed with his daughter. He's probably going to leave you and take his kid."

"No way. I won't let that happen."

"What?—The husband or the baby?"

I bite the inside of my cheek. It's obvious what I mean.

153

"He won't believe it—if I start acting all supermom. He sees through shit like that."

Sam raises an eyebrow.

"He won't leave me. He thinks I'll fall apart if he does."

"Is that how you want to keep him? By manipulating his emotions?"

I shrug. "I try not to think about it, honestly."

"Yeah, that's kind of apparent. Why not just let him go? You could find someone else."

I have the urge to slap him across the face. I light up a Slim instead.

"I won't ever let him go. I love him too much."

Sam smirks at me and plucks it from my fingers, stubbing it out on my granite. "Never?"

"Never," I say. "Never ever."

Sam points a finger at me. "That's not love."

I roll my eyes at him. "What do you know? You're gay."

TWENTY

Daddy called me his right hand. It should have been considered an honor, but it felt more like I'd pinned a scarlet letter to my dress. Everyone knew his rigid policy on not bringing family into the company, so my sudden appearance was a cold, drizzly raincloud over the other employees. Had my father recruited a spy? Was he downsizing the company, using me to report who was and wasn't doing their jobs? They shuffled papers when I walked by, pretending to be busier than they were. Some were radically pleasant, hoping to gain my friendship to secure their jobs, while others were openly hostile. The *Why is she here?* question was the ever-ringing bell that preceded me down the halls. It was miserable. What was more miserable was the size of my office. Other than Daddy's, mine was the most coveted in the building. One wall made entirely of glass, it offered a view of downtown Ft. Lauderdale. If I stood just right, facing the ocean, I could see Caleb's building in the distance. Its previous owner, who was well loved by everyone at OPI-Gem, was fired a week before I arrived. He'd been with the company for twelve years and had earned the office I'd been handed. My door plaque might have just read Entitled Brat in pink bubble letters. I was making five times the money I'd made at the bank. On the surface, my already privileged life had just landed down Licorice Lane. On the inside, under the shiny new office and title, I was warping.

My father gave me a prestigious job at his company to prove how little he thought of me. My boyfriend gave me smiles that didn't reach his eyes. My mother gave me love so thin it felt more like sugarcoated contempt. If someone had cared enough to say: Leah, it's all in your head…all I would have to do was refer them to the three people in my life who didn't really want me there.

My assistant peeked her head in. "Ms. Smith, everyone is waiting for you in the conference room."

Shit. I'd forgotten about that. I grabbed my MacBook and Jamba Juice and bolted out the door. I was so wrapped up in my pity party that I was ten minutes late for an uber-important meeting. I hated that. I strolled in casually, avoiding my father's eyes, and sat down in my seat.

I looked up, expecting to see Bruce Gowin, who normally sat next to me, but instead I was greeted by a blonde with blindingly white teeth.

Where was Bruce? Bruce was my partner in snark. My head swiveled around the table looking for him, until my father caught my eye.

"Leah, I'm so pleased you finally decided to join us. If you are looking for Mr. Gowin—he is no longer with us. Cassandra Wickham is his replacement."

"You can call me Cash," she said, extending her hand. Cash…how Hollywood.

Cash had edgy, trying-too-hard chin-length hair and lips that had seen about five rounds of the collagen needle. She was striking…sexy. I immediately felt threatened. I gave her the most genuine smile I could muster and turned back to my father who was watching me closely. Cash was his new pet, I could already tell. I wondered if Bruce had been fired just to make room for her.

"Let's begin, shall we…" He turned on the projector and every head swiveled toward it, like we were programmed to do so. And we were. Charles Austin Smith verbally berated anyone who dared speak or nod off during his meetings. He verbally berated my mother for speaking her opinions so often that she no longer had any. King Smith. Formerly Smitoukis, but that was part of his poor life. When the King spoke, his subjects lost their tongues and listened.

The meeting was a way for all of the OPI-Gem departments to touch base. Since I was head of Internal Affairs, it was my responsibility to coordinate Cash's new position as Pharmaceutical Formulation Chemist. Since most formulation chemists were either self-taught or had in essence been apprenticed under experienced researchers, Cash was an immediate important person in the company. A pharmaceutical rock star, if you will. I didn't know how I felt about my new charge. I wanted Bruce back.

After the meeting, I headed to my father's office to find out where he went. Closing the door behind me, I took the only available seat opposite his desk. I waited for him to look up from his computer before speaking.

"What happened to Bruce, Daddy?"

My father took off his reading glasses and set them on his desk. "Mr. Gowin was not performing. I have big projects emerging that are going to set us on the map as a pharmaceutical company. We needed a new set of eyes. I trust that you will take Ms. Wickham under your wing."

I nodded…too eagerly. He frowned. "You will be working closely with her while we formulate and test a new drug. I'm putting you in charge of the entire project."

My jaw dropped. I quickly recovered, wiping the silly smile from my face, trying to be Vice President of Internal Affairs.

It was a big deal. Whatever my father's motives were for bringing me into the company were all cast aside by this one bit of news. He trusted me with the launching of a new drug. That was huge!

"Thank you, Daddy. I'm so honored."

He dismissed me with a wave of his hand, and I had to restrain myself from skipping out of the office. The first thing I did was call Caleb.

He was breathless when he picked up the phone. I imagined he'd just come back from a run.

"Wow, Red. I'm so proud of you. I'll pick you up from work tonight and we'll celebrate."

I glowed under his praise. I agreed to be ready by seven. I hung up the phone and smoothed my skirt. I was going to have to take a trip down to the lab where Cash would be setting up her office. Since we were going to be working together, it was in my best interest to get to know her. When I turned toward the door, she was already there.

"Leah," she said. "May I come in?"

I nodded and motioned for her to take a seat.

"I thought we could maybe get lunch, get to know one another a little bit."

I decided not to tell her that I was about to do the same thing. Let her think she was chasing me. I was the boss; I should maintain a professional air. I studied her features as she sat across from me. We were around the same age. She was a little leathery, like she'd been best friends with a tanning bed for the last few years. And, I could respect a nice C-cup, but when you delved into the double D's you were emulating a little too much Jessica Rabbit. Cash was definitely double D'ing it.

"I don't really know my way around," she said, crossing her legs. "I just moved here from D.C."

What did one say to something like that? I really didn't care where she was from. I smiled.

"You can ride with me. Tomorrow?"

She nodded and stood up. She had a tattoo of a dolphin on her ankle. Strange for someone from D.C.

"Great, see you tomorrow." She lingered at the door. I thought she was going to say something else, but at the last minute she sped out and turned the corner as if she were running from something.

I watched her walk down the hall and push the button for the elevator. There was something so shady about her. Caleb would probably be able to figure her out. He was good at shit like that. I was almost tempted to let them meet, but then I thought of the way women reacted to Caleb, and I trashed the idea. The last thing I needed was that bottle blonde flirting with my boyfriend. I'd just have to keep a close eye on her myself.

When six o'clock came, I slipped into the bathroom to freshen up for my date with Caleb. Luckily I was wearing my new, white Chanel suit. I pulled the pins from my hair and let it tumble down my back. The red was striking against the white. I was beautiful. I knew that; men told me all the time, and most women were jealous of me. So jealous it was almost impossible to maintain friendships.

Caleb walked into my office ten minutes early, smelling of pine needles and looking edible. He was always early. I acted surprised, like I hadn't spent the last twenty minutes primping in the bathroom. I stood up to kiss him and my stomach fluttered when his tongue slipped into my mouth.

"I like this," he said, running a finger along the material that topped off my cleavage. He was referring to my suit, but with Caleb there was always underlying meaning.

"Why don't you take it off and see if you like what's underneath," I said into his mouth. I liked the idea of christening my new office.

He was considering my offer, when there was a knock on my door.

I pushed away from his chest, annoyed.

"Come in."

Cash opened the door. Her face flushed when she saw us.

"My God, I'm so sorry," she said, backing away. "I was coming to ask you if you knew how to get to the nearest Panera."

Her eyes traveled over us, pausing on Caleb's face.

I didn't like the way she was looking at him. I pressed myself closer, wrapping my arms around his neck like a possessive sloth.

Mine.

She seemed to understand my body language. The corners of her mouth turned up slightly. There was an uncomfortable pause, during which I was waiting for her to go away. Caleb cleared his throat. Introductions, of course.

"Cassandra Wickham, this is my boyfriend, Caleb," I said, giving the mandatory introduction. Caleb broke away from me to shake her hand. I didn't want him touching her. She held onto his hand for a few seconds too many, smiling coyly.

Did she not see me standing right there?

"Are you new to the area?" Caleb asked, letting go of her hand. He leaned into me, and I pressed myself against his side. He knew my weaknesses, one of them being insecurity. Whenever he picked up on those vibes, he overcompensated in the attention department. Perfect, he was perfect.

Cash nodded. "Just moved here a week ago."

"Cassandra is going to be working with me on the new project," I said, tightly. I didn't feel like calling her Cash anymore.

I knew what was coming next. Caleb was a gentleman. If someone didn't know their way around and was proclaiming hunger—

"You should join us for dinner. We were going out to celebrate."

I flinched. She didn't appear to notice, maybe because her eyes were glued to my boyfriend.

"I'd hate to impose…"

Yeah, fucking right.

"Of course you wouldn't be imposing," I said, quickly. "We'd love it if you tagged along."

Her eyes shot to mine, and I had no doubt she heard what I was really saying.

"Well then, I'll just grab my purse."

As soon as she was out of my office, Caleb kissed me on the forehead…then the lips. He was drawn to kindness, turned on by it even—which is exactly why I was insecure. I wasn't exactly on Santa's Nice List. Either he hadn't figured that out yet, or he was too distracted by my boobs to care. Admittedly, I had a really nice set.

We met Cash in the lobby and she insisted on driving with us. I just about had to nudge her out of the way to get to the front seat. Caleb took us to Seasons 52. We ordered wine and one glass later, Cash found out more about my boyfriend than I had in a year.

"So, this girl—your ex—wouldn't sleep with you. Excuse me for saying this, but you're so fucking sexy, how is that possible? Was she a lesbian?"

Caleb smiled crookedly, and I wondered what secret he was hiding behind his sensual lips.

He ran his tongue along his bottom lip and regarded Cash with what I called the "laughing eyes."

"Someone hurt her emotionally. Unfortunately, I hurt her as well."

"Unfortunately?" she mimicked, her eyes darting to where I sat.

I felt the sting without seeing his face. Caleb wore his emotion on his jaw. I could imagine he was clenching it pretty hard at this point. I reached for his hand under the table, and our fingers entwined. He thought I was offering support, but really I just needed to know he was still mine. I wanted to remind him that I was the one sitting at this table with him, not her.

He shifted in his seat. Cash had given him the third degree about how we'd met. As soon as she'd latched onto the idea that he'd been reluctant to go on the blind date with me, she'd wanted to know why.

"What about you, Cash? What's your story?" Cash's eyelashes tried to fly away. I bit down my smirk and prepared for a wild ride. Caleb had a knack for rooting out information. I was fairly certain that by the end of our meal, we'd know her whole life story.

She reached a manicured finger up to swipe her hair behind her ear. She was hiding something. I knew what a woman with a secret looked like; I stared at one in the mirror every day. Women wore their secrets in their eyes, and if you paid attention, you would catch glimpses of sharp emotion pooling through in regular conversation. Caleb asked her if she'd moved to Florida alone, and I caught a quick downward glance, before she cheerfully answered, "Yes."

I'd taken a psychology class in college that studied body language. One of the lectures had been called The Art of Lying. We had been required to run an experiment along with reading the chapter, in which we'd ask a person who was not in the class a series of questions. Much to my delight, I'd discovered that a person who is recalling a real memory looks up and to the right, whereas a person who is utilizing the creative part of their brain—to lie—looks down and to the left. Cash was doing a lot of downward dogging with her eyes. Filthy. Little. Liar.

"Where does your family live?" Caleb asked. He was running a piece of my hair between his fingers. Cash looked on enviously.

"Oh, they're around," she said, waving off his question.

"Around here?"

"My father lives here. My mother lives in New York."

"Do you see him often?"

She shook her head. "Not really."

Another fucked-up family, no doubt. I almost nodded in support.

"I wish I had more time," she said quickly. "I've just been so busy with the move. We're very close."

Her mouth was open to deliver another lie, when our server arrived with the food. A shame. I wanted to hear it. The rest of the meal was accompanied by small talk. So, she was close to her father? Must be nice.

TWENTY-ONE

Caleb had hidden the boat from me. What else is he hiding? The knowledge that there could be more is rusting my brain. It's all I can think about, until I am practically choking on my suspicion. I've been frowning so much I'm going to need a Botox shot at the end of this. One thing is certain: I need to find out if there is more, even if that means breaking his code of privacy. Caleb hates anyone in his office if he isn't there. I've always given him his space, seeing that the entire rest of the house is mine, but tonight calls for snooping. I let Sam go home as soon as he puts Estella down. Normally, I make him stay for a few hours and watch TV with me, but as soon as seven o'clock comes, I practically shove him out the door.

I open the door to Caleb's office, still chewing on my celery stick, and flick on the light. I hardly ever come in here. The whole room smells of him. I breathe deeply and immediately feel like crying. I used to get to cuddle up to that smell every night, and now…

I eye the stacks of books piled everywhere. I don't really know when he finds the time to read. When he is home with us, he is cooking and interacting. Despite the fact that there is always a book lying around the house, I've never actually seen him read. Once, I'd been tidying up, putting the books that he scattered around the house back in his office, when his bookmark had fallen from one of the novels I was carrying. Bending to retrieve it from the floor, I'd found what looked like a penny—or at least it used to be a penny. Now, it had a message about kissing stamped on it. It was an odd shape too, bent slightly and elongated. I'd stuck it back in his book and the next time I was out, I'd picked him up a real bookmark. It was leather, imported from Italy. I paid fifty dollars to the salesman, thinking Caleb was going to be so impressed at my thoughtfulness. When I'd presented it to him that night at dinner, he'd smiled politely and thanked me, showing none of the enthusiasm I'd expected.

"I just thought you needed one. You use that weird penny, and it keeps falling out—"

His eyes had immediately snapped to my face. "Where is it? You didn't throw it away, did you?" I'd blinked at him, confused.

"No, it's in your office." I couldn't hide the hurt from my voice. His eyes had softened, and he'd come around the table to kiss my cheek.

"Thank you, Leah. It was a good idea—really. I needed something better to use to remind me of my place."

"Your place?"

"In the book." He'd smiled.

I'd never seen the penny again, but I had the feeling he'd stowed it somewhere for safekeeping. Caleb was strangely sentimental.

Pushing aside a pile of books on the floor, I go to his drawers first and begin pulling out papers. Bills, work crap—nothing important. The filing cabinet was next. I browse through each file folder, reading them out loud.

"College, Contractors, Deeds to houses, Discover Card..."

I flip back to Deeds to houses. We only had one house, aside from Caleb's condo, which he insisted on keeping. There were three. The first address was for our house, the second for his condo, and the third…

I sit down as my eyes rove over each word…each name. I feel like I am trying to dig through glass. My brain is at a disconnect with my eyes. I force myself to read. By the time I am done, my eyes can no longer focus on anything. I lay my head on his desk, the papers still clutched in my hand. I'm having trouble breathing. I start to cry, but not self-pitying tears—tears of anger. I cannot believe he did this to me. I cannot.

I stand up so filled with rage. I am ready to do something reckless. I pick up the phone to call him—to scream at him. I hang up before I dial. I double over, clutching my stomach and a moan rumbles from my lips. How can this hurt so much? There have been worse things done to me. I hurt. I hurt so much. I want someone to cut my heart out just so I don't have to feel this. He promised he would never hurt me. He promised to take care of me.

I knew he never loved me like he loved her, but I wanted him anyway. I knew his love for me was conditional, but I wanted him anyway. I knew I was second choice, but I wanted him anyway. But, this was too much. Stumbling from his office and into the foyer, I look around my mansion, my beautiful little world. Had I created this to cover up the stench of my life? A filigree egg sits on a table near the door. It's an antique that Caleb bought for me on a trip we took to Cape Cod. It cost him five thousand dollars. I pick it up and fling it across the room, screaming as I do. It smashes against the tile, skittering every way, like my life.

I walk to our wedding picture, which is hanging above the sofa. I consider it for a moment, remembering the day—supposedly the happiest day of my life. I grab the broom, which is leaning against a wall, and smash the handle as hard as I can into the glass frame. The picture comes off the wall, crashing over furniture and landing face down on the coffee table.

Estella starts to cry.

I wipe my leaking face with the back of my hand and move toward the stairs. I'm kind of glad she's awake. I need someone to hold.

TWENTY-TWO

My wedding day looked more like a coronation than an actual wedding. It *was* a coronation for me in a way. I had won my crown. I had, quite possibly, the sexiest, most endearing man the world had to offer. I'd beaten out the evil, raven-haired witch to get him. I felt triumphant. I felt validated. It felt like a long time coming.

I thought all of these things, as I stood in front of the mirror in my ivory dress. It was a heart bodice, mermaid skirt. My hair was up, curled into what looked like a seashell, with a stunning white flower pinned to the side. I'd wanted to wear my hair down, but Caleb asked for it up. I'd do anything for Caleb.

I peeped out the window at my parent's sprawling backyard. The guests were starting to arrive; ushers were leading them to their seats. The sky was dimming and the thousands of lights I insisted be strung in the trees were finally beginning to show.

A huge tent sat off to the left, where the reception would be. To the right was the Olympic-sized swimming pool. My parents had ordered a glass floor to be placed over the pool, where Caleb and I would take our vows. We'd be walking on water. It made me giddy just to think of it. Chairs were set up to circle the pool. We'd have an audience all around us. Caleb had laughed when he'd first seen it the day before. He hated the way my family tried to outdo the Joneses.

"Love is simple," he'd said. "The more pomp you add to a wedding, the less sincere it becomes."

I hated that. Weddings were the frosting for the rest of your life. If the frosting wasn't good, who wanted to stick around for the cupcake?

We'd stared at that glass floor for a good fifteen minutes, before I eventually said, "I wanted to be the Little Mermaid." He laughed at first, and then his face had turned serious. He tugged on one of my curls. "It'll be beautiful, Lee. You'll be the Little Mermaid. I'm sorry, that was the jackass in me speaking."

My mother bustled into the room ten minutes before the wedding. It was the first I'd seen of her all day. She leaned over me as Courtney applied my lipstick. Katine, who was across the room putting the final touches on her own makeup, met my eyes in the mirror. She was all too familiar with my mother and her antics. I quelled rising nausea as Courtney dabbed at my lips with a tissue.

"Hi, Mom," I said, turning to smile at her.

"Why did you choose that shade, Leah? You look like a vampire."

I glanced at myself in the mirror. Courtney had been applying my signature shade of red. Maybe it did look a little too goth for a wedding. I reached for a tissue and wiped it off, pointing to a rose-colored tube instead. "Let's try that one."

My mother watched in satisfaction as the new lipstick was applied. "Everyone is almost here. This is going to be the most impressive wedding of the year, I can guarantee you that."

I beamed.

"And the most beautiful bride," my sister said, brushing blush across my cheeks.

"And the sexiest groom," Katine threw over her shoulder.

I giggled, grateful for their support.

"Yes, well, let's hope she can hold onto him this time," my mother said. Katine dropped her mascara wand.

"Mother!" Courtney snapped. "So inappropriate. Can you lay off the bitch mode?"

I'd never get away with saying something like that. My mother frowned at her favorite daughter. I could sense a rising argument.

I put a hand on Courtney's arm. I didn't want there to be fighting today. I wanted everything to be perfect. I swallowed my hurt and smiled at my mother.

"We love each other," I said confidently. "I don't need to hold onto anything. He's mine."

She raised her perfect eyebrows at me, her lips pulling tight. "There's always something they love more," she said. "Be it a woman or a car or…"

Her words dropped off, but I finished them in my head—*or another daughter…*

Courtney, oblivious to our father's favoritism, swept more blush over my cheekbones. "You're so cynical, Mother. Not every man is like that."

My mother smiled indulgently at her younger daughter and swept a hand across her cheek. "No, my love," she said, "not for you."

I heard the implication. Courtney did not. I eyed her hand on my sister's cheek, and I hurt. She rarely touched me. Even when I was little, I was lucky to get a hug on my birthday. Turning away from them, I thought of Caleb and immediately felt better. We were starting our own family today. I would never, ever treat my child the way they treated me. No matter what the situation. Caleb was going to be the best dad. I would be able to look back at my old life with sadness as I glowed in the rosy haze of my new one. Caleb.

I had him. Maybe no one else, but he was enough for me.

Five minutes before things were scheduled to start, there was a knock on the door. My mother had already left and only Katine and Courtney were with me.

Courtney ran to see who it was, while Katine helped me into my shoes.

She came back half smiling. "It's Caleb. He wants to speak to you."

Katine shook her head. "Hell, no! He can't see her yet. I'm divorced, and you know what? I let the asshole see me before we got married." She said it matter-of-factly, like that was the sole reason her marriage had fallen apart.

I looked at the door, my heart rate spiking. I didn't mind. "You two go downstairs. I'll see you in a minute."

Katine folded her arms across her chest like she wasn't going anywhere.

"Katine," I said, "Brian left you because you slept with his brother, not because he saw you in your wedding dress. Now get out."

Courtney grabbed Katine's arm, before she could retort, and dragged her from the room.

I smoothed my dress, glancing quickly in the mirror before heading to the door. What could he want to speak to me about? Suddenly, I felt sick. What if he wanted to call things off? Was there ever a good reason a groom demanded to speak to the bride before he married her?

I cracked it open.

"You're not supposed to see me," I said.

He laughed, which immediately set me at ease. A laughing man didn't come to break up with his fiancée.

"Turn around," he said. "And I'll back in."

"All right."

I turned my back to the door and took a few steps away. I heard Caleb shuffle in. He came to stand with his back pressed against my back. He reached for my hands, and we stood there like that for a good minute before he spoke.

"I'm gonna turn around…" he said.

"No!"

He started laughing, and I knew he was teasing.

I squeezed his hands. He squeezed back.

"Leah," his voice touched my name in a way that made me close my eyes. Everything that rolled off his tongue sounded beautiful but especially my name.

"Yes?" I said softly.

"Do you love me or the idea of me?"

I stiffened, and he stroked the tops of my fingers with his thumbs.

I tried to pull my hands away because I wanted to see his face, but he held them firmly, not letting me go.

"Just answer the question, love."

"I love you," I said with certainty. "Do you…do you not feel the same?"

Oh God. He was going to call off the wedding.

I felt my throat constricting. I dropped my head, pulling in deep breaths.

"I love you, Leah. I wouldn't have asked you to marry me if I didn't."

Then why are we having this conversation?

"Then why are we having this conversation?" I had sounded surer in my head. My voice quivered.

"Love isn't always enough. I just want to make sure…"

His voice trailed off. Was he talking about Olivia? I wanted to scream. She was here with us on our wedding day. I wanted to tell him that she was gone! She'd moved on. She was…she was…a worthless bitch that didn't deserve him.

Did I love him?

I lifted my chin. Yes, I did—more than she did, anyway. If he needed me to talk him through this, I would.

"Caleb," I said, my voice soft. "There is something I've never told you. It's about my family."

I took a breath and allowed the truth to seep from my lips. It was now or never. My words were laced with shame and hurt. Caleb, sensing something, gripped me tighter.

"I'm adopted."

He made to spin around, but I held him in place. I couldn't look at him just yet. I just needed to get this out. Any minute they were going to come looking for us, and I needed to finish before they did. "Just, don't turn around, okay. Just…listen."

"Okay," he said.

"After my parents got married, they tried for three years to have a baby. Doctors told my mother that she couldn't have children, so they reluctantly decided to adopt. My father is Greek, Caleb. He needed a son. They decided not to wait for a domestic adoption, which would have taken years. My father had connections in the Russian embassy."

"Leah…"

My heart almost caved at the sound of his voice. "Just shut up," I said. "This is really hard; just let me say it."

I fought the tears. I wouldn't sacrifice my makeup for this.

"My real mother was sixteen and she worked in a brothel. I wasn't the boy they wanted, but they brought me back with them. I was six weeks old. A month later, my mother found out she was pregnant. She had a miscarriage…I guess it was a boy. My father blamed the stress of the miscarriage on me. I was apparently very difficult—colicky and whatnot. She got pregnant with Courtney a few months later, but my father had lost his boy. I guess he's hated me ever since. I went from the baby they wanted to the baby that killed the wanted baby…to the inconvenience—a prostitute's baby."

There was a loud rapping on the door. "A few more minutes," I called out. I spun around and made Caleb face me. He took me in his arms, his eyebrows drawn. I felt his warmth seeping into me. He was quiet for a long time.

"Why didn't you tell me?"

"God, Caleb. It's my family's dirty little secret. I was ashamed." I had to bend my head all the way back to look into his face. He made me feel small and protected.

"You have nothing to be ashamed of. It's them—I can't even imagine."

He shook his head. "Is that why your father won't walk you down the aisle today?" He narrowed his eyes, and I blushed. I'd told him that my father's gout was acting up. No holds barred. I nodded. My father had told me a week earlier that he would not be escorting me down the aisle. I hadn't really expected him to.

Caleb swore. He hardly ever swore in front of me. I could see how angry he was. "That's why he gave you the job." It wasn't a question. He was piecing things together. I nodded. He looked so enraged; I knew my plan was working.

"Caleb…don't leave me," my lip quivered. "Please…I love you."

He grabbed me almost roughly and pulled me into his arms. I clutched him, not caring about my makeup or my hair. This was the way into his heart. I played on his compassion, and I played on his need to protect things that were broken and lost.

The knocking on the door resumed. Caleb held me at arm's length and looked at me. Something had transitioned in his eyes. I'd become something else to him in the moment I'd shared my secret. Had I known that would happen? Had I intentionally held off on telling him the truth in case something like this ever happened?

He lightly ran a finger from my hairline, straight down my forehead across my nose, over my lips and down my neck.

"You're stunning," he said. "Can I walk you down the aisle?"

My heart skipped, skidded, flew…did a fucking happy dance. He was going to marry me.

"Yes, please."

"Leah…"

"Yes?"

"I won't hurt you. I'll take care of you. Do you believe me?"

"Yes," I lied.

TWENTY-THREE

She looks the same. Raven hair hanging wildly to her waist. She looks almost gypsy-like in her teal linen pants and a cream sheath shirt that hangs casually off one defined shoulder. I eye her gold hoop earrings, which are big enough to fit my entire hand through. They make her look exotic and slightly dangerous. She has always made me feel plain.

Her eyes rove over the handful of occupants in the diner, searching for a face she recognizes: an old man, a couple who share the same side of a booth, two servers folding silverware into napkins...and me.

I see the shock overcome her features—the parting of her lips, the slight spreading of white around her irises. Suddenly, she stiffens. Her eyes chase to the four corners of the room, and I know she is looking for him. I shake my head to tell her he's not here. I take a sip of my coffee and I wait.

She moves with purpose toward my table. When she reaches where I am sitting, she doesn't sit but stares at me expectantly.

"An old client?" she says dryly.

"Well, I am, aren't I?" I motion for her to sit. I'd sent an anonymous message to her office, claiming I was an old client in desperate legal trouble. I'd asked her to meet me at a diner named Tiffany's. I had no idea if she'd come or not, but it was better than showing up at her office.

She slides cautiously into the seat across from me, never taking her eyes from my face.

"Well, what the fuck do you want?"

I flinch. Louboutins or not, she's still the same crass piece of white trash she used to be.

"I thought maybe you could look over this document for me." I reach into my purse and pull out the papers I'd stolen from Caleb's filing cabinet. Placing them on the table, I slide them toward her.

"What is this?" she asks. She eyes me distastefully. How dare she look at me that way? She has singlehandedly ruined my life. I'd have everything if it weren't for her devious, overreaching hands.

I'd probably also be in prison. I push that thought away. Now is not the time for gratitude. Now is the time for answers. I poke the document in front of her.

"Take a look. See for yourself."

Without moving her head, she looks at the papers then back to me. It's a smooth, hard, impressive piece of intimidation. The art of her body language is something to be admired.

"Why would I want to do that?" she says.

She's making me feel chilled. I get a flashback of being on the witness stand, and my heart rate spikes. I practice to see if I can do it too.

"It's Caleb's," I say, only moving my lips.

I don't know whether it's the mention of his name or if my imitation of her body language is working, but she tenses.

A server approaches our table. Olivia reaches for the papers.

"Get her a coffee, two creamers," I say, waving him away. He hurries off. Olivia, who is reading, briefly glances up at me. I spent almost every day with her for nine months. I know what she likes.

I sip my coffee as she reads, watching her face.

Her coffee arrives. Without looking up, she pulls the lids from the creamers and dumps them into her cup.

She lifts the mug to her lips, but halfway there her hand freezes. Coffee spills onto the table as she slams the mug down. Abruptly, she stands up.

"Where did you get that?"

She is backing away from the table, shaking her head. "Why is my name on there?"

I run my tongue across my teeth. "I was hoping you could tell me that."

She bolts for the door. I stand up, tossing a twenty on the table, and go after her.

I follow her into the parking lot and corner her by the newspaper stand. "You are not getting out of explaining why your name is on this deed along with my husband's!"

Her face is washed of color. She shakes her head. "I don't know, Leah. He never—I don't know."

She covers her face with her palms, and I hear her sob. That only makes me angrier. I take a threatening step toward her.

"You're sleeping with him, aren't you?"

She pulls her hands away and glares at me.

"No. Of course not! I love my husband." She is clearly insulted that I would even accuse her of such a thing.

"I love mine!" My voice cracks. "—So, why does he love you?"

She looks at me with true loathing.

"He doesn't," she says simply. "He chose you." It pains her to give me those words. I can see the emotion spilling from her skin.

I hold up the deed and shake it. "He bought you a house. Why did he buy you a fucking house?"

She snatches the deed from my fingers and points to a date. "Did you miss this little detail? Long before you, Leah—but, you know that. So, why did you really trick me into coming here?"

I swallow—a nervous reaction. She sees it and smiles cruelly.

"I should have let them throw you in prison, you know that."

She turns away, walking toward her car door. Her statement infuriates me. I follow her, digging my fingernails into my palms. I breathe through my nose.

"So you could have him?" I blurt. My blood pounds in my ears. I ask myself that question all the time. I say it again. "You should have lost the case so you could have him?"

She freezes, looks at me over her shoulder.

"Yeah."

I didn't expect the truth. It frightens me. I open my mouth—force the words out. "I thought you loved your husband."

She blows air through her nose. The action reminds me of an agitated horse. Her eyes rove from my shoes and land in disgust on my face.

"I love yours too."

TWENTY-FOUR

B efore Caleb and I were married, I rarely allowed my parents to be around him out of fear that their opinions would rub off on him and he'd start looking at me like they did. Most of my other boyfriends hadn't caught on to their veiled insults and cold parenting. Caleb was smart; he'd see right through them, right through me—and start asking questions. I didn't want the questions or the eventual resignation it would bring: Leah is a disappointment. She's not the real deal, just the secondhand daughter.

I didn't like anyone knowing my shit. So, for the two years of our courtship, I herded him in and out of social events with my family with meticulous precision. It was exhausting for the most part—making sure no one said too much, the conversations didn't dip too deep. After the wedding, that changed. Maybe I felt more comfortable since I had the commitment, or maybe it was the fact that I had finally told him the truth about where I came from.

We were formally invited to attend dinner at their house a week after we got back from our honeymoon. Caleb was still bristling over the fact that my father wouldn't walk me down the aisle.

"I don't want to go, Leah. What he did was disrespectful to you. He's lucky I didn't call him out at the wedding. I won't let him treat you like that."

I loved that. I felt more valuable in those five seconds than I had in years.

"Please," I reached up on my tiptoes and kissed his chin. "Let's just keep the peace. I love my sister. I don't want to cause a rift."

He grabbed my upper arms and squeezed gently, narrowing his eyes. "If he says one word, Leah, one word that I don't like…"

"You're going to punch him in the face," I said firmly.

He grinned crookedly and kissed me roughly on the mouth—just the way I liked it.

"I'm going to punch him in the face if he serves duck. I hate duck."

I giggled against his lips. "What about if he tells the scuba-diving joke?"

"That too—he's getting hit for the joke…"

We were moving toward the bedroom, our feet shuffling together, our lips never far apart.

I laced my fingers in his hair, the edges of my thoughts fraying until they fell apart, and all I could think of was his touch and his husky voice in my ear.

Later that evening, we walked to my parents' door hand in hand. Two weeks in the Maldives had left us tanned and relaxed, and we were still floating in our vacation lull, laughing and kissing and touching like one of us might disappear. Caleb was finally mine. As my hand sought out the doorknob, my thoughts fleetingly went to my arch nemesis. My lips found a smile so rooted in triumph that Caleb cocked his head at me quizzically.

"What?" he asked.

I shrugged. "I'm just happy, that's all. Everything is perfect."

I wished I could say: Dum, dum, the witch is dead…

But, the witch wasn't dead. She was in Texas—which was good enough.

My parents and sister were in the family room. They looked at Caleb expectantly when we walked in, almost like they were waiting for him to announce he was leaving me. There was an awkward thirty seconds of silence before my sister jumped up to hug us.

"How was it? Tell me everything." She grabbed my hand and led me toward the couch. I glanced at Caleb, who was shaking hands with my father. Daddy liked Caleb. He liked him so much that I wondered what he'd think about the fact that Caleb hated him. I felt a sick satisfaction knowing that I'd turned Caleb against him. My father thought he could have anyone, and he truly wanted everyone's adoration…except mine.

"It was beautiful," I assured her. "Very romantic."

A quick glance at Caleb.

She leaned close to me. "They've been bitching all morning about how much the wedding cost them," she said. "Don't bring it up."

I felt my cheeks grow warm. This was typical behavior for my parents. Of course they'd pay for their eldest daughter's wedding. Of course it would be extravagant and over the top to impress their friends. Of course they would bitch afterward about how much money they'd had to shell out for someone who wasn't really blood. But, what else could they do? No one knew I wasn't really theirs. To do anything less would cast a shadow over their perfect image as loving parents.

Please, God, please don't let them say anything in front of Caleb.

My sister was holding a glass of red wine. I took it from her and swallowed a mouthful.

My mother was walking toward us, each of her birdlike steps tugging a fresh strand of dread to the forefront of my mind.

"You should really stay out of the sun, Leah," she said, sitting down across from me. I looked down at my bronze-colored arm. Despite the fact that I was fair-skinned and had red hair, I tanned like an Italian.

"You look silly with color—it looks like you went for one of those spray tans."

"She looks fine, Mother," my sister snapped. "Just because you're afraid of the sun, doesn't mean we have to be."

I shot my sister a grateful look and tensed for the next biting comment.

"Caleb looks well," she said, glancing over to where he was still speaking with my father. "So handsome. I always thought he'd be a good match for you, Courtney."

My head swam, my vision blurred. Courtney made an angry sound in the back of her throat.

"That is so wildly inappropriate," she hissed. "Not only is perfect *not* my type, but Leah and Caleb go together better than any couple I know. Everyone says so."

My mother raised her eyebrows. I found my tongue.

"Why would you even say something like that?" I said to her. "After everything you did to help me…"

She sniffed and took a sip from her own wine glass. "A woman shouldn't have to fight that hard to be with a man. He should just want her…"

My sister was looking from one of us to the other. "What are you talking about?"

My mother's eyes locked with mine in a silent warning. "Dinner should be ready," she said. "Why don't we head over to the dining room?"

Mattia still made most of my parents' meals. She'd been with my family since I was a little girl. I always looked forward to her cooking. Tonight, it was salmon with a honey mustard glaze and rice pilaf. She squeezed my shoulder as she set my plate down in front of me.

"Congratulations," she whispered in my ear. I smiled at her. I'd wanted her to come to the wedding, but my parents thought it was inappropriate.

"I have something for you," she said, "just a small something. I'll leave it in the kitchen for you."

I nodded at her, hoping my mother hadn't heard. My mother had a gift for making heartfelt gestures seem silly and comical.

Mattia left the room after the last plate was laid, and I turned my attention to the conversation my father was having with Caleb. Despite his current feelings toward my parents, Caleb was composed and respectful, answering questions and delivering them in perfect sequence.

He was a social genius. I attributed it to the fact that he seemed to be able to get to the core of every person he met in one meeting, and from there on out, he automatically knew how to manipulate their moods. I'd seen him ask a stranger question after question until he broke down their defenses. Initially, the subject of his interest looked mildly guarded, giving him censored answers. He timed his probing questions with jokes and self-deprecating comments that set the person at ease. He never judged. He narrowed his eyes when it was the other person's turn to speak—a charming bit of body language that said: you are so interesting, keep speaking. I loved watching him speak to people. I loved watching them fall for him. By the end of a conversation with Caleb, people were so taken with him, they looked disappointed when the interaction ended. He really cared—that was the difference between Caleb and someone who was just being nosy. People picked up on that quickly.

Caleb was mine. He was finally all mine. I smiled at my salmon, and my sister kicked me under the table.

"What?" I mouthed to her.

She shook her head, smiling.

After dinner, we moved back to the living room. My father was old school; he pulled out the snifters and cigars as soon as we sat down. Caleb politely declined the cigar, but took a finger of Scotch.

I sat next to him, while my mother and sister disappeared into another part of the house. This was the man time, but I wasn't leaving mine alone with my father. Not when he was angry with me about the money he'd shelled out for the wedding.

"What are your plans?" Daddy asked, pointedly ignoring me and looking at my husband. He blew a bit of tobacco from his lip, and I looked away. His mannerisms were beginning to annoy me.

Caleb licked his lips. "We put in an offer on a house. We're waiting to hear from them."

"I hope you don't intend on keeping Leah at home. I need her to come back to the office."

Caleb stiffened. I could read his body language as if it were my own. I wanted to hear what he would say to the great, powerful Smith strong arm.

"I don't intend on keeping her anywhere," he said. "Aside from my bed, she's free to come and go as she pleases."

I choked on my spit. I wanted to laugh at the look on my father's face. He was crude, I'd heard him make all manner of jokes, but Caleb's comment had disarmed him. Caleb probably knew it would—the brilliant little manipulator that he was.

My father cleared his throat, a slight smile on his lips.

Caleb turned toward me. "Do you plan on going back to work, Leah?"

Daddy wasn't used to this. I wanted to sneak a look to see how he was handling his *not* daughter being asked her opinion.

"I don't know," I said. "I could think about it…"

Why did he want me back? He had an entire horde of employees to play his corporate game. Maybe this was him trying? To what…be my dad? My boss? I was surprised he was even suggesting I go back to work, since he believed that after a woman got married, her place was in the home.

My father switched tactics at the last minute; pivoting his body toward me, he angled himself away from Caleb, making me the sole receptacle of his attention.

Nice.

"What do you say, Leah? You've been such an asset since you arrived. We need you to finish this project."

As much as I wanted to say no, I couldn't. Blame it on the alcohol, or my nagging addiction to please the only man who didn't want me, but I couldn't walk away when he was asking me to come back. I had a need to prove that he was wrong about me. That I wasn't the child of a worthless slut, but a valuable asset to his family.

I nodded, feeling weak for bending. He was using me for something. I couldn't figure out what yet. My goddamn soul hurt. Caleb was watching me. I smiled at him, my eyes no doubt betraying my uneasiness. He could see all the way down my throat, right to the place where my heart beat. Thank God he was classy enough not to mention it.

On the way home, Caleb asked me if I really wanted to go back.

"You said you were done."

I looked fretfully out my window, counting the car lights that passed us.

"I know."

"So why are you going back? You don't owe him anything, Leah."

"Just let me do this without psychoanalyzing my motives."

He looked at me out of the corner of his eye. "All right. Just promise me one thing."

I looked at him. Caleb didn't really ask for promises.

"If he pulls a stunt like he did at the wedding, you walk away and you don't look back."

"Okay," I said.

I glanced down to my lap where Mattia's present sat, wrapped in pearly white paper with embellished bells on it. Sliding my fingernail under the tape, I pulled the wrapping away to reveal a sugar and creamer set. It was cheap—the kind you get at Marshalls, with glass bodies and silver handles—but it was from Mattia and I loved it.

Mattia had been the only one in my house to give me hugs. I counted on her hugs.

I was just about to turn down the radio when Caleb turned it up.

Coldplay, he listened to them as if they were whispering truths to him. I never understood his fascination. They were always trying to dress up big concepts with piano vamps. I drummed my fingers on the armrest as I waited for the song to be over. Like anyone could fix anyone else. If that were true, Caleb wouldn't like Debbie Downer music; he'd listen to happy crap that represented our relationship. When I met him, he was drowning in his emotion for some woman who had broken his heart. I spent years trying to pull him out of it, only to get a sort of floating contentment that came and went depending on the day. We'd go weeks at a time being happy with each other, and then suddenly, the wind would change direction, and Caleb would turn into the brooding, dark person I'd first encountered at the yacht party.

Right now…at this moment…on this day—he was happy. I looked at his face as he sang the lyrics to the song and linked our fingers. He said I could trust him.

TWENTY-FIVE

As I drive home from my meeting with Olivia, I intermittently sob and swear. The whole world is swimming in and out of focus as I weigh the chances of losing my husband. Olivia's words mingle with my thoughts until I almost crash into a garbage truck. As soon as I walk through the front door, I beeline outside to where Sam has Estella on a blanket. I pick her up and hold her against my chest. She wiggles and lets out a wail of protest. Sam takes her from me, and she stops crying. I take her back from Sam.

"Take the day off," I say, studying her scrunched-up face. "It's about time she learns to fucking like me."

Sam raises his eyebrows. I'm about to tell him that I don't like the look on his face, when he turns and walks away.

I can see him through the French doors. He grabs his keys from the kitchen counter and strides off without a backward glance. I look back at Estella.

"Maybe we can try this again. If we can figure out how to like each other, your daddy might stay."

She flails her fists and blinks at me. She really is kind of cute.

I stretch my legs out and lay her on my thighs. I talk to her for the next thirty minutes about life until she starts screaming at me. Then we go into the house for dinner. After I've put her to bed, I put on my sexiest piece of lingerie and wait. Forty minutes later, I hear his key in the lock.

When I rush into the foyer, Caleb is closing the front door behind him. I freeze, and when he looks up, I'm not sure who looks more flustered.

"I'm just here to pick up some of my things."

He won't look at me. I take a few steps toward him. I want to touch him, tell him I'm sorry.

"Caleb, talk to me…please."

He fixes his eyes on me, and I see none of the warmth that used to be there. I flinch back. Has everything between us disappeared?

"I'll be back for her tomorrow. There are just a few things I need to pick up," he repeats.

I place a hand on his chest and he freezes.

He grabs my wrist. "Don't." This time he looks me in the eyes. "You use sex like it's a weapon. I'm not interested."

"It's okay when Olivia uses it, just not me?" The words are out before I can stop them.

"What are you talking about?"

I think about my conversation with Sam. If I want to know about his relationship with Olivia, now is probably the time to ask, since he's already mad at me.

"Why didn't you ever sleep with her?"

Caleb reacts instantaneously, grabbing me by the shoulders and moving me out of his way. He heads for the stairs. I follow behind him.

"Come on, Caleb. You let her use sex—or lack thereof—as a weapon. Why?"

He glares at me. "You don't know what you're talking about."

"Maybe. But that's because you never talk about her. And, I want to know exactly what happened between the two of you."

"She left me," he says. "End of story."

"What about the second time?" I challenge. "During your amnesia?"

"She left me again."

His admission cuts me, deeply.

"Why didn't you ever talk to me about what she did? When she came back and lied to you?"

"Why didn't you ever ask?" he counters.

"I didn't want to know…"

He starts to turn away.

"But, I do now," I say.

"No."

"No?" I follow him up the first few stairs. "I want to know why you hired her as my attorney…why you weren't angry with her for lying to you."

He turns around so quickly I almost topple over.

"I hired her as your attorney because I knew she'd win. I was angry with her…I still am."

"Why?" I yell after him, but he's already gone.

TWENTY-SIX
PAST

One thing to know about me: I dig. If I can't find it—I dig deeper, harder. I dig until I find it. The only thing I couldn't dig into was my own mind. I didn't want to see it.

My father was acting strange, even for him. Twice, I'd caught him swallowing a handful of pills. The only pills I'd ever seen him take were vitamins. These were not vitamins. I found the bottle in the top drawer of his desk.

The bottle said it was a Vasodilator—a high blood pressure medication, but also mixed in the same bottle was a pill I recognized—Klonopin, an anti-anxiety pill. My father had anxiety. I wanted to know how long he'd been taking them and *why* he was taking them. My father had always been the healthiest man I'd ever met. He was sixty and he had a six-pack. It was an old man six-pack, but still. He made fun of people who suffered from things like depression and anxiety, ironic since he supplied them with medication.

I called my mother.

Her voice warbled across the line when I asked her about the pills.

"He's fine," she affirmed. "You know how things get in the office. He's under stress with this new drug he's testing."

I held the receiver closer to my ear. Whatever I said from here could either end the conversation or tell me exactly what I needed to know. I opened my copy of Manipulating Mother 101.

As far as I knew, the testing of our newest drug, prenavene, was successful. Daily, I had to sign off on paperwork that Cash or my father delivered to my office. The drug had been in its testing phase for more than five years. We were on the final leg toward marketing it. Why would my father be having anxiety over a successful project?

"I bet he's a mess," I said, trying my hardest to sound sympathetic. I could almost see her nodding on the other end of the line.

"I wish I could just smack that terrible man," she whispered into the receiver, "claiming prenavene induced his heart attack. Your father hired a private investigator, you know. The man was a walking heart attack. He has a history of it in his family and he weighs three hundred pounds."

She said *three hundred pounds* like it was a swear word. It took me a few seconds to wrap my mind around the words *heart attack*.

Holy fuck.

Why hadn't I heard about this? A heart attack during a trial run of a drug was huge! It was enough to shut down the testing until the drug could be re-formulated. It was hard to say anything after that announcement. Why? Why would he risk everything? Not wanting her to know she'd just outed something I obviously wasn't already privy to, I listened to her babble for a few more minutes. I needed to use her for more information. I swallowed the betrayal in my throat and told her that I had another call coming through.

Why would he keep something like this from me? Why hadn't they shut down the testing? I thought about calling Cash, but her loyalty was obviously to my father if she hadn't told me already. I was going to have to dig this out myself. Money. That had to be it. At the last sales meeting, he'd mentioned a drop in our sales. Prenavene was a way to bring the company back. Were we really that desperate for a new drug that he would do something like this? Risk everything?

The next morning, I went into the office early. My father arrived promptly at six o'clock every day. I had an hour before he would show. I had a set of spare keys to his office. I unlocked the door and flicked on the light. Stepping around to his computer, I powered it on, drumming my fingers on his desk. His level of access in the system was higher than mine. I would need his passcodes to access his files. Swearing, I typed in my parents' wedding anniversary. Incorrect Code popped up on the screen. That was a terrible guess on my part—he wasn't exactly the sentimental type.

I tried birthdates, my sister's and mine. Nothing. Finally, I tried the coordinates to his hunting cabin in North Carolina. The system magically opened, and I had the vast grid of OPI-Gem in front of me. I clicked on the icon marked Prenavene and went to town.

It was true. Oh God, it was true. By the time I locked the door to his office, I had enough information to shut down my father's company and put him in prison for the rest of his life. The worst part was I wanted to. No, I didn't. He was my father…well, kind of. He'd raised me. Or maybe Mattia had raised me. I wasn't even sure anymore.

My head throbbed as I made my way to the elevator. I was going to call in sick. I couldn't look all of those people in the face when I knew what I knew. I had to figure this out. Find a way to know exactly who was involved and who was being kept in the dark like me. My head was down as the doors opened. When I looked up, he was standing in front of me, a newspaper tucked under his arm. Shit, why hadn't I thought to take the stairs?

I threw my shoulders back, forcing a smile.

"Good morning, Daddy."

He nodded at me, exiting the elevator. Then all of a sudden, he stopped. "Why are you here so early?"

The lie rolled off my tongue easily. "I'm not feeling well today. I just came in to pick up some work. I'm taking the day off."

He narrowed his eyes. "You look fine. Go home and change and come back in. I need you here today."

"I'm sick," I said, like he hadn't heard me the first time.

"This is a pharmaceutical company, Johanna. Go get some samples out of storage and medicate yourself."

I watched the empty hallway for a good minute after he'd disappeared into his office. Did that really just happen? Of course it did. My father hadn't taken a sick day in twenty years of work; what would make me think it would be okay to offer him illness as an excuse? I stepped into the elevator and the door closed. If I hurried, I could be back in forty minutes.

TWENTY-SEVEN

Caleb took the baby to his condo the day after he came to pick up his clothes. His face was grim and determined as he stood at the door and let me say goodbye. I kiss the red fuzz on her head and smile casually. I am treating this whole situation as if they are going to the supermarket rather than moving out. *Bide your time. Let him see how hard it is to take care of a baby by himself.* I feel smug as they pull out of the driveway. Sometimes a little separation is good for the soul. Caleb is a family man. In a few days, he'll be back, and I'll try harder. Everything will work out. Estella is my sure thing. She'll keep us tied together no matter how bad things get.

When his car lights disappear, I open the freezer and pull out two bags of frozen vegetables. Carrying them to the table, I poke holes in the plastic with my finger and start thumbing peas into my mouth. There are things I could do to make the situation better. Katine takes her kids to Mommy & Me classes. They sit in circles and sing and bang fucking tambourines. I could do that.

The doorbell rings. I shove a handful of lima beans into my mouth and dance toward the door. Maybe Caleb has changed his mind already.

My husband is not standing on the doorstep. I eye the man who is.

"What do you want?"

"I came to see if you were all right."

"Why wouldn't I be all right?" I snap. I make to close the door, but he pushes past me and walks into the foyer.

"You shouldn't be here." My words might as well be vapor. They don't reach him, or he has his own agenda, per usual.

He looks over his shoulder at me, his smirk so familiar I feel my vertigo slip.

"Of course I should be here. I'm checking up on my sister-in-law. It's the family thing to do, especially since my brother has left you."

I throw the door closed and the pictures on the wall rattle.

"He hasn't left me, you abhorrent prick." I march past him and sit at the table with my peas.

He strolls in a moment later and starts examining the photos on the wall like he's never seen them. I eat my peas one by one and watch him.

Finally, he sits down across from me, folding his hands on the tabletop.

"What did you do this time?"

I look away from the smug expression on his face. "I didn't do anything. Everything is fine. He hasn't left me."

"I heard they passed you up for the Mommy of the Year award."

I bite the inside of my cheek and refuse to respond. Seth gets up and ambles over to the liquor cabinet, pouring himself a finger of Caleb's Scotch.

"If you keep it up, my baby brother might actually file the papers this time. A man can only take so much of your never-ending antics."

I throw him a dirty look. "And then what, Seth? You move in and take over his life?"

This time I've thrown him off balance. He lifts the glass to his lips, never breaking eye contact with me.

Unlike his brother's, Seth's eyes are grey. At the moment, I can almost see the smoke coming out of them.

"Did I hit a nerve, big brother? Wanting what Caleb has again?"

I stand up and make to walk past him, but he grabs my upper arm. I struggle to free myself, but he squeezes until I still.

His mouth is next to my ear. "Maybe I should tell him that I've already had what's his."

I yank myself free.

"Get out of my house."

He sets his glass down and winks at me, heading for the door. "I think I'll go visit my baby niece today. Buh-bye, Leah."

The door closes. "Son of a bitch," I say. I mean this literally. I march back to the kitchen and pick up the phone. I needed to get out, do something, but…not something destructive. I pass by Katine's name and pause over Sam's.

"What's up, gay man?" I say into the receiver.

"That's kind of offensive, Leah."

"I was thinking we could do a little shopping today. Maybe lunch?"

"Just because I'm gay doesn't mean I'm going to be your flaming sidekick."

"Oh, come on. You like wine! We could get some wine…go to Armani…"

"I'm busy today," he says. "I have to run errands."

"I'll come with you. Come pick me up."

He sighs. "All right. But, you better be ready when I honk."

"You will come to the door like a gentleman," I say, before hanging up.

I go upstairs to change and come back downstairs just in time to hear the obnoxious wail of the horn on his Jeep.

I sit on the couch and smooth out my dress. I will not be summoned outside. I wait for a minute or two, expecting to hear his knock, but instead, I hear the Jeep pulling out of the driveway. Before he can leave, I jump up and race outside.

"You're such an asshole," I say, throwing myself into the front seat. He pulls a face at me to show his displeasure.

"I'm not playing games with you, Leah. Don't you get tired of always trying to win?"

"No," I snap. "That would make me a loser."

He shakes his head and turns up the music to drown out anything else I might want to say. I sit quietly and smoke. I don't know where we are going, but I'm glad to be out of the house that's saturated with way too many memories. I want...I *need* to be Caleb-free for a few hours. Get back to my roots.

I turn down the radio. Fuck Coldplay. What the hell type of spell do they have on everyone? Artsy-fartsy juju. When Caleb comes home I'm going to make him throw away all of their CDs.

"Let's do something fun."

Sam runs a hand down his face. "I will take you home right now, and you can sit in your big, empty house and stew about your small, empty life. Do you understand?"

"God, you're a killjoy." I pluck a piece of tobacco from my tongue and flick it out of the Jeep.

His words hurt me. Sam is a straight shooter, but right now I need to be coddled and told that I'm pretty.

Ten minutes later, we pull into the parking lot of a Walmart.

My feet, which are resting on the dash, immediately come down. "Oh, hell no! I am not going in there."

He shrugs and gets out of the car. "Sam!" I call after him. "Walmart gives me hives."

After a few seconds, I scramble out of the car and chase after him. I follow him to the back of the store where he throws a dozen green light bulbs into a cart and wheels maniacally toward the food section.

"Why do you need all of those Perriers?" I watch as he loads bottle after bottle into the cart, arranging them along the bottom so they won't break.

"They're for Cammie," he says.

My eyes bug. "You—are you…do you have to take them to her?"

"Yes, we're going there next."

I skip behind him in a panic as he makes his way toward the register. "Can you drop me at home first?"

The last thing I want to do is see that smug blonde face of hers. Bitch.

"We're going there after this. She's throwing a party and forgot to pick this stuff up."

"Aren't you the good, little cousin," I grumble under my breath. Why did I let him convince me to come? I should have just stayed home like I wanted to.

As the stuff rolls along the conveyor belt, I toss on a package of mints. When Sam looks at me, I shrug.

I sit in coiled anxiety for the entire fifteen-minute drive. I eat mint after mint until the box is empty and my tongue is raw. Sam snatches the container from me, his eyes wide.

"Are you crazy? These are Altoids, not chocolate."

I sit on my hands and look out the window. We are in Boca. Cammie's house is in an upscale, gated neighborhood. Sam stops outside of a house with flowerboxes on the windows and jumps out. I scoot lower in my seat, though the open-aired Jeep provides little place to hide.

"Hey." He kicks the side of the car where I am sitting. "A little help."

I glance over at him in disbelief. Did he really expect me to help him carry bags in there? He did. Oh shit.

He carries the bags to the side of the house and opens a gate that I presume leads to the backyard. I can do the backyard. I lower myself to the ground and grab a couple of bags from the trunk. I am mildly curious about what this party is for, anyway. As soon as I round the corner into the backyard, I walk into Cammie.

She gives me one wide-eyed look and screams Sam's name. He comes running, his arms loaded with boxes.

"What is this?" Her voice is high-pitched. "What is Dirty Red doing here?"

I shove the bags at her. Sam drops his boxes and gives Cammie a dirty look. "Caleb left her," Sam says, putting an arm around my shoulders. "Be nice."

"He did not leave me," I assure Cammie.

Cammie puts her hands on her hips. "I don't care who left whom. Put those damn bottles over there." She points to a table, and I carry them over. I sneak a look around. The yard is spacious. There is a pool in the shape of a lima bean and a hot tub. Men are setting up rented tables across the lawn, shaking out white linen tablecloths.

"Hi."

I jump. A man comes up beside me carrying a huge speaker. He sets it on the table and smiles at me.

I eye him uncertainly. I'm not sure if I'm going to get yelled at for talking to him. Cammie is mildly insane. He is attractive. Everything about him is dark, aside from his blue-green eyes. I wonder idly if he's part of the set-up crew for the party.

He extends his hand toward me, and without thinking, I take it.

"And who are you?" he asks when I don't offer my name. He's smirking at me like he thinks I'm funny.

"She's no one." Cammie comes up beside us and yanks our hands apart.

"Cammie!" he chides. He looks at her fondly and then back at me. Her boyfriend? No. Cammie is not this guy's type.

Cammie screams Sam's name. He comes trotting around the corner, eating a bag of chips. "Take her home!" she says, giving me a dirty look.

The man cocks his head. He points to Sam and seems to be trying to make some kind of mental connection. When his eyes return to my face, he appears to have put the pieces together. His whole face lights up.

"You're Leah," he says in amazement. He's wearing eyeglasses. I want him to take them off so I can see his eyes better.

"And you are?"

He's re-extending his hand. Before I can re-take it, Cammie smacks it away.

"Dude," she says, pointing at him. "Let's not play this game."

He ignores her. "I'm Noah," he says.

I'm overtaken by his kindness. I'm overtaken by his— Oh, God! Olivia's husband!

I compose myself before I audibly groan. This is a party for Olivia. I am at her best friend's house, staring her husband in the face. Oh. My. God.

"I better go," I mumble to Noah's delighted face. Cammie is vigorously nodding her head. Noah is shaking his.

"You don't look half as crazy as I thought you'd look."

Did he really just say that?

"Olivia said something about a redheaded gargoyle with fangs."

I blink at him. So, she'd told him about me. I wonder if she mentioned the little apartment-trashing stunt…or the driving-her-out-of-town stunt…or the trial? For some strange reason, I don't want him to think I'm a bad person.

"Noah," Cammie says, shaking his arm. "Can you not engage with the enemy? We have things to do."

"She's not the enemy," he says, never taking his eyes from mine. "She's a dirty fighter." Yup, he knows. I feel like I'm in a trance. If this guy told me to drink the Kool-Aid, I would probably do it. Fuck it. I would *absolutely* drink the Kool-Aid.

Olivia married sexy Ghandi. No wonder she loves her husband. I clear my throat and look around the yard. "So, is this party for her?"

Cammie squeals somewhere in the background; Noah nods. "Yes, her birthday. It's a surprise."

How nice. No one throws me birthday parties. I swallow hard and step away from the table.

"It was nice meeting you," I say. "Sam?"

He's at my elbow in a second, steering me toward the gate. I glance over my shoulder at Olivia's husband. He's messing with the speaker. Cammie's hands are flailing about, no doubt expressing her sentiments about me as he ignores her.

Hot damn. What does this woman have that I don't? Why do men like Noah and my husband fall in love with her?

TWENTY-EIGHT

The pressure at work changed after I found out about the doctored prenavene results. It was like he knew I had unfurled his secret, and he was out to make me pay. The attention I had always desired from him was suddenly there. Except it wasn't the warm, fatherly love I'd hoped for. He became hostile and demanding, often insulting me in front of people. There were a few times I'd look up to see him staring at me; the look on his face so acutely angry I'd feel lightheaded. I longed for the furrow I'd hidden myself in when he hadn't known I existed. It was safer out of his eyesight. The most important question was: how had he found out?

It was Cash. It had to be. I'd asked her detailed questions about the trial run. She must have squealed to my father. And what made it worse was the way my father was treating her—like a long-lost fucking daughter.

The caca hit the fan a week before my birthday. My father called an emergency family meeting at the house. Caleb thought it was weird, but I knew what was coming. I thought about prepping him in the car on the ride over, but thought it would be better coming from Charles Austin, the pharmaceutical fraud. That way I could play innocent and pretend I knew nothing about the shenanigans.

When we arrived at the house, everyone was waiting for us in the family room. I slid into a love seat with Caleb, who was surveying the gathering with mounting suspicion. He looked at me to see if I knew anything and I shrugged. My sister, who was sitting next to my mother, looked at me with sudden realization on her face.

"You're pregnant, aren't you? That's what this is about."

I shook my head, shocked at her lack of emotional thermostat. Nothing bad ever touched my sister. I felt a moment of jealousy that reached twenty shades of green.

"Johanna's not having a baby," my father said. "This is something more serious, I'm afraid."

For a minute, I wondered what could be more serious than a baby. Would he even let my baby call him Grandpa? Caleb was tense beside me. When Daddy said the bit about the baby, Caleb grabbed my hand and squeezed.

My father looked at Caleb when he spoke. That's the way it was with him. If there was a man in the room, that's who he'd look at—even if he was about to inform his wife and daughter about his imminent demise.

I listened to the whole thing, clutching my husband's hand as if it were the only thing tethering me to my sanity. Despite the anger I felt for my father, I hoped he wouldn't be in too much trouble. Was that possible when you did something like that?

He took us through the trials, and when he admitted to doctoring the results, I felt Caleb go rigid. He ended his story with a nice fist to my stomach.

"I've been indicted. They are going to look at Johanna as well."

Caleb jumped up. "What? What does Leah have to do with this?"

"Her signatures are all over the paperwork. None of the testing could have been done without her signature. The same goes for the releases."

I made a noise that sounded like strangled fear. Caleb looked down at me, his eyes lit like two burning amber balls. He narrowed them. "Is this true? Did you know what was going on?"

I shook my head. "I just signed what he told me to sign. I didn't know anything about the real results."

His head whipped back to my father. "You're going to tell them—" he pointed a finger. I don't think I've ever seen Caleb point his finger at someone.

My father was already shaking his head. "It won't make a difference, Caleb."

I felt my worth at that point. A penny. I was a sidewalk toss away—a grimy piece of metal stuck to the bottom of the cup holder, couch cushions, old wallets, and under the fridge between a shriveled grape and an unidentified hair—that was me. He saw no value in me, except to use me when he came up short.

Fuck. fuckfuckfuck.

Caleb's voice was hard rock grinding itself into gravel. I couldn't make out what he was saying until it was too late. I heard the words *She's your daughter*, right before he lurched forward. I saw the tremor of shock pass across my father's face, as my beautiful, russet-haired husband threw a punch that would have had Tyson nodding in approval. My sister and my mother started screaming. I covered my ears. You'd swear they had never seen a man get put in his place. I wanted Caleb to hit him again, mostly for not loving me, but also because I was officially in a barrel of deep trouble.

"Caleb!" I grabbed him, hauled him back. His body was still twisted toward my father like he wanted to hit him again. "Let's go. I want to leave."

His jaw was scary. Truly. Put me in a room with a hundred hungry mountain lions before you put me in a room with Caleb's jaw.

Caleb grabbed my hand. My father, the great Charles Austin Smith, was flopped face up on the chaise lounge, his nose bleeding through his fingers and his face the color of raw liver. Before we walked out, I stopped. My breath was keeping time with my heart. Caleb looked at me questioningly, and I shook my head. I faced my family. The three of them were huddled together around my father's bleeding face. My mother's eyes were terrified as she tried to mop up the blood with a beverage napkin. My sister was saying *Daddy* over and over as she cried. I felt repulsed and terrified as I watched. For the first time, I didn't want to belong with them. I didn't want to be a part of their bleeding, cowering trio.

"Daddy?" He lifted his head and I saw his bloodshot eyes find me. My mother and sister stopped wailing to look at me, too. "Daddy," I repeat. "I'm never going to call you that again. You probably don't care, and that's okay, because I don't either. I'd rather be the bastard daughter of a prostitute than ever share your blood."

Caleb squeezed my hand, and we walked out.

Two days later he was dead.

TWENTY-NINE

I stalk Cammie on Facebook. I swear all that dumb blonde does is post pictures of her lunch. I hate that. I keep hoping to catch some snippet of Caleb or that slut, Olivia. I sign on to my barely used account and type in Cammie's name. I want to see if she posted pictures of Olivia's birthday. I want to see if Caleb was there. *That's stupid*, I tell myself. Olivia is married to sexy Ghandi. There is no way Caleb would be invited. I comb through all of the pictures anyway, searching for a piece of his hands or feet or hair. All I see are pictures of Olivia. Someone had snapped a photo of her walking into the surprise party. Her mouth is open and if you didn't know better, you'd think someone was pointing a gun at her instead of shouting *Happy Birthday*. She is wearing skinny jeans and a tube top. I sniff as I click through the pictures. Olivia hugging Noah, Olivia laughing with Cammie, Olivia blowing out candles on a cupcake tower, Olivia shooting someone with a water gun, Olivia getting pushed into the pool...

The very last picture is of Olivia opening a present. She is sitting on a chair with the box open in her lap. The look on her face is anything but happy. Her eyebrows are drawn together and her mouth is puckered into one of her famous side frowns. I eye the box, trying to see what's inside of it, but all I can see is the metallic blue paper. Cammie has captioned the picture: Don't know who this one is from?? Own up or you don't get a thank-you card.

I look at the package suspiciously. What could be inside that would cause her to look so horrified? I click to the next pictures, but Olivia is in none of them. It's like she disappeared after she opened that package. I shove a handful of barely thawed carrots into my mouth. Scooting my chair back, I go in search of Sam. I find him folding laundry in the nursery. Caleb has the baby, but Sam has been coming in anyway to help me live.

"You were at that party, right?"

"What party?" He opens a drawer, deposits a pile of onesies, and closes it without looking at me.

"Olivia's party, Sam." His eyes travel from my crossed arms to my tapping foot.

"I will not feed into your stalker tendencies."

"What was in that blue box Olivia opened?"

Sam's eyes snap to my face.

"How do you know about that?"

"I was on...uh...Facebook."

Sam shakes his head. "I don't know. The box didn't have a card. She took one look inside that sucker and ran into the house. I didn't see her again after that. I think Noah took her home."

"What happened to the box?" Why am I so interested?

"I think Cammie has it."

I grab his arm. "Ask her."

He shakes himself free, his brow creased into three deep lines. I point to his forehead.

"You should really consider Botox for that."

"I am not digging around in the Olivia obsession box for you."

"I'm not obsessed with her," I counter. "I just want to revel in what made her upset."

"Don't you and Nancy do enough Olivia bashing as it is?"

I screw up my nose. Could there ever be enough Olivia bashing? That woman should have to wear a sign on her back that says "White Trash Boyfriend Stealer."

"Say what you like, Sam, but she didn't try to destroy your life."

I am walking toward the living room when his voice catches up to me.

"From what I hear, she saved yours."

I spin and glare. I can't believe he just said that. How completely untrue. I am sick, sick, sick of being forced to feel grateful to that sly-looking bitch for something anyone could have done. I could have hired any attorney I wanted. Olivia was forced on me.

"Is that what Cammie told you?"

He puts the last clean bottle in the cabinet and faces me.

"Isn't that what happened? She took your case and won it?"

"For God's sake! That was her job."

"Why did she take your case?"

I am already pale, but when someone asks me that question, e.g., my mother, my sister, my friends…I can always feel the color in my skin peel back. Why did she take the case? Because Caleb asked her to. Why did Caleb ask her to? At first, I thought it was because she lied to him. He was collecting on her guilt, making her pay up for the deceit by defending his wife. But, then I intercepted a look. A look. How long can a look be…truly? A look can be a second long, a freaking, harmless second, and it can tell long, complicated stories. You can see three years in a second-long look. You can see longing, too. I hadn't known that until I saw it for myself. I wish I hadn't seen it. I wish I could never see another look transferred between two people with history.

"It seems to me, you give loyalty to all of the wrong people," he says.

"What are you talking about?" I snap.

"Oh, I don't know. You almost take the fall for that father of yours, when he obviously treated you like crap, and then you shove your baby off to the side like she's an inconvenience to you."

I balk.

"You can have the rest of the day off."

Sam raises his eyebrows. "I'll see you on Monday, then."

I don't acknowledge him when he leaves. I go upstairs to check on Estella and then realize that she's gone. I'd been doing that lately, expecting to hear her or see her when I walk into a room. Unlike a few months ago, I don't feel relief that she's not here. I feel…

What do I feel? I hate that. I definitely don't want to think about my feelings.

I go to the freezer and pull out the lima beans. Weighing the bag in my hand for a few seconds, I suddenly toss them back like I'm pitching for the Marlins.

I grab my car keys from the hook in the kitchen and head for the garage. My fast car is in the garage: my pre-baby, lots of fun, cherry-red convertible. I pat the hood before I get in. Then I'm zipping past my mommy-mobile, past the mailboxes, and down the street.

I feel lost. I feel lost and incredibly angry. I jerk to a stop in the parking lot of the grocery store. Marching inside, I don't miss a beat as I snatch up a basket and head for the candy aisle. I empty the shelf of chocolate-covered raisins and grab an armful of Twizzlers. When I dump everything on the belt at the register, the kid ringing me up looks at me with wide eyes.

"Will that be—"

"That's all," I shout. "Unless you want to give me a new life."

He's still gaping at me when I snatch up my load and run for the car.

The first thing I do when I get home is empty my freezer of vegetables. I cut the bags open, one by one, and send the colorful little niblets down the garbage disposal. I hum as I work. Then I take a swig of vodka, straight from the bottle, kick off my heels, and open the first box of chocolate-covered raisins. It all goes downhill from there. I eat every last box until I am sick. I call Caleb at two a.m. His voice is slurred when he picks up.

No two a.m. feeding, I think. Lucky him.

"What is it, Leah?" he asks.

"I want my baby back." I chew on a Twizzler and wait.

He's quiet for about ten seconds.

"Why?"

I sniff.

"Because, I want her to know that it's all right to eat candy."

"What?" His voice is clipped.

"Don't you 'what' me. Bring my baby back. First thing tomorrow." I hang up the phone.

I want my damn baby. I *want* my damn baby.

THIRTY

The trial was the most surreal experience of my life—not just because my husband's ex-girlfriend was my attorney, but also because I had never been called out on anything before. I was in real trouble for the first time in my life.

I didn't agree to Olivia being my attorney. I fought it until Caleb got right in my face and said, "Do you want to win or not?"

"Why are you so sure she can win this case? And why would you think she'd want to? Are you forgetting how she pretended not to know you when you lost your memory? She wants you back—she'll probably lose on purpose."

"I know her," he said. "She'll fight hard…especially if I ask her to."

That was it. Case closed. Except mine was still open and dangling like a glass Christmas ornament from my archrival's fingertip. I had to trust him via her; there was no one else. My father was usually the one to get me out of trouble, and this time he was the one who had put me there before dying of a heart attack.

I didn't trust her. She was snappy with me. Attorneys were supposed to make you feel good—even if they were lying about your chances at winning. Olivia made it her sole mission in life to make me believe I was going down. It was not lost on me, that whenever my husband was around, she was sour and tense. She wouldn't look at him either. Even when he directed a question at her, she'd pretend to do something else when she answered him. I hated her. I hated her every day for the year it took her to clear me of the charges. There was only one day during the entire thing when I did not hate her.

The day she put me on the stand was the worst day of my life. No one wanted her to do it—they thought it would ruin the case.

Let her plead the fifth was the consensus at the firm. Olivia had gone against every piece of advice offered as she prepped me for the stand. I saw the looks that were being exchanged at my expense. Even when Bernie, the senior attorney, had approached her, Olivia had shot her down.

"Dammit, Bernie! She can handle herself," she'd said. "This is my case and I'm putting her on the stand."

I was terrified. My fate was in the hands of an evil, conniving woman. I couldn't decide if that was a good thing or a bad thing. Most of me was convinced that she was trying to lose the case on purpose. When I told Caleb my theory, he was sorting mail in the kitchen. He barely glanced up at me.

"Do what she says."

What?

"What do you mean, do what she says? You're not even listening to me."

He tossed the mail down and walked to the fridge.

"I heard you, Leah."

"I don't trust her."

He had a beer in his hand when he turned toward me, but he was looking at the floor.

"I do."

And that was it. My only ally was the woman who would gain the most from my imprisonment. She prepped me for the stand by drilling me with questions that the prosecution would ask, drilled me with her own, yelled at me when I wasn't sedate enough, swore at me when I faltered in my answers. She was hard and she was tough, and a part of me appreciated that. A very, very small—I hate this bitch and I want her to die—part. But, I trusted Caleb. Caleb trusted Olivia. I was either going to go down in flames or walk out of the courtroom a free woman.

The day I took the stand, I was threadbare. I wore what Olivia brought for me: a dress with soft peaches and lilacs, my hair in a low ponytail, pearl stud earrings. As I secured them in my ears, I wondered if they belonged to her. They were fake pearls, so probably. My hands were shaking as I smoothed out my dress and looked at myself in the mirror. I looked vulnerable. I felt vulnerable. Maybe that was her plan. Caleb said to trust her.

I searched for her eyes as I took my seat on the bench, my knees weak beneath my folded hands. In the weeks of prepping, I'd learned to read her eyes. I'd learned that if she held them wide, her eyebrows slightly raised—I was doing well. If she stared right through me, she was mentally cussing me out, and I needed to change course, quickly. I hated that I knew her so well. I hated it, and I was grateful for it. I often found myself wondering if Caleb knew how to read her eyes like I did. Probably. I didn't know what was worse—being able to read Olivia so well, or actually feeling proud that I could do it.

She stood in front of me, instead of pacing back and forth like they did in the movies. She looked relaxed in her tan suit. She was wearing a striking, cobalt blue necklace that made her eyes glow.

I took a breath and answered her first question.

"I worked at OPI-Gem for three years."

"And what was your active job title?"

I looked at the necklace, then her eyes, the necklace, then her eyes…

It wasn't really cobalt. What was that shade?

"I was Vice President of Internal Affairs…"

It carried on like that for forty minutes. Toward the end, she started asking me questions that made every sweat gland on my body weep. Questions about my father. My mother was sitting next to Caleb, watching me intently, her hands pressed beneath her chin in what looked like a silent prayer. I knew it to be a silent warning.

Don't humiliate your family, Leah. Don't tell them where you come from. She was begging the gods of illegitimate, fucked-up daughters.

Olivia hadn't wanted her there for fear of her intimidating me into not telling the truth. But, she had insisted on coming.

"What was your relationship like with your father, outside of work, Ms. Smith?"

My mother's chin dropped to her chest. My sister swiped her hair behind her ears and gave my mother a sideways glance. Caleb pressed his lips together and looked at the ground. The gods of illegitimate, fucked-up daughters rumbled in the clouds.

I straightened up, pressing back the tears—those hateful tears that exposed my weakness.

I recalled what Olivia had said to me when we were arguing about some of her questions just a week ago. I told her that I wasn't going to blacken my father's name from the witness stand. She'd gotten grey in the face and her dime-sized hands had balled into fists.

"Where is he, Leah? He fucking threw blood at you and died! You tell the truth or you go to prison."

Then she'd sidled up close to me so no one else could hear and said, "Use your anger. Remember how it felt to destroy my things when I was trying to steal something from you? If you lose this case, I might take him from you again."

That had done the trick. I had been so angry I'd answered all of her questions—even the hard ones. She'd had a smug look on her face for the rest of the day.

Now, I had to channel some of the anger back. I pictured her with Caleb. That was all I needed.

She repeated her question. "What was your relationship like with your father, Leah, outside of work?"

"It was nonexistent. He only interacted with me at work. At home he considered me somewhat of a nuisance."

It all went downhill from there.

"Your father had a reputation for never hiring a member of his family, is that correct?"

"Yes," I said. "I was the first."

I risked a glance at my mother. She wasn't looking at me.

Olivia's opening argument had included this information. She had stood in front of the jury with her hands behind her back and warned them that the prosecution was going to paint me as cunning and manipulative, but really all I was, was a pawn in my father's desperate plan to save his company from going bankrupt. "He used and manipulated his own daughter for financial gain," she'd asserted.

Those words had unzipped my controlled exterior. I started crying immediately.

She cleared her throat, bringing me back to the present.

"Did your father ever ask you to sign documents without you looking at them?"

"Yes."

"What did he say to prevent you from looking at the documents?"

There was an objection from the prosecution. Olivia rephrased her question.

"What was the typical procedure your father used in obtaining your signature?"

"He would tell me that he needed the signatures quickly, and then wait in the room until I had signed everything."

"Did you ever mention to your father that you were uncomfortable signing the documents without reading them?"

Another objection. Leading the witness.

Olivia looked annoyed. The judge allowed it. She repeated her question, one eyebrow arched. I didn't want to answer that question. It made me look irresponsible and foolish. *Better a fool than an inmate*, Olivia had snapped, when I'd voiced my concern the previous day. I swallowed my pride.

"No."

I wiggled around in my seat, darting my gaze to Caleb to see what his reaction was. He was staring at me stoically.

"So you just signed the documents? Documents that would potentially release a deadly drug onto the market and kill three people?"

I opened and closed my mouth. We hadn't rehearsed this. I was on the verge of tears.

"Yes," I said softly. "I wanted to please him."

"I'm sorry, Ms. Smith, can you speak louder so the jury can hear you?"

Her eyes were glowing like her goddamn necklace.

"I wanted to please him," I said louder.

She turned toward the jury so they could see the *Wow, that's fucking important* look on her face.

By the time Olivia took her seat, my mother had a hand covering her mouth and she was crying.

She was probably never going to talk to me again. At least I had my sister. She had been a daddy's girl, but she wasn't blind to the strained relationship my father and I had. As I stepped down from the stand, I sought out my attorney's eyes. They weren't glowing anymore. They just looked tired. I realized how hard it must have been to do what she just did—especially when she wanted me behind bars so she could score my husband.

Fierce, she was so fierce. It was probably the white-trash background that made her such a good fighter. I gazed at her earnestly to see if she approved. She did. I had a second—no—a fraction of a second when I wanted to hug her. Then, it was gone and I wanted her to die and rot in the ground.

I wanted to gloat after I won the trial. I wanted her to know that he was mine and always would be. She needed to know. We were celebrating the win at a restaurant. Olivia arrived late. Honestly, I don't even know why she came. Whatever debt she felt that she owed Caleb was paid. She'd won me my freedom and I would have gladly parted ways, content to never see her again. Yet, here she was, at my celebration, walking on my happy home with her short dress and spiked heels.

I made my way over to her, intent on expressing my displeasure with her being there. I glanced at Caleb who was preoccupied across the room. I didn't want him to see me speaking to her. I wanted her to leave before he saw that she was there.

When she saw me coming, the smile dropped from her face. I had to give it to her—the bitch was exotic. One dark eyebrow rose as I strolled up, champagne in hand. Her mouth pulled into a pucker. She looked down her nose at me. I'd gotten used to it during the trial, but tonight it made me furious. Tonight was mine...and Caleb's.

I hadn't gotten four sentences in when she looked at me and said, "Leah, go be with your husband, before he realizes that he's still in love with me."

Shock.

Why

Did

She

Think

That?

It wasn't true. She was hung up on him. Who could blame her? I looked at Caleb. He was everything I wanted to be. He protected me. He stood with me. He was the only man who said he'd never hurt me.

He laughed at something someone in his group said. My heart swelled at the sight of him. Olivia was jaded, and he was mine. I looked at my Caleb, so sure in that moment of our strength as a couple. It was as if he could sense my eyes on him. I felt the beating of butterfly wings in my stomach, just as his head came up. I smiled. We'd shared intimate looks like this in the courtroom. When I was afraid I looked at him, and he'd meet my eyes, and I would feel better immediately. This time was different. I felt a groundswell of confusion. The room tilted. The beating wings stilled. He wasn't looking at me.

As suddenly as he looked up, the smile was gone from his face. I could see his chest rising and falling beneath his suit like he was taking deep breaths. In those five seconds, I saw every piece of Caleb's mind splayed across his face like someone had made a thousand little cuts and everything was coming out at once: anguish, love, belief. I turned to see where he looked. I knew I shouldn't. But, how could I not? The answer was too bright for me. It made me want to shield my eyes and duck back into the cover of darkness. Olivia was the target of his eyes. I felt like he'd dropped me from the highest building. Shattered. Every part of me. He was a liar. He was a thief. I wanted to crumble to the ground right there, admit my defeat. Die and die again. Die and take Olivia with me. Die.

I opened my mouth to scream at her. To regale her with every insult and name I'd collected over my twenty-nine years. They sat on the tip of my tongue, ready to hurl toward her. I was going to throw my champagne in her face and rip at her eyes until they bled. Until Caleb thought she was so ugly and deformed, he would never look at her like that again.

Then she did the most dumbfounding thing. She set her glass down, her wrist wobbling like it couldn't handle the weight of the dainty glass. Then she tucked her chin to her chest and left.

I took a breath—a deep, satisfying breath—and went back to Caleb's side.

Mine. He was mine. That was that.

THIRTY-ONE

I rock back and forth after I get off the phone with Caleb. What is wrong with me? How did I worship the ground my father walked on after all those years of neglect? It was pathetic. I hate myself for it, and yet I know I'd do it all over again. And this baby—she is my only blood family and I do everything to stay away from her. She hasn't done anything wrong. What type of person am I to isolate my own child?

How can chocolate-covered raisins bring such clarity? It isn't the chocolate-covered raisins. I know that. It's what Sam said to me, the part about me giving my loyalty to all the wrong people. The only person who really deserves it is the little girl I grew in my body. And yet, I can't assemble the right feelings for her. I open my computer and search *postpartum depression*. I read through the symptoms, nodding. Yes, that has to be it. There's no way I am this bad of a person. I need to get on medication. There is something very wrong with me.

In the morning, Caleb brings my baby back. I clutch her to my chest and smell her head. He has her shock of red hair tied up in a little pink bow. I eye her gingham dress and give him a dirty look.

"Why are you dressing her like she's Mary Poppins?" I say sourly. He deposits her diaper bag and car seat next to the door and starts to leave.

"Caleb!" I call after him. "Stay. Have some lunch with us."

"I have somewhere to be, Leah." He sees the disappointment on my face and says in a much gentler voice, "Maybe another day, yeah?"

I feel like someone has reached out and slapped me across the face. Not with his rejection of my lunch offer, but with that very simple "Yeah?" dripping off the end of his sentence. That *yeah*, is an acidic memory, burning painfully across my hippocampus. I think of Courtney and her summer in Europe. The way she came back, speaking as if she were born a Brit.

Wanna go to the mall tomorrow, yeah?
You have that shirt you borrowed from me, yeah?
You're the worst sister in the world, yeah?

I am the worst sister in the world. Courtney, who always stuck up for me with my parents, reminding them that I was alive...where is my loyalty to Courtney? I haven't been to visit her once since...

I kick the door shut with my foot and carry Estella to her nursery. I take off the Mary Poppins dress. She gurgles and kicks her legs like she's glad to be free of it. "Yeah," I coo. "Let Daddy dress you in middle school and you might not have any friends."

She smiles.

I start screaming Sam's name. I hear his heavy footsteps as he charges up the stairs. "Wha—?" he says, breathless. "Is she breathing?"

"She smiled!" I clap my hands.

He peers over my shoulder. "She's been doing that."

"Not at me," I argue.

He looks at me as if I've grown another head. "Wow," he says. "Wow. You grew a heart, and all it took was seven boxes of chocolate-covered raisins."

I flush. "How do you know about that?"

"Well, I took out the trash this morning, for one thing. And I've been finding them all over the floor."

I'm quiet for a long time as I dress Estella in something more fashionable. It's like dressing an octopus, all the limbs moving at the same time. I contemplate telling Sam that it was his words that shook me up a little, but decide not to. I tell him about Courtney instead. "Sam, I have a sister."

He raises an eyebrow. "Great. So do I…"

"I'm having a serious moment here, Sam!" He motions for me to carry on.

I brush Estella's hair. "I haven't seen her in a very long time. She's never even met Estella. Do you think that might have something to do with my…postpartum?" I test the word out, glancing at him sideways to see his reaction.

"I'm not a doctor."

"Yet," I say.

"Yet," he smiles. "But, anything is possible. You *are* a pretty vile human being."

I ignore him and continue brushing Estella's hair.

"So, take Estella and go see her," he says, finally.

"Yeah," I say. "Will you come with me?"

"I don't see why—"

"Okay, great. Get your things. Also, I need you to make an OB/GYN appointment for me. I need drugs."

"I'm not your secretary. We've had this discussion before."

"See if you can get something for Tuesday."

I walk out of the room.

"Leah," he calls after me. "Your baby…"

"Oh, yeah." I head back for Estella and pick her up.

She looks so cute. "We're going to see your auntie," I say.

We don't go see Courtney. Cash calls. Normally, I don't take her calls. Or her e-mails…or her Facebook messages. But since I am reforming my life, I pick up when her name flashes across my screen.

"What do you want, Cash?"

"Oh, you picked up!"

"Would you rather I not have?"

There is a pause. I assume she's gathering all of her words together. God knows she's been saving them up for two years.

"Leah, I'm so sorry," she says. I hear her sniff and wonder if she's crying.

"That's a given," I snap. "You are a liar."

"I was just doing what he asked," she says and then pauses. "How is Courtney? I've tried to see her. They won't—"

"Stay away from her," I interrupt. "She doesn't want to see you."

I wrap my free arm around my waist. I suddenly feel very vulnerable. Why did this woman think she could talk to me about *my* sister?

"Courtney is my family," I say firmly. "And I will do everything I can to protect her."

I hear Cash sob and feel a pang of pity. Maybe I'm being too harsh. I wonder what Courtney would say to her.

"I need to tell her I'm sorry. I need—"

I cut her off. "I have to go. Don't call me again, Cash. I'm serious."

I hang up and immediately go to the closet and pull out Courtney's umbrella picture. I hold it against my chest, gnawing on my bottom lip. How could I stay away from her as long as I had? What was wrong with me? We used to be so close.

I start to laugh, covering my mouth at first, trying to stifle the hyena-like noises. I can't control it. The laughter rolls out of me, climbing in volume. It's the easiest thing I've done all day. When Sam comes to stand in the doorway of my closet, I abruptly stop.

"What are you doing?"

"Nothing."

I straighten up, stashing the painting away before he can see it.

THIRTY-TWO

He left me after the trial. Not right after. We had three months of silence during which I learned what it was to be married and utterly alone. Caleb went back to work right away, leaving me at home alone for most of the day. I roamed the house and watched daytime television, feeling depressed. I had expected things to go back to normal after the trial was over, never considering that I would be out of a job and my high-profile case would tarnish my name, despite my not-guilty verdict. My father's company was dismantled. What was left of it was used to pay settlements to the families of the deceased and my attorney's fees. Caleb's moods were remote. He wouldn't look at me anymore. It was the stress of the trial, I decided. I suggested we take a vacation together. He said he had already taken too much time off of work for the trial. I suggested marriage counseling. He suggested time apart.

One name kept ringing in my head over and over: Olivia. Louder and louder and louder.

She had driven a wedge between us. Again. She was like a disease that came along every few years, contaminating everyone in her path.

Caleb lost a lot of weight the first month. I thought he was sick. I made him go to the doctor, but his blood work came back normal. There was nothing wrong with him. But, there was something very wrong. He hardly smiled, hardly spoke. When he was home, he spent hours alone in his office with the door closed. When I asked him about it, he blew me off.

"I can't always be perfect, Leah. Sometimes, I get to have bad days too."

What did that mean? Had he always had bad days and just never told me? I tried to think about the last time I remembered Caleb having a bad day, and I couldn't. He was always smiling, teasing, encouraging. Did that mean he never had bad days? Or that he hid them from me? I didn't want to think about it. I didn't want to think.

"Why aren't you eating?" I asked.

"I don't have an appetite."

"You're under a lot of pressure. Let's go away for a few days."

"I can't," he said, without looking at me. "Maybe next month."

I asked again the following month. He said no. He was having more than a few "bad days."

Finally, I'd had enough. I had lunch with his mother. If anyone would know how to handle Caleb, it would be Luca.

Or maybe Olivia…

No, I wasn't going to give her that. She had some sort of power over him, yes, but he'd been mine for five years. I knew him. Me!

Luca arrived to our lunch ten minutes late. I was on my second glass of wine when she gracefully lowered herself into the seat across from me. It was rare that we both had free time to get together. After we ordered and got through ten minutes of small talk, she looked me right in the eyes, like she knew something was up.

"So, what's wrong? Tell me…"

I avoided her sharp, blue eyes and concentrated on my chewed-down fingernails.

"It's Caleb," I said. "Ever since the trial, he's been… different."

She took a sip of her drink. "Different how?"

I caught the edge in her voice. I had to be careful what I said about him. I needed her insight without her jumping all over me for criticizing her son.

"Distant. It's like he doesn't want to be around me anymore."

She tapped her fingernails on the table and studied me.

"Have you spoken to your mother about this?"

I shook my head. "Our relationship is strained. Plus, she gives terrible advice."

Luca nodded. She'd never really cared for my mother. Caleb told me once that she thought my mother was cold and unapproachable.

"Do you know anything, Luca? Has he said anything to you?"

She reached out and patted my hand. "No, honey, he hasn't. But, he was like this once before, do you remember?"

I did remember. It was during his amnesia.

I nodded, slowly, not sure what she was suggesting.

"You brought him back," she said. "Can you do it again?"

Her eyes were just like Caleb's when she zoned in on you: intense, searing.

I wanted to snort. She was giving me way too much credit. The last time I had to drive Olivia out of town to bring him back. But, no one knew that except Olivia and me. What would it take this time?

"I don't know how. I've tried everything."

"What does my son value more than anything?"

I leaned back as the server arrived with our salads. I waited for him to leave before answering her.

"Family," I said picking up my fork.

"Yes," Luca agreed. "So give him one."

I balked. Was she really saying what I thought she was saying?

"Children? You think Caleb wants to have a baby?" We hadn't spoken about children since before we were married. I hadn't even thought about the possibility. I wasn't sure I even wanted them. Caleb was enough for me. Caleb wanted them. He always had.

"Children have a way of bringing people together," she smiled. "Especially, when they've fallen apart."

We ate in silence for a few minutes before she spoke again. "You shouldn't have let him hire that woman."

I choked on my food. "Olivia?" I asked.

Luca nodded. "Yes, Olivia. She's trouble. Always has been. Keep the past in the past, Leah. Do what you have to do. I fully support you."

For the first time, I wondered how much Luca knew about Caleb's months of amnesia. Did she know something about the time he spent with Olivia? Had he told her?

I went home ready to talk to Caleb about the possibility of starting a family. Before the words were out of my mouth, he told me he was moving back to his condo.

"You're leaving me?" I said, in disbelief. "We were happy...before the trial. We stopped working on things, Caleb. We can get counseling."

"You were happy. I'm not sure what I was."

"So you were lying to me?"

"You never asked, Leah. You close your eyes to what you don't want to see."

"Is this about prenavene? Those people who died?"

He flinched. "It's really hard for me wrap my head around the decisions you made."

"Did it make you look at me differently?"

He laughed coldly. "I knew when I married you that there were issues." He sighed and looked almost sad. "It made me look at myself differently."

I didn't understand. My father manipulated me. Surely, he realized that. What exactly did he mean by "issues"?

Twenty-four hours later, Caleb was gone.

Depression doesn't even begin to describe what I went through. I'd lost my father, my career, and my husband all in the span of a year. I curled up in a ball and wept for days…weeks. No one came. I tried to call my sister, but she hardly picked up her phone anymore. Katine was seeing some new guy and couldn't be bothered. My mother moved to our summerhouse in Michigan as soon as the verdict was read.

I called Seth. I shouldn't have.

THIRTY-THREE

I agonize over Cash's phone call. I eat more chocolate-covered raisins. I watch more *Nancy Grace*. I search the Internet for pictures of cats with funny captions underneath. No one knows I like those; it's a secret. Sam catches me.

"Are you kidding?"

I close my laptop. "You can't tell."

"Who am I going to tell? Your book club?"

"I have friends," I insist. "And none of them read." I'm pretty strung out on sugar, so I giggle. Sam raises his eyebrow. "And you're proud of this?"

I turn away, hugging my knees to my chest. The manny turns everything fun into a criticism. "No, Sam," I sigh. And then as an afterthought, I add, "I used to read a lot…in high school."

"*Cosmo*?"

He's folding laundry—he's always folding laundry. "Don't you ever get tired of doing that?"

"Yup. But, it's my job."

Oh yeah.

"I read novels. But, then I got too busy."

I ease a few more candies between my lips and stare at the muted TV screen. *I got too busy fucking boys*—I wanted to say.

"Sam?"

"Hmmm?"

"What was in that box Olivia opened on her birthday?"

He shakes out a blanket and folds it expertly into a small square. "Why do you care?"

"What if it was from Caleb?" I say softly.

He won't look at me. "Cammie says it was," he says. "But, I don't know what it was, so don't ask."

I eat a lot more chocolate-covered raisins. I pretend to bite my tongue and yell *Ouch!* to cover for the tears that spring to my eyes.

"Leah," he says, "it's okay if it hurts you. You should tell him that it does. Also, if you're considering a career in acting—don't."

"Why would he buy her a birthday present?"

When Sam doesn't answer, I start thinking about Cash again. It's an endlessly unhealthy reel of thoughts: *Cash...Caleb...Olivia...Cash...Caleb...Olivia.*

The last time I had spoken to Cash was right after my trial. After seeing her on the prosecution's witness list, Olivia did some impressive detective work and discovered that Cash was actually Charles Smith's bastard. Olivia had taken no pleasure in telling me, much to my surprise. She'd even said that she was sorry. I'd reeled for a day, fitting all the pieces together in my mind until they made perfect sense. I had not told my mother what I knew. I waited until Olivia exposed Cash's paternity while cross-examining her, completely discrediting her testimony. I'd looked at my mother's face when my attorney dropped the ball. It had registered nothing. *She knew,* I thought. *She knew and she stayed with him.* The prosecution was mortified. Olivia won another round. Courtney began sobbing hysterically in the courtroom. I glared at Cash from where I sat, my blood boiling for all of the wrong reasons. She had knowingly betrayed me. For him. I should have been mad at him, but all of my anger was directed at her tacky, blonde hair and pink lipstick.

After the debacle in the courtroom, she called my cell phone, pleading with me to meet with her. But, she had allowed my father to use her to destroy my life. When I wouldn't respond to her begging, she mailed me a handwritten ten-page letter, detailing her life from the moment she was born to the day my father asked her to come work for him. I ate an entire bag of frozen peas and smoked three cigarettes while reading that damn letter.

Her mother had been my father's secretary in 1981, and according to Cash, she was conceived on his desk. When my father couldn't convince her mother to have an abortion, he reluctantly agreed to pay her a monthly dividend to make her and her unborn child go away. But, despite his initial feelings, he'd made yearly visits to see Cash and had even paid her way through college. He told her about Courtney and me when she was little. She had grown up knowing her daddy had two other little girls, and when he was gone from her, he was with them. Cash had admitted that she developed a fascination with us early on. She used to daydream about what it would be like to have sisters. My father had even shown her pictures of us, which she kept taped to her wall. I was more surprised by the fact that my father carried pictures of us, than anything else. Since when had Charles Smith developed an affinity for fatherhood? After I read the last word, I burned the letter. I couldn't let Courtney see it. She wasn't dealing with things well as it was. Courtney was too much like my mother. She had an addictive personality, and she emotionally collapsed under stress.

"Leah…Leah?"

I jerk back to Sam, who is still folding the damn laundry.

"What?" I hiss. I wish he'd do that in another room and stop stressing me out.

"Your phone is ringing," he says.

I look down at my cell and see Caleb's name flashing across the screen. I grab it so quickly, I drop the phone. Snatching it off the floor, I answer with a breathless "Hello?"

"Hi," he says. "I'm calling to check on Estella."

"She's taking a nap. She smiled at me!"

There is a ten-second pause before he says: "She looks like you when she smiles."

I instantly feel warm all over. I want to know if that makes him like me more.

"I miss her," he sighs.

"Well, you can come over if you like. But, you're not taking her again until the weekend."

"I understand. She has a doctor's appointment next week. I was hoping to take her to that. I want to be there when she gets her shots."

I sigh. "Fine, you can take her." I think better of it. "But, I want to be there too."

His turn to sigh.

"I'm thinking about taking her to see Courtney."

Caleb clears his throat. "You should. Are you all right to go by yourself?"

"I'm taking Sam," I rush. "It's just…time."

"Are you still angry with her?" he asks.

"No," I say, but oddly enough, I am nodding my head.

THIRTY-FOUR

Seth was Caleb's older brother by four years and two days. They were nothing alike. Cain and Abel, if you will. I was shocked the first time I met the dark-haired, dark-eyed police detective.

"You're Caleb's brother?" I blurted. He had barely smiled at my surprise.

"Yup, last time I checked." He held on to my hand for a little too long, his eyes boring into me. "I guess we don't really look alike, huh?"

I shook my head. Seth shared none of Caleb's features. He was the anti-Caleb with his small button nose, thin lips, and eyes so dark they looked almost black.

Weird, I remember thinking. He was a recluse. During family gatherings, you'd find Caleb in the middle of the action, surrounded by people who were all hanging onto his every word. You'd be lucky to find Seth at all. He didn't show up to most of the barbeques and dinners, and if he did, he lurked in the garden or went for a walk by himself. If caught alone, he was surprisingly engaging and darkly intelligent. He reminded me of Holden Caulfield. I read the book in high school and remember Holden giving me chills. Sometimes, Seth would look at me in a completely unguarded way, a small smile playing at the corners of his lips, and I would get chills.

Once, before Caleb and I were married, we were at his mother's house when Seth turned to me out of the blue and said, "You remind me of a cheap reality show, Leah. You're shallow, and you pretend to be stupid for God only knows what reason."

I'd stared at him in complete mortification, hoping no one else had heard. I darted my head around the room. Caleb was preoccupied with a game on television, and his mother was in the kitchen finishing up dinner.

"What the hell, Seth?"

He'd shrugged. "I know you're not really as stupid as you put out. Shallow, maybe. You have the type of eyes that have claws in them."

I'd stared at him for a long time, wondering if that was how everyone else saw me. Wondering if that was how Caleb saw me.

"It's sexy," he said. "I don't think my brother appreciates it."

I'd flushed and looked away. That was the most he'd ever said to me up until that point. I wasn't sure if he was hitting on me or insulting me. It occurred to me that it might be both. I'd never seen him with a woman. I figured he was one of those asexual men and more concerned with his career than finding someone to warm his bed.

"Why don't you ever date?"

"Who says I don't?"

"You never bring anyone over...or talk about anyone."

He snorted. "Have you seen the welcome my mother gives to women we bring home?" He was somewhat right. I'd heard about the reception she gave Olivia from Luca herself. She detested the woman almost as much as I did. But, Olivia was easy to hate, and Luca was really nice once you got to know her.

I dismissed his comment with a wave of my hand. "She is always nice to me."

He laughed. "That's because you're a lot like her. She probably has a healthy fear of a fellow bitch."

My mouth dropped open. "What is it with people in this family saying exactly what they're thinking? It's so rude."

He leaned over the arm of the sofa and winked conspiratorially at me. "You should try it. Though, it's quite fascinating to sit back and watch all of your thoughts boil behind your eyes and never make it to your mouth."

I had no words. Seth saw the look on my face and started to laugh. "Don't worry, Leah. Your secret's safe with me. No one needs to know there is a brain underneath all of that pretty hair."

I glared at him, clutching tightly to the arm of my chair. I was angry...and I was incredibly turned on. Caleb always said just enough to leave you feeling both incredibly charmed and wondering exactly what he was getting at. Seth spewed truth like it was Old Faithful: too much, too fast, too hard. No wonder no one ever spoke to him.

"You're an asshole, you know that?"

He shrugged, turned back to the TV. "I've been told. But, at least I see you. My brother only sees your hair."

I got up, but his next words pulled me back down.

"I've been waiting for you to remember," he said.

"Remember what?"

He looked at me with such directness, I flinched.

"That you and I have slept together."

If I had been holding my glass, I would have dropped it. My eyes darted to Caleb. Thankfully, he was tuned out to our conversation.

"What are you talking about?" I hissed.

"Relax," he said, lightly. "It was a long time ago."

I searched my memory for his face. Wouldn't I have instantly recognized him if we'd slept together? Probably not. I'd had a lot of sex with men I barely knew. But, if we had...why would he wait so long to tell me?

"You're messing with me," I said.

"Nope." He shook his head so casually I wondered if we were talking about sex or what he had for lunch.

"You definitely came up to my hotel room. It was the weekend after the Fourth of July, six years ago. We met at that little bar in the Keys."

I almost fainted. Six years ago, I had indeed gone on a trip to the Keys with my sister and a few of my friends. It was a combined birthday/holiday weekend celebration.

"How can you remember that if I don't?"

"You were pretty wasted from what I can remember."

Oh God. I did remember meeting a guy in the bar. He danced with me, and then we went across the street to his hotel. Had that really been Seth? What were the fucking odds?

"Don't—"

"Tell my brother," he finished. "Yeah, I figured you wouldn't want him to know. My lips are sealed." He pretended to lock his lips and throw away the key.

How could this be happening? If Caleb found out...

He wasn't going to find out. Seth and I both had something to lose. I nodded at him. "Thank you."

After that day, I tried to keep my interactions with Seth to a minimum. He sought me out whenever we were at the same event. I was partially mortified and partially flattered. He always had a hushed quip ready about my claw eyes or my censored thoughts. Sometimes, he'd call me out when we were in a group and say, "What do you think about that, Leah?" or "I'd like to hear Leah's take on this." To which I'd be forced to answer. He always made inappropriate comments when no one else was paying attention. Sometimes, I'd blush so fiercely at the things he said that Caleb would look at me in alarm and ask me what was wrong. Only Seth could make me blush. It made me feel like we had a secret camaraderie. It made me wonder if he was right, if Caleb really saw me—if anyone did.

During my trial, Seth showed up to almost every hearing. I was pleased by his unexpected support as much as I was confused by it. It was quiet, but it was there…always on the left side of the back row. It made Caleb happy that he came. Their relationship had always been strained. I expected the chasm was forged by Luca's obvious favoritism of her youngest son.

"He must really like you, Red," Caleb said, after a grueling day of listening to the prosecution question their witnesses. "No one can get him to show up to anything, but for you, he's here."

"He's a sergeant in the police force, Caleb. I'm sure this sort of thing interests him."

I really wondered if he was playing his own jury, trying to decide if I was as wicked as he was always insinuating I was. It was exhausting trying to hide yourself from everyone. Watching them watch you. Wanting to know everyone's thoughts and deathly afraid that those very thoughts were condemning you. I was so angry with the man I had called my father for my whole life. I constantly found myself wondering what would have happened had he not died. Would he have scrounged up enough decency to protect me from this? Or would he have asked me to take the fall for him? And most importantly: would I have done it?

Seth asked me that very question the day I called him, after Caleb left me. He stopped by after work with a box of French pastries in his hand. He knew I liked them. I took them from him smiling, and he followed me into the kitchen.

"Where's my brother staying?" he asked.

"His condo." I opened the box and took out an almond croissant. Seth watched me bite into it before speaking.

"That father of yours was something else."

My chewing stilled.

"According to that hot little attorney of yours, he completely framed you. Is she right?"

I wasn't sure whether I was more offended that he'd called Olivia "hot" or that he was questioning my innocence.

I forced myself to swallow what was in my mouth and glared at him. "He didn't do it on purpose," I said. "I don't exactly think he expected to die."

"So, if he hadn't had a heart attack and conveniently left you with this mess, you think he'd be taking the fall for this?"

"Yes, I do."

It was a lie.

"According to Caleb, his signature wasn't on any of the documents you signed."

"What's your point, Seth?" I snapped. "Did you come here to goad me?"

He pursed his lips and shook his head. "No, Leah. I came to see if you were all right. Truly."

"I'm fine." I slammed the lid to the pastry box closed and walked toward the fridge. I could feel him behind me before I turned around. The suddenness of my turn caused him to slam into me. He didn't pull back. He kissed me. Right on the mouth.

"Seth!" I shoved him away. He stumbled back a step. "What the hell do you think you're doing?"

"You called me," he said. "I thought…"

"You thought what? That I wanted you to kiss me? I called you because Caleb left me, and I don't know what to do! You didn't have to come over here and take advantage of me."

He kissed me again. Harder this time. I responded a little before I pushed him away.

"Get out," I said, pointing to the door.

I cried after he left. How long had it been since Caleb kissed me? I tried to remember. Was it before the trial started? I think about all the months of preparation and can't pull up a single memory of being kissed. How had I missed that? How had Seth's abrupt kiss made me remember?

THIRTY-FIVE
PRESENT

A few days after Cash's phone call, we pull up to a tan stucco building around one o'clock. Sam jumps out first and has Estella out of the car before I've even checked my makeup. My hands are shaking when I open my door. We meet in front of the car.

"You okay?" Sam asks.

I nod without looking at him. I haven't been able to take my eyes off the building. I wish I hadn't worn heels. Sometimes, they make me feel confident, but today they make me feel pretentious. We walk in silence, or as much silence as my heels will allow.

At the front desk I give my name: Johanna Smith. I see Sam quirk his eyebrow. I don't look at him. God, I hate that name. I only told Sam we were coming to see my sister, not where she was. We are led down a long hallway that smells of antiseptic. I glance over at the baby, wondering if the smell will bother her. She is asleep. *Such a good sleeper.* I smile.

We are taken to the very last room. I stop in the doorway, and Sam places a hand on my shoulder. I suddenly feel very sick. He nudges me. He's so damn pushy.

I walk through. She is sitting in a wheelchair facing the window. Bright sunlight streams onto her face. She seems impervious to it, staring straight ahead, not really seeing anything. I walk to her slowly and crouch down in front of her.

"Court," I take her hands. They are limp and cold. "Court, it's me." She stares past me. I look around the room—a bed, a television, two chairs. There are no personal touches—no flowers or pictures on the walls just like the rooms we passed on our way here. I look back at Courtney.

"I'm sorry I haven't come before now," I say. "I brought Estella to see you."

Sam, who has already taken her from her car seat, hands her to me. She holds her neck stiff as I take her, her large eyes looking around with innocent curiosity. I place her in Courtney's lap and hold her there. My sister doesn't move, doesn't blink, and doesn't register the tiny presence pressed against her body. Estella fusses after a few seconds, so I take her and hold her.

My sister's hair is greasy and limp. It is too short to tie back and hangs in her face. I reach up and push it behind her ears. I hate this. I hate this place, and I hate that my sister is here. I hate myself for not coming to see her sooner. She doesn't belong here. I make my decision right then and there.

"Sam," I say, standing up, "I want to bring her home…to my home. I can have someone come in to help."

"Okay," he says. "Are you clearing this with me or…" He shakes his head, and I want to slap him for the tenth time today.

"I'm just telling you, idiot."

He grins.

"Courtney, I'm going to bring you home. Just give me a few days, okay…to get everything ready."

I touch her face lightly. Beautiful, vibrant Courtney—I can see her in this person's features, the high forehead and aquiline nose. But her eyes are lifeless. I reach around the back of her head and press my lips against her forehead. I can feel the scar beneath my fingertips, thick and hard. I swallow a sob and straighten up. Estella clings to my shirt, her little fists grabbing the material tightly. I march out without looking back, my heels clipping with new purpose.

Sam waits with Estella while I speak with the director of the facility. When we leave, I have a handful of pamphlets for in-home care.

We are back in the car when he speaks for the first time since leaving Courtney's room.

"So...Johanna?"

"Shut up, Sam."

"It's a valid question, Your Majesty. If you don't tell me why you hate it, I'm going to call you Johanna from now on."

I sigh. How much to tell him? Caleb was the only one who knew. What the heck, right? I didn't even know why it was a big secret anymore. My father was dead, his empire fallen, and my mother was a drunk. Whyyyyyy not tell the manny?

"I was adopted. No one knows. It's been a big secret." I shake my head, quirking my mouth to the side like it's nothing. Sam lets out a low whistle.

"So, anyway, I was born in Kiev. My birth mother worked in a brothel—yada yada."

"Yada. Yada," Sam repeats. "Seems like a little more than yada yada."

I give him a stern look before continuing. "My birth mother was reluctant to give me up. She was young. Sixteen. When she was little, her mother used to read to her from an American book called, *Tales of Johanna*. She agreed to give me up, but only if my parents would name me Johanna. They wanted a baby so badly that they did."

"So that's kind of great," Sam says. "It's like she gave you something of herself."

I snort. "Yeah, well...my parents only told me I was adopted when I was eight. You can imagine my shock.

They sat me down in the formal dining room—just tiny little me and them in this imposing room. I was so afraid I was in trouble; I was shaking the entire time. As soon as I found out about the origins of my name, I didn't want it anymore."

Sam reached out and squeezed my shoulder. "Man, I thought my parents sucked."

I grimaced. "So, that's why I go by my middle name. The end."

"Is Courtney their birth daughter?"

I nodded.

"What happened to her?"

"When my father died, she got sick."

He interrupts me. "Sick?"

"In the head," I say. "She was always that way. She was diagnosed with bipolar disorder. She'd go into these depressions and no one would hear from her for months. She didn't tell anyone this time. We were all so wrapped up in our own lives, no one checked on her. I guess my father's death and everything that happened around my trial just sent her over the edge."

"So, did she—?"

I brake a little too hard at a red light, and he jerks forward.

"She shot herself. The bullet grazed her brain, and they were able to save her in time. But, there was too much damage."

"God," he says. "And this is the first time you're seeing her since…"

"Since the hospital after it happened."

His eyes are wide.

"Don't judge me," I snap. "I was pregnant. I was on bed rest."

"You were a selfish, self-centered bitch."

I glare at him. "I was afraid."

"Of what, Leah? She's your sister. God, I can't believe I work for you. I feel sick."

I glance at him. He does look pretty disgusted. "I'm making it right," I say.

We drive in silence for the next few minutes.

"Ooh! Jamba Juice. Want one?" I swerve into the parking lot, and to my satisfaction, Sam's head hits the passenger-side window with a nice little thud.

"Sorry," I smile.

He rubs his head, seeming to forget his question.

"I'm going to ask Caleb to come home," I say as I pull into a spot. I check his face to see his reaction.

"I don't want a fruit juice," he says.

"Come on, Sam!"

He shakes his head. "Bad idea. You're going to get hurt."

"Why?"

Sam sighs. "I don't think he's ready. Caleb is the type of man who has an agenda."

"What does that mean?"

Sam scratches his head like he's uncomfortable.

"What do you know?" I narrow my eyes at him.

"I'm a guy. I just know."

"You're gay! You don't have special insight into straight men."

He shakes his head. "You are the single most offensive woman I have ever met, you know that? And, I'm not gay."

My mouth pops open. "What are you talking about?"

He shrugs, embarrassed. "I just told you that so you wouldn't hit on me."

I blink at him. He cannot possibly be serious. "Why would you think I'd want to hit on you? Ew, Sam! I can't believe this!"

He sighs. "Are we getting a juice or not?"

I fling myself out of the car. "I'm not getting you anything. Stay here with the baby."

I am so angry, I completely miss the Jamba Juice store and have to backtrack. Men are such worthless liars. I should have known he wasn't gay. He wears way too much polyester to be gay. And, I haven't once seen him check out Caleb. Caleb is freaking gorgeous.

I am sipping my juice and halfway back to the car when I start laughing.

When we get home, I call Caleb's cell three times before he finally picks up.

"When you pick Estella up tonight, I was hoping you could stay a while so we can talk."

There is a long pause before he says. "Yes, I need to talk to you, too." I feel a surge of hope.

"Okay, it's all set then. I'll have Sam stay a little bit later than usual."

I hear him sigh into the phone.

"Fine, Leah. I'll see you tonight."

He hangs up. I don't even think about the fact that he never hangs up without saying goodbye, until a few minutes later.

THIRTY-SIX

Four months after Leah was acquitted, I filed for divorce.

Olivia

—That was my first thought.

Turner

—That was my second thought.

Motherfucker

—That was my third thought. Then I put them all together in a sentence: *That motherfucker Turner is going to marry Olivia!*

How long did I have? Did she still love me? Could she forgive me? If I could wrestle her away from that fucking tool, could we actually build something together on the rubble we'd created? Thinking about it set me on edge— made me angry. We'd both told so many lies, sinned against each other—against everyone who got in our way. I'd tried to tell her once. It was during the trial. I'd come to the courthouse early to try to catch her alone. She was wearing my favorite shade of blue—airport blue. It was her birthday.

"Happy Birthday."

She looked up. My heart pounded out my feelings, like they did every time she looked at me.

"I'm surprised you remember."

"Why is that?"

"Oh, you've just been forgetting an awful lot of things over the years."

I half smiled at her jab.

"I never forgot you…"

I felt a rush of adrenaline. This was it—I was going to come clean. Then the prosecutor walked in. Truth was put on hold.

I moved out of the house I shared with Leah and back into my condo. I paced the halls. I drank Scotch. I waited.

Waited for what? For her to come to me? For me to go to her?

I walked to my sock drawer—infamous protector of engagement rings and other mementos—and ran my fingers along the bottom. The minute my fingers found it, I felt a surge of something. I rubbed the pad of my thumb across the slightly green surface of the kissing penny. I looked at it for a full minute, conjuring up images of the many times it had been traded for kisses. It was a trinket, a cheap trick that had once worked, but it had evolved into so much more than that.

I put on my sweats and went for a run. Running helped me think. I went over everything in my head as I turned toward the beach, dodging a little girl and her mother as they walked along hand in hand. I smiled. The little girl had long, black hair and startling blue eyes—she looked like Olivia. Was that what our daughter would have looked like? I stopped jogging and bent over, hands on my knees. It didn't have to be a *would have* situation. We could still have our daughter. I slipped my hand in my pocket and pulled out the kissing penny. I started jogging to my car.

There was no time like the present. If Turner got in the way, I'd just toss him off the balcony.

I was one mile from Olivia's condo when I got the call.

It was a number I didn't recognize. I hit *talk*.

"Caleb Drake?"

"Yes?" My words were clipped. I made a left onto Ocean and pressed down on the gas.

"There's been an…incident with your wife."

"My wife?" *God, what has she done now?* I thought about the feud she was currently having with the neighbors about their dog and wondered if she'd done something stupid.

"My name is Doctor Letche. I'm calling from West Boca Medical Center. Mr. Drake, your wife was admitted here a few hours ago."

I hit the brakes, swung the wheel around until my tires made a screeching sound, and gunned the car in the opposite direction. An SUV swerved around me and laid on the horn.

"Is she all right?"

The doctor cleared his throat. "She swallowed a bottle of sleeping pills. Your housekeeper found her and dialed 911. She's stable right now, but we'd like for you to come in."

I stopped at a light and ran my hand through my hair. This was my fault. I knew she took the separation hard, but suicide? It didn't even seem like her.

"Of course—I'm on my way."

I hung up. I hung up and I punched the steering wheel. Some things were not meant to be.

When I arrived at the hospital, Leah was awake and asking for me. I walked into her room, and my heart stopped. She was lying propped up by pillows, her hair a rat's nest and her skin so pale it almost looked translucent. Her eyes were closed so I had a moment to rearrange my face before she saw me.

When I took a few steps into the room, she opened her eyes. As soon as she saw me, she started crying. I sat on the edge of her bed and she latched onto me, sobbing with such passion I could feel her tears soak through my shirt. I held her like that for a long time.

"Leah," I said finally, pulling her from my chest and settling her back onto the pillows. "Why?"

Her face was slimy and red. Dark half-moons camped around her eyes. She looked away.

"You left me."

Three words. I felt so much guilt I could barely swallow.

"Caleb, please come home. I'm pregnant."

I closed my eyes.

No!

No!

No...

THIRTY-SEVEN

I send Sam upstairs with Estella and wait for Caleb.

Flick

Flick

Flick

Things have to go my way tonight. He knocks instead of using a key. That's a bad sign. When I open the door, his face is grim. He won't look at me.

"Hello, Caleb," I say.

He waits for me to invite him in and then heads upstairs to see Estella. I follow him to the nursery. Sam nods at him in greeting, and Caleb takes the baby from him. She smiles as soon as she sees him and shakes her fists. I feel a little jealous that he gets smiles so easily.

Caleb kisses both her cheeks and then under her chin, which makes her giggle. He repeats this again and again until she's laughing so hard, both Sam and I smile.

"We should talk," I say, standing in the doorway. I feel like an outsider when he's in the room with Estella.

He nods without looking at me, makes her giggle one more time from his kisses, and hands her back to Sam. She immediately starts to cry.

I hear Sam say "Traitor" as we leave the room and head downstairs. Caleb looks once over his shoulder, as if he's tempted to go back.

"You can see her after…" I say.

I had the kettle on before he got here; it is just starting to whistle as we walk into the kitchen. I set about making him tea while he sits on a barstool with his hands clasped in front of his mouth. The fact that his leg is bouncing is not lost on me. I dunk a tea bag into the mug of hot water and avoid his eyes. I am transferring the tea bag to the trash when he says—

"You went to see Olivia?"

My hand freezes, tea drips on the tile and onto my pants.

"Yes."

Now I know why his leg is bouncing.

"You forced me to do it." I step on the lever that opens the trash can and drop the tea bag in. I can feel his eyes on me.

He cocks his head. "You really believe that, don't you?"

I don't know what he's talking about. I fiddle with my thumbnail.

"Did she call you?" *That tattletale bitch*, I think bitterly. And then in an almost panic—*What else did she tell him?*

"You had no right, Leah."

"I had every right. You bought her a house!"

"That was before you," he says calmly.

"And you never thought to tell me? Really? I am your wife! She came back when you had your amnesia and lied to you! You couldn't tell me that you bought that woman a house?"

He looks away.

"It's more complicated than that," he says. "I was making plans with her."

Complicated? Complicated seems like too good of a word for Olivia. I definitely don't want to know about the plans he made with her, either. He needs to see the truth. I need to make him see the truth.

"I found out on my own, Caleb. How she lied to you when you had the amnesia."

He cocks his eyebrow at me. Maybe if I tell him the truth, he will finally see how loyal I am, how much I love him. "I paid her to leave town. Did she tell you that during my trial? She was willing to sell you out for a couple hundred bucks."

I once watched a natural dam break on television. I remember seeing a scenic picture of a river surrounded by trees. All of a sudden, the trees disappeared—sucked away by the collapse of the riverbank. A swell of angry water rushed around the corner, wiping out everything in its path. It was sudden, and it was violent.

I see the dam break in Caleb's eyes.

Human eyes are the sign language of the brain. If you watch them carefully, you can see the truth played out, raw and unguarded. When you are the bastard child of a prostitute and you need to know what your adoptive parents are thinking, you learn how to read eyes. You can see a lie prod the truth, a hurt be swept into a cranial recess, happiness as a wide luminescent light. You can see the crushing of a soul beneath a terrible loss. What I see in Caleb's eyes is a leftover hurt—hurt with mold growing on it. Hurt so profound that blood and tears and regret cannot possibly do it justice.

What does she have that I don't have? She owns the deed to his house and to his hurt. I am so jealous of his hurt that I throw my head back and open my mouth to scream in rage. He won't hear me. No matter how loudly I scream his name, he will not hear me. He only hears her.

"She wouldn't do that," he says.

"She did. She is a deceiver. She is not what you think."

"You did that to her apartment," he says. His eyes are wide, bleary.

I look away, ashamed. But, no, I am not ashamed. I fought for what I wanted.

"Why her, Caleb?"

He looks at me blandly. I don't expect him to answer. When his voice breaks the tense air between us, I stop breathing to hear him.

"I didn't choose her," his voice breaks. "Love is illogical. You fall into it like a manhole. Then you're just stuck. You die in love more than you live in love."

I don't want to hear his poetic analogies. I want to know why he loves her. I finger the gold hoop earrings I'm wearing. I bought them after I met her at the diner. They don't have the same effect on me. Where they made her look exotic, I look like I'm playing dress-up. I yank them from my ears and toss them away from me.

But, I can be what he needs. He just needs to give me the chance to prove it.

"You need to come home."

He drops his head. I want to scream—*LOOK AT ME!*

When he does, his eyes are raw.

"I filed the papers, Leah. It's over."

Papers?

I say the word. It whispers from my lips—burns them. "Papers?"

My marriage is worth more than something as thin and insubstantial as papers. You cannot end something with that vile word. Caleb is a man used to getting his way. Not now. I will fight him on this.

"We can go to counseling. For Estella."

Caleb shakes his head. "You need someone to be able to love you the way you deserve to be loved. I'm so sorry—" He clenches his jaw, looks at me almost pleadingly, like he needs me to understand. "I can't give you that. God, I wish I could, Leah. I've tried."

I think about that, I do. I think about the time I caught him looking at Olivia like she was the only fucking thing that mattered on the whole fucking planet, and the time he kept her ice cream/finger in the freezer for two years. What type of love was that? Obsessive? What had she done to get his brain wired to her circuit board? I am so out of breath after I am done thinking these things that I spin for the doors that sit off the kitchen and shove them open. The air outside is thick and still. It feels like Jell-O, and I feel like every part of my heart is breaking. I pace the patio, and in seconds, I can feel my shirt sticking to my back. Out of the corner of my eye, I see Caleb follow me outside. He has his hands in his pockets, and he's biting his upper lip.

I rifle through my bag of tricks. I look at his face: hard, determined, sorry. I don't want his sorry. I want what Olivia has. I want to be enough for him.

Honesty is sticky, and I hate it. It always has consequences that fuck up your life… God, I'd rather just wade around the truth and find a lie I can live with. That's what I call compromise. Knowing that my husband loves someone else and living with it…that's a truth you don't look in the eye, and now he was forcing me to.

I stop pacing and stand in front of him with my hands squared on my hips.

"I won't sign the papers. I'll fight you."

I want to slap him when he narrows his eyes and shakes his head at me.

"Why do you want that for yourself, Leah?"

What I want for myself is the family I put together through blood, sweat, and toil. I want it all to mean something. I won, fair and square. The bitch had him between her fist, and I took him back. Why is my fucking prize trying to divorce me? I collect myself, all the shredded angry pieces, and I rope them back together so I can take control. Vicious doesn't work with Caleb. You can reason with him. He has stout British honor and American practicality.

"I want what you swore to give me. You said you'd never hurt me! You said you'd love me for better or worse!"

"I did. I didn't know…" He covers his face with his hands. I'm not sure if I want him to go on. His accent, his goddamn accent.

"You didn't know what, Caleb? That you were still hung up on your first love?"

His head comes up. I've caught his attention.

"I found the ring. After you had the accident. Why did you buy me a ring if you still loved her?"

His face is ashen. I keep going.

"It's not real. Those feelings that you have are for someone and something that no longer exist. I am real. Estella is real. Be with us."

Still he says nothing.

I take a minute to sob. Where does he come off thinking that he has the answer to happiness? I thought I had the answer, and look where it got me. Caleb once told me that love was a desire and desire was an emptiness. I remind him of this. He looks shocked, like he can't believe I was capable of even understanding those words. Maybe I've played stupid with him long enough.

"It's not that simple, Leah."

"You do the best you can, with what you have. You can't leave us. We are your truth." I slam my fist into my palm.

He swears, laces his hands behind his neck, and looks at the sky. I don't feel bad for using the guilt card. The guilt card is solid. It always pays out with interest. When he looks back at me, he's not wearing the contrite face I was hoping for.

"You and I don't know how to play the truth game." He blows air through his nose.

I would have let that comment slip by in abeyance, but I can sense an underlying meaning beneath his words, and I am compelled to dig.

"What are you talking about?"

Caleb's eyes park on my face. I squirm. "Why did you do those things? Blackmailing Olivia…trashing her apartment?"

I don't hesitate. "Because I love you."

He nods, seeming to accept it. I feel hopeful. Maybe he will see what I did as a fight for love.

"You and I are not so different." He scuffs the toe of his shoe against the tile and smiles like he's just swallowed a mouthful of grapefruit. His eyes are clear and wide when he looks up at me: maple syrup without the sweetness.

"Leah…" he sighs and squeezes his eyes shut. I brace myself for what he's about to say, but nothing can prepare me for what comes out of his mouth.

"That ring was hers, Leah."

I feel the shock move through me, as if it is a physical thing like blood. It rushes and pulls and tears. Then, he says the words that change everything.

"I faked the amnesia."

I hear each word separately. I have to mentally latch on to each one and put them back together so I can understand. But, I don't understand. Why would he do that?

"Why? Your family…me…why would you do that to us?"

"Olivia," is all he says.

It's all he needs to say for me to put all of the pieces together. I decide that I hate the color of maple syrup. I'd rather choke and die on a mouthful of dry pancakes, than ever eat maple syrup again.

"Fuck you," I say. Then, I say it again. And again. And again. I say it until I am in a fetal position on the ground, and all I can think about is throwing every bottle of fucking maple syrup out of my fridge and out of my life forever.

My head spins. I've never felt anything so painful. My heart heaves and contracts. It feels heavy and then it feels like it's not there at all—like he stuck his hand through my ribcage and squeezed until it burst. It feels like I have a thousand-ton elephant sitting on my chest. I weakly try to hold on to my reserve, but I feel it being torn away from me. Something inside of me uncoils. With an awkward jerk of my head, I glare up at him with all the hatred I am feeling.

He stands with his back to me until I am done crying, and when I stand up, he faces me.

"I know that to merely say *sorry* would be an insult. I am more than sorry for what I've done. I married you when all along I belonged to someone else. I have been lying to everyone. I don't even recognize myself anymore."

I am emotionally inebriated. I don't know whether to make him watch me slit my wrists or slit his and put an end to my misery. My face has become a swamp of tears and mascara and nose leakage. I want to hurt him.

"You think you can leave us and be happy? She's gone, Caleb," I sneer. "Wedded…bedded—" I see him flinch, and my rage climbs higher.

I lick my lips and taste wine. I've had too much of it, and my tongue is ready to curl around every ugly secret I own and spit them at him, one by one, until he's asphyxiated from the incredible weight of them. I want to take away his breath, crush his windpipe, and with what I know, I surely can.

Where to start? I contemplate telling him that I've met Noah and that he's fucking sexy Ghandi—that I understand why Olivia was able to move on.

I shake my head; tears burn like lemon juice in my eyes. I need to know it all. What he did during those weeks that I thought she was taking advantage of him.

"Did you sleep with her—during your pretend fucking amnesia?"

There is an uncomfortably long pause, which I consider answer enough.

"Yes." His voice is suddenly raspy.

"Have you ever been in love with me?"

He dips his head as he thinks.

"I love you," he says, "but, not in the right way."

My heart plummets as realization sets in. He loves me—he's never been *in* love with me.

"You don't love me the same way you love Olivia."

He flinches like I've hit him. For a moment, his guard is down, and I see so much hurt on his face that I am taken aback. He covers it quickly.

He looks sorry, he really does—or maybe it's just my vision that is blurred because of my tears. I collapse in a heap again and pull my knees up to my chest.

I hear him slide down next to me. For a long time, neither of us says anything. I am mentally replaying the year he spent pretending to have amnesia, revisiting the conversations and doctor's visits. I cannot find a single crack in his story. I fight through the memories, trying to find at least a moment in that year when I sensed he was being untruthful, but there is nothing. I feel like such a fool. So used. How could I be so in love with a man who was so willing to deceive me? I feel like a piece of trash, disposable and unwanted. I know that I am a mess; my tears have caught strands of my hair and plastered them to my face—a face that always gets blotchy and red when I cry. I have never let him see me like this, not even when my father died.

There are so many questions, so many things that I need to know, but my tongue stubbornly stays glued to the roof of my mouth. Caleb tried to get Olivia back. Not once, but twice—first when he faked the amnesia, and the second time when he hired her to be my attorney. If he wanted her so badly, why hadn't he left me when he had the chance? It wasn't in his nature to drag his feet.

I shake at his honesty. The stinging truth of how I had pressured him into proposing to me after I chased Olivia out of town echoes in my head. No. This is not my fault. He didn't have to marry me. I may have played fiercely to keep him, but I thought that he loved me, that he wanted to spend his life with me. He never showed me otherwise. Then I realize something else: Caleb is not as good as I have always thought him to be. His integrity, his honesty, the pure and selfless way he takes care of the people he loves…it all evaporates in light of this new, deceitful Caleb. My God—he did everything in his power to get to her, and I did everything in my power to keep her away.

Have I always known in the back of my mind that I am second choice? Lots of people have first loves that they never really get over, but how could I have grasped the degree of his obsession with Olivia? What kind of woman am I if I knowingly married a man who didn't love me? He is a thief. He stole my life; he stole hers. Goddamn, why am I even thinking about her life?

My first clear thought is that I want to make him pay. I flash to an irrational thought, where I picture myself hogtying Olivia and dumping her in the Everglades for the gators to deal with. Of course I would never do that—I would hire someone to do it for me. I file through all of the other emotional bombs I can drop on him. I have told so many lies that I have an entire buffet of shadiness to choose from. I pluck out the worst one and rub my chin on my shoulder. This one will hurt him, probably deeper than anything that I could do or say about Olivia. Ready…set…

"Estella isn't yours."

EPILOGUE

Hate is such a prodigious feeling. It's hot and oppressive like fire. It starts by burning through your God-given reason until there is nothing left of it but a mound of ash. It moves on to your humanity next, hot tongues flicking across the few remaining threads of innocence until they melt into each other and morph into something ugly. Then, in the rubble of what you were, hate plants a seed of bitterness. The seed grows to a vine and the vine chokes what it touches. That's where I am—the vine wrapped so tightly around my neck I can barely breathe. One hand is on that vine, the other is pressed against my chest to keep everything from falling out.

He told me he loved me. He was supposed to protect me from hurt, not inflict it in the cruelest of ways. He betrayed me. I'm dying. I'm dead. Why am I still breathing? God, I don't know how to make the hurt stop.

I still have a backbone. I've been crippled in other ways, but I still have a backbone. His arms were warm. Now, the only warmth I feel is from the blood still pounding through my veins. That's how I know I'm alive. I've faked orgasms. I've faked smiles. I've faked happiness. Caleb faked amnesia and then he faked an entire relationship. I took a hammer to his shins for it. He thought Olivia could hurt him, I'll hurt him worse. I'll keep hurting him. And if he goes after her again, I'll rise up and do everything in my power to keep them apart. Some people never change. I guess I'm one of them.

THANKS BE

I'm defiant by nature. My defiance evoked *The Opportunist*. My defiance pressed the self-publishing button on Amazon. But, no matter how spunky I think I am, it took a hell of a lot of people to push me through this process. I'd like to thank some of them.

Mom, for telling me beautiful lies and nurturing the writer in me. Your stories and "only child" indulgences fueled what I am today.

Dad, for thinking I'm the greatest thing ever. It's important for your dad to think you're the greatest thing ever.

Rhonda and Mark Reynolds, for believing in me and sacrificing for my story.

Jeff Capshaw, for giving me that initial shove to publish, and for the constant stream of books and music suggestions that fuel my creativity. (Rainer Maria Rilke rocks!)

Tosha Khoury, for possibly being the biggest *Opportunist* fan and supporter. Thank you for loving me and for sharing Snow White.

Melissa Brown, Kerry Ann Ramey, Calia Read, and Rebecca Espinoza for being the first eyes to see this book. Thank you for your thoughts and encouragement. Maria Gowin, for your sharp eyes and willingness to help clean up my text.

To all of the readers! Cheers to you! Your enthusiasm and red-hot anger kept me writing.

Luisa Hansen, one of the best moments of 2012 was when I found out someone created a fan site for me. A damn fan site! The Pressed Penny rocks! So do the Passionate Little Nutcase shirts.

Sarah Hansen (not related to Luisa), thank you for your beautiful cover. You are a giving and talented wench. I love your angry eyebrows.

Tricia Tulchin Boozer, so glad you are the face of my villain. You are beautiful and funny and honest.

My intense and hands-on agent, Andrea Barzvi. Thank you for your expertise and your questions about the story, which made it better. I feel lucky to be in your capable hands. Most of all, I appreciate your willingness to love a villain.

James, not a day since I met you have you doubted that I would sell books. Thank you for pushing me out the door every night so I could go write. Thank you for believing I could do this, more than I believed it.

And finally, Lori Sabin and Jonathan Rodriguez, my two closest friends. You both allow me inside your respective brains, where I pillage and steal all of your good ideas. Your grey matter makes me a better writer and a better person. Thanks for saving my story and my sanity and everything else in between. I hate you for your sheer artistic brilliance. I love you for your kindness. I bow.

CONTACT

www.tarrynfisher.com

www.facebook.com/authortarrynfisher

www.instagram.com/tarrynfisher

http://twitter.com/DarkMarkTarryn

True ~~Love~~ Story

By

Willow Aster

1 Layover in Hell

It has been a year, two months and seventeen days since I last saw him. Two years, ten months and five days since he broke my heart—well, since I *knew* that he had broken my heart. Technically, he began breaking my heart the moment I met him, five years, eleven months and one day ago. I've traveled across the country to get away from him, changed my phone number so neither of us will be tempted to call the other, had one botched relationship after another, all in an effort to forget.

And now I'm 1,600 miles from home, waiting on another flight to head 500 miles further south, and he's walking toward me in DFW airport.

Ian Sterling is oblivious to the fact that our lives are going to crash in…five, four, three, two…

I can't move as he walks up to my gate and begins talking to the agent. I've seen the puddle-jumper we're about to get on together. There is no escaping him.

Caving to the inevitable, I take him in. He is perfection, and I'm not the only one who thinks so. The ticket agent looks all aflutter as she gazes up at him and stutters. His thick hair is sticking up in every direction, just the way I like it. He looks sleepy and obscene; I want to slap him and wrap my arms and legs around him and breathe his air—me and every other woman who lays eyes on him. The guitar by his feet is like another appendage; I've rarely seen him without it.

Before I even know what I'm doing, I am on my feet and sprinting through carry-on bags and travelers' feet. I have to get out of here. If he sees me, I can't guarantee what will happen. I just don't think I can risk it. My heart can't take any more.

I avoid his general direction and am making progress when I get snagged on a zebra print suitcase with purple trim. The hem of my mini catches on the handle of the bag and one yank doesn't do the trick. My skirt *will not* budge. Panic begins to overtake me; my hands are a shaky mess. I am just about to rip a hole in the material so I can keep moving when I hear him.

His raspy voice cuts through the chatter around us. I've missed that voice. "Sparrow?"

My whole body goes still. Except for the tremors in my hands and knees and guts. I grab my skirt again, and this time it miraculously comes loose. *Traitor!*

Ian is clutching the counter in front of him and for a moment, I think he's going down.

"Sparrow?" He says again and gives his hair a nervous tug. His eyes swallow me up and I know I have to sit before I'm the one that goes down.

I put on my calmest face and give a polite, but cold smile.

"Don't get any ideas," I say.

He nods and reaches out to touch my face.

I back up. If he touches me, it's over. I pretend to not see the hurt in his eyes.

"Sit with me?" He asks.

I collapse in the first open seat. So much for getting away.

Ian sets his guitar in front of me and sits on the higher end: elbows on his knees, knees against mine, his eyes trying to read me. Those eyes have been the death of me many a time. I sink into them far too easily. He has the eyelashes that all women envy and I study them instead, remembering all the times I've teased him about being so pretty. He leans in even closer. I cannot bury any further into my seat than I already am.

All of a sudden, he backs up and looks around. "Is your mom with you? I knew I should have shaved," he mutters.

A surprised laugh pops out. "No, Charlie isn't here. Settle."

"Whew." He rubs the stubble along his jaw and grins. "I can't believe you're here in front of me. You look good, Sparrow. So beautiful."

He reaches over and gently pulls one of my curls, watching it boing back into place. He places a hand on each cheek, his eyes studying me until they stop on my lips. He always had a thing for my mouth. And my hair. He used to list what he loved about each of my body parts, going into such detail that my neck would get splotchy. And then he'd tease me about all the splotches, while kissing each one.

I have to stop my brain.

"I see this face every night when I close my eyes. All day long, I think I see you, everywhere I go…" His eyes cloud and he drops his hands. "I've dreamed this so many times, I'm not even sure you're real right now. *Are* you really here?"

A thick lump burns in my throat, making it harder and harder to swallow. I know all about seeing his face everywhere. And not sleeping. And how long it took me to even eat again after he tore my heart out and stomped on it with the black combat boots I bought him that hellish Christmas. Shoving the ache down, I take a deep breath and fix my face as a blank slate, void of all feeling. Except the hate I wish I could have for him.

In our stupor, I think we've missed a few of the boarding calls because the ticket agent looks pointedly in our direction as she loudly makes the FINAL CALL TO BOARD. All the other passengers are sitting and waiting on us when we get on the plane. I sense some hostility. I don't want to make a Texan mad at me.

"Well, what do you know, our seats are next to each other," he smirks.

"I'm sure it helps that we're the last ones on," I snap out of the side of my mouth. I sit down and yank the neckline of my shirt up higher when I see his eyes wandering.

He sits down and laughs. "Come on, Baby, I have you for one hour. Let me look at you." The way he says *have you* makes me feel feverish.

"Don't call me that."

"Let me see your ticket," he grabs it before I can say no. "4B." He holds his up so I can see *4A*. "I couldn't have planned this any better myself..."

I lean my head back on the seat and close my eyes. It's not even two minutes before we're rolling and taking off. Now I know why there is a general glare in our direction from the other passengers; we held up the flight.

The air is thick with sorrow and desire. I have always known the minute he is in a room. It didn't matter if it was a room of a hundred people or across thousands, I could spot his inky black hair and swagger from a mile away. To be in such close proximity after so long apart is threatening to make me sick. Ian is watching me, his head leaning on the seat and his whole body shifted toward mine.

A flash of color catches my eye—no, surely those things aren't still in circulation.

"Tell me you're not still wearing the elephant socks."

His grin takes over his entire face, stopping my heart in the process.

"They're a little holey now."

I snort. It's a good thing my mom isn't here, she'd be mortified. "Yeah, I bet."

"I've never stopped loving you, Sparrow Fisher."

I focus on breathing and not losing my coffee and muffin all over him. That would serve him right.

"I've never loved *anyone* but *you*." He goes on, seemingly unfazed by my silence.

I turn my head and the look on my face seems to scare him. His eyes widen.

"It doesn't matter, Ian. Love…it means *nothing*, at this point. And I'm the only one in this non-relationship who can truly say that I've never loved anyone but YOU. So don't even give me that nonsense about only loving *me*. That's a load of crack." I huff and look out the tiny window, trying to forget he's there.

He chuckles and I whip my face around to see what could possibly make him laugh.

"You still love me," Ian whispers, stroking my cheek. "And you said, *crack*." He smiles sadly at me; his eyes searching mine, pulling me in…deep.

"We don't say *Crap*; we say *Crack*." I recite.

"We don't say *Shi*—" I clamp his mouth shut before he can say the rest. "We say *Shoot*." He finishes, muffled. He kisses my hand and I am sinking, sinking fast. My stomach is back on the ground, and my heart is in my throat. I'm not sure how long his mouth mesmerizes me. His tongue flicks around my middle finger and I'm jarred awake. I rip my hand away.

"Oh, Spar…" he begins.

"You know what? We're stuck on this flight together. I don't want to talk like this anymore. We can talk about other things. Like—what's new with you? Or, what's happening with your career? How is your mom? Things like that…the rest, I just do not even want to hear come out of your mouth. Got it? And if you can't keep your end of the bargain, I can ignore you the rest of the flight. Deal?"

His eyes are dancing and I want to smother him with the airsickness bag. Yeah, I can't say *barf bag* either, okay? I have this thing about words. Sometimes it feels like a disease; other times, it feels close to a gift when I'm writing and come up with meaningful words instead of slang drivel. Disease or not, my editor appreciates it.

"Deal," he says and he reaches out to shake on it. His rough hands feel like home, laying claim on me all over again.

I gradually thaw just enough to carry on a conversation. I figure for all the times I've wanted to know where he was, what he was doing…this is my chance. I can pick up the hurt again later. The rest of the flight breezes by in fast-forward. We talk about the details of his career, although I'd kept track of a lot of it online. Ian's a professional musician and has spent time in both L.A. and New York playing on any and everyone's projects. He's considered the best guitar player out there; guitar companies vie for him because Ian Sterling playing their guitar *one* time will increase their sales by insane percentages. But even more than that, his songs…he can write a song like no other. And then there's his voice; it's *exceptional*. He tells me about his new friendship with J. Elliot, his lifelong idol.

"Working with Elliot has been a dream. He's really pushed me to do a solo project with the songs I've written the last few years." He does his anxious hair tug thing and looks at me, watching for a reaction.

I know what this means, but don't acknowledge it. I've known it would come to this. The songs he wrote for me a couple years ago will be playing every time I go to the mall, every time I turn on the car radio and probably in a cute romantic comedy that I need to avoid. Ian Sterling has been successful for years, but with Elliot behind this project, he will explode. And I'll be the roped up ball of sadness. That's what my future holds right there. Little prickly threads of devastation hanging out of my gnarly, ransacked heart.

"You deserve all the royalties. Every single song is about you." He leans over and rests his forehead on mine. "God, I want to kiss you."

My eyes close and for a moment, I just inhale him. How many times have I dreamed of being this close to him? I feel the pull he's always had on me and am tempted to give in one more time. Sanity fortunately returns. I shove him off and he holds up his hands as I stare him down. "Fine, fine! I'll behave!"

Relentless. I'm torn between throwing up and making out with him in this tiny airplane.

"What are you doing in New Orleans? Besides being by my side day and night?" He smiles as my eyes narrow. "What?" He asks with a shrug. "It's a reasonable question."

"Tessa's getting married on Saturday. I'm the maid of honor. There's a lot to do in the next five days."

"Ah, Tess. I've missed her."

"Me too."

I lean my head back on the seat again. Ian is staring me down and I'm exhausted.

"Sparrow, we don't have much time left on this flight." He presses his eyes with his fingers and takes a deep breath. "Give me your number. Please. I promise I won't…well, I can't really promise that. Just say you'll see me again while you're here."

"It's not a good idea." I shake my head, as much to myself as to him.

"Well, my number is the same. I will never change it. You know, hoping one day you'll call and say you're taking me back," he says earnestly.

"You're impossible."

"You're delectable."

"You're incorrigible."

"You're edible."

I sigh, frustrated and turned on.

"You know it's true." He inches closer.

"No, I can't really say that I do."

"Well, I can."

"Ian!"

His eyes are distraught when he looks at me. "Sparrow, I know you've already heard me say I'm sorry, about a thousand times...but if you can't hear anything else, hear this...you changed me. Please let me..."

I hold my hand up and look straight ahead. It helps to not see his face. "Don't. Just...don't."

His face crumbles and I think I see his hand tremble as he runs his hands through his hair. His eyes fill and for a moment, he doesn't look nineteen. He doesn't look thirty. I see what he will look like at sixty and it makes me sad.

The plane is already beginning its descent. I look out and see the lights of the city and think about how I'd give anything to get lost in Ian's words. It's a powerful feeling, to know this magnetic, dangerous, quirky, beautiful, sexy...man wants *me*. Agony is almost worth it if I could just be with him.

It's as if no time has passed at all. I see with sickened clarity that I will never be over Ian Sterling. Never.

He's watching me, waiting for me to say something. Just one word to give him hope and we will be back in our own little world of love and lust and banter.

I turn to face him and he looks at me with expectancy, willing me to let him back in. Willing me to say yes...

I shake my head and the cobwebs clear. I remember. I remember it all. I want him to hurt.

"How's Laila?"

True ~~Love~~ Story

Made in the USA
Columbia, SC
15 March 2020

89220445R00159